THE CIRCLE CAST

THE CIRCLE CAST

THE LOST YEARS OF MORGAN LE FAY

Alex Epstein

VANCOUVER   LONDON

Distribution and representation in Canada by
Fitzhenry & Whiteside • www.fitzhenry.ca

Distribution and representation in the UK by
Turnaround • www.turnaround-uk.com

Released in the USA in 2011

Mixed Sources

Cert no. SW-COC-001271
© 1996 FSC

FSC

Inside pages printed on FSC certified paper using vegetable-based inks.

Manufactured by Sunrise Printing
Manufactured in Chilliwack, BC, Canada in October 2010

2 4 6 8 10 9 7 5 3 1

Cataloguing-in-Publication Data for this book
is available from The British Library.

Library and Archives Canada Cataloguing in Publication

Epstein, Alex
The circle cast : the lost years of Morgan le Fay / Alex Epstein.

ISBN 978-1-896580-63-0

I. Title.

PS8609.P77C57 2010   jC813'.6   C2010-902919-4

To Angel

for when I knew her

Omnia mutantur, nihil interit.

Tradewind Books thanks the Governments of Canada and British Columbia for the financial support they have extended through the Canada Book Fund, Livres Canada Books, the Canada Council for the Arts, the British Columbia Arts Council and the British Columbia Book Publishing Tax Credit program.

 Canada Council for the Arts **Conseil des Arts du Canada**  BRITISH COLUMBIA ARTS COUNCIL
Supported by the Province of British Columbia

  LIVRES CANADA BOOKS

Acknowledgment

This book owes a tremendous debt to my editor, Kim Aippersbach.

I'd like to thank Michael Katz and Carol Frank who had faith enough to publish it. I'd also like to thank Emma Bull, Will Shetterly and the other members of the Sacred Flying House who gave me many wise words of advice early in the book's journey.

This book was inspired by my love for T.H. White's *The Once and Future King*, which my father read to me when I was a boy, and John Boorman's film *Excalibur*, which made Morgan le Fay real to me.

I owe my understanding of post-Roman Britain and King Arthur partly to Geoffrey Ashe—in particular his book *The Discovery of King Arthur*. A visit to Butser Ancient Farm in Hampshire, England gave me the four-horned sheep and the chimney-less huts.

Morgan's magic arose from a spiritual questing I did many years ago. I want to thank Christine R. and the other members of Homecoming for the spiritual gifts they gave me.

The Celtic cult of the war goddess, reconstructed in the Din Tagell chapters, comes out of my first wife Angel Gulermovich's UCLA dissertation— *War Goddess: The Morrígan and her Germano-Celtic Counterparts*. It's pretty cool stuff.

Contents

PROLOGUE

She had been born of the sea, and now the sea was trying to claim her. The air was salt and wet, half brine in her mouth. She would try to cough it out, but to cough she had to breathe in first, and she could never get her lungs clear. The cold wet air battered her face, while the ship's deck either slammed up against her legs or dropped out from under her.

She had been born of the sea, and all the world around her was sea. The horizon was lost in the grey confusion between churned water and rain-swept air.

She could hear the ship boom as it slapped down onto the water, and sometimes she thought she could hear the Greek slaves cry out in the hold as the waves tore the long oars out of their hands. The wind made the ropes sing, a low banshee moan that never ceased. She wondered if the mast would snap.

She had been born of the sea, and in the savage dimness before night fell, she thought of letting it reclaim her.

The round black ship yawed and pitched wildly in the giant waves, and Morgan could hear the moans of a hundred men below deck. The waves were far too brutal for the men to use their oars; they cowered in the hold.

A few of the captured Greeks struggled with the sail, while three of her bravest warriors held tightly onto the ropes and kept an eye on them.

She had given up green lands for this. She had been a queen; a chief had loved her, and begged her for children. She had walked away from all that, to be here now, in this world of brine and foam and fear. She had given up grace.

But the storm was what she was. She was nothing if she was not this ship full of shields and spears and the arms to wield them and the legs to propel them and the mouths to roar fear into enemies. She had never been an Irish chieftain's wife, not really. She had never really been a holy Christian woman. She had never really been a wise woman's slave in a lake village. She had been born of the sea so that she could return by sea, to reclaim who she really was.

And she was the sea too. She was this air and this salt and the wind that drove the storm. The waves were around her, but she was the waves too.

She closed her eyes and held on to the rigging, and she reached out into the heart of the storm. The storm was a tremendous unsatisfied longing. Huge volumes of air were not where they belonged. The winds would howl until they reached where they yearned to be.

She could not calm the fury of the storm. But she didn't want to. She let her name blow away in the wind, and her tears run away in the brine. She reached into its heart and welded her discontent to its longing, and lashed them both to the mainsail.

With a great heaving shudder, the gale changed direction until the ship was running before it. Its bow cut the water, smashing the waves apart like a wolf scattering geese. The storm no longer beat upon the ship. The ship was hers, and the storm was her, and the ship was one with the storm.

And she was herself again, Morgan, who had once been named Anna. As the storm drove the ship toward Britannia, toward her destiny, she gave thanks for this gift, the gale that was taking her home.

Chapter One

THE COUNCIL OF WAR

It began with a look. Anna had never seen two people look at each other like that. Uter, the war leader of the British, was looking at Anna's mother, Ygraine. He was asking for something with his eyes. Her mother was flushed and frightened. Then she whirled and pushed her way into the crowd to get away, but she kept looking back at Uter. Uter was watching her the way a wolf watches a lamb.

It was a look Anna had never seen before. One day it would be the destruction of Britain.

UTER had been nice to Anna when she'd met him in the big tent. He hadn't seemed nearly as fierce as the stories her father, Gorlois, had told about him: the battles he had won against the Saxons, or the villages of theirs he had burned. He wasn't tall, like her father, and his nose was a small pug nose, not long and Roman like her father's. But when he looked her in the eyes, he was really looking at her, as if she mattered. As if, she thought, he liked looking at her.

It was a huge tent, bigger than her father's villa back home, almost sixty yards long, and it was filled with hundreds of soldiers and warriors drinking and boasting. The governors of all the provinces of Britain had sworn to send their soldiers to drive the invading Saxons back across the sea to the Continent. Outside, there was a city of tents, thousands of them, and more soldiers and warriors from all over Britain. You could hear the murmur of their voices and the roar of all their campfires. And Uter had been picked to lead them all in the war against the Saxons.

Anna's father was talking with Uter as a few tall Picts walked past in a knot, gawking at everything. They were wild barbarians from the north, beyond Hadrian's Wall, with strange tattoos all along their arms, and long beards. They made respectful but strange gestures at Uter as they walked past. They were the enemy, as bad as the Saxons.

"What are they doing here?" Anna whispered to her father.

Uter grinned at her, as if she was very smart for asking. "I guess they're hoping to pillage the Saxons instead of us, for a change."

"And if we lose?" asked her father. "Who's going to make them go back home?"

"Who said anything about losing?" Uter said, and his grin got wider, so that it was a little scary. Anna could see why people wanted him to lead them into battle.

"Is that Marcus Cunomorus?" her father said, and got up abruptly. People were throwing their arms around a tall scarred man with grey hair who'd just come into the tent. "I'd better go talk to him."

"Have you two been fighting?" asked Uter, amused.

"I caught his men moving boundary stones," said her father. He meant the stones that marked out the lands he governed. Marcus Cunomorus had been trying to nibble away at his lands by moving them.

"If I caught men stealing my lands, I'd have them flayed alive," Uter laughed.

"It's stupid and pointless," said her father. "They're not his lands or mine. We're not kings. We govern in the name of Rome." He turned sharply and walked off. That was his way. He wouldn't argue with you. He'd tell you his point of view and then head off before you could make a fool of yourself trying to contradict him.

"Rome died," Uter called after him. "Haven't you heard?"

It was true. The last Roman soldiers had marched out of Britain a hundred years ago. Barbarians had sacked Rome a few years before Anna was born. Still, her father insisted that he was the governor of a Roman province. His departure left Uter grinning at Anna. "Looks like he forgot you," he said. He didn't seem to mind being stuck with an eleven-year-old girl. "Have you ever seen this many soldiers?" he asked.

"You must have almost a whole legion," she said, anxious to show Uter that she knew what she was talking about. Her father liked to talk to her about strategy and tactics. "How many cavalry do you have?"

But suddenly Uter wasn't paying attention to her anymore. He stood up, staring. Anna followed his gaze.

It was her mother, smiling graciously in the centre of a circle of laughing soldiers. She was wearing robes of Syrian silk that fluttered as she moved. "That's my mother," Anna said.

Uter didn't seem to have heard her. "Who in the name of Venus is that?" he asked.

"That's my mother," Anna said again. "Her name is Ygraine."

"Go find your father," Uter said. Then he surged into the crowd toward her mother. What was he doing? There was something wild in his expression.

Anna scrambled after Uter. She saw her mother through the thicket of arms. Ygraine had stopped moving. Her smile had faded. Her face was flushed red. She spun away.

What did Uter want from Anna's mother? Why was Ygraine so upset?

Anna left the pavilion where all the soldiers and warriors were feasting and drinking, and walked out into the tent city that sprawled across the hill. Around the hilltop were the remains of a legionary fortress, from when the Roman legions still garrisoned Britain a hundred years ago. Now the rotting wooden walls held soldiers gathered from all over Britain: from the Cantaccii in the southwest, whose lands the Saxons had already taken, to her father's soldiers from Trigos on the Cornish peninsula in the far west, to the Brigantes in the north. There were hundreds of tents laid out in neat rows. The muddy lanes between them were bustling with men. Below the hill-fort, the tents of the Picts spilled into the river valley, in no particular order; they weren't proper soldiers, only warriors.

Anna found her mother in their tent, alone. She seemed worried. "Is something wrong?" Anna asked.

"No," her mother said. "Are you scared about the war?"

Anna shook her head. She'd never seen so many soldiers and warriors in one place. Her father had said there were mobs of Saxons flowing into Britannia, but surely no mob could defeat all these tough-looking soldiers.

"I am," said Ygraine. "You never know what will happen in war."

But Anna's mother wasn't telling her what was really wrong. There was something strange in her voice.

ANNA'S father stayed out for hours, maybe plotting strategy with the other governors. Anna wanted to wander through the tent city. She'd never been this far from home, and it was exciting. But her mother said she couldn't. She just wanted to comb Anna's hair, so Anna let her. Ygraine sang to her, and in the heat, Anna got sleepy lying on her blankets on the soft grass.

Her mother began to sing a lullaby. Anna wanted to wander around the camp, to hear men tell war stories—she could hear them out there, laughing and boasting. But her mother's voice was a spell that wove the soft grass and the warm blanket into an embrace. She wasn't sure if she was asleep yet. And then she was.

SOMETHING was rustling right outside the tent. It was dark; the crickets were out in force. And there was her mother's voice, and a man's. Was her father back? The murmuring was quiet, low, but it had a kind of urgency to it. Her father was like that.

But why were they talking outside the tent? They didn't want to wake her. That was it. They were thoughtful that way.

No. Something was wrong. Anna opened her eyes. From the firelight outside, she could see their soft shadows against the tent canvas. The man was shorter than her father. Stocky. And very close to her mother. They had stopped talking.

Where was her father?

Suddenly her mother turned away. She seemed to be wrestling with the man.

"Ygraine," the man said. It wasn't her father's voice, and it was urgent, and something in it scared Anna.

Then she heard a slap.

"Mama?" she called, and she got up from the blanket. "Mama!" Somehow she got tangled in the blanket and fell down again.

She ripped the blanket off her feet and ran out, slapping the tent flap aside. The man was already striding away. He was wearing Roman armour. She saw soldiers nodding their heads respectfully as he went by until he disappeared into the shadows.

"Are you all right?" Anna asked. Her mother's face was pale in the firelight. "Who was that?" Her mother didn't answer. "Did he kiss you?"

Ygraine pulled Anna into the tent, and sat down abruptly on the grass, trembling.

"What's wrong, Mama?" Anna asked. She ran her fingers through her mother's hair, trying to comfort her, but Ygraine didn't seem sad, just upset. "Who was that?" Anna whispered again.

After a long time, her mother finally spoke. "Please don't tell your father," she said, her voice cracking.

BUT Ygraine must have told him, because only a little later, Gorlois was whispering to his wife in harsh low tones.

Anna was frightened. She wanted to wedge herself under the folding table, but she wasn't a little kid anymore. The name Uter burst out more than once, and she heard her father curse, though he never cursed.

So Uter had been the man in the shadows. Anna had liked him. But he had tried to kiss her mother.

Why?

Her father burst out of the tent, but there was no shouting. That was his way. He just started waking his centurions up, going into their tents or rousing them from their campfires. And, long before the dawn broke, Bretel, her father's senior centurion, was rushing everywhere whispering orders. The men were tightening saddles and shoving bags back onto carts, stepping carefully, holding the horses' bridle bits from jangling, looking every few minutes at the brightening east.

BEFORE the sun even broke the tree line, her father's army was marching away from the old legionary fortress, its rotting battlements looming black against the pale red sky.

On the way here, Anna had ridden on her own pony. But now she had to ride in one of the supply carts. Its iron-ringed wheels made a racket on the stones of the road. Her mother was far ahead, at the head of the column. Her father was riding back and forth, barking orders to the men.

What had happened? The Saxons were not in this direction. The men hadn't eaten. Her father had them pass loaves of bread down the line, so they could tear off pieces and eat while they marched. Why were they running away? She didn't understand.

When they finally stopped, it was midday. The sun was hot. Eight hundred men had covered a score of miles. They were exhausted. Anna was ashamed. It wasn't like her father to sneak away in the middle of the night. Anna felt humiliated, and she hadn't even done anything wrong.

Three riders came up the road. Everyone tensed, but soon Anna recognized the riders on the left and right as her father's. The centurion in the middle carried a long lance pointed up, a white pennant flapping from its tip. His brass breastplate was polished and gleaming.

The horsemen guided the rider to Gorlois. The centurion dismounted and put his fist against his chest in a salute.

Her father saluted back. He gestured for the rider to follow him to the shade of some trees. Then he stopped and gestured at the centurion's sword. The centurion looked surprised, but he unstrapped his sword and handed it in its sheath to the horseman to his right.

Anna slipped off the cart and snuck into the shadows along the edge of the woods. She made her way quietly toward the men.

Her father was leaning against a tree, his face set in frustration. She knew that look.

The centurion was standing ramrod straight.

"You can't leave," he was saying. "We all swore an oath to stay with the army."

"I didn't break my oath first," her father said sharply.

"An oath is an oath," said the centurion, barely moving a muscle. "You know me, Gorlois. I don't love Uter any more than you do. But if you leave us—wearing that—" he said, gesturing at her father's legionary armour, "then what will those half-naked barbarians make of their own oaths? There goes the whole war."

Anna could hear the man's discomfort. As if he hated being the one to say it. But it was about honour. Honour was what made men better than they were. Without honour, a man was nothing. With honour, he sometimes had to do things he hated.

Her father's voice was edgy. "Don't talk to me about honour. I could have called him out. That would have been the honourable thing to do."

"Why didn't you?" asked the centurion.

"You tell me," Gorlois said. It was his habit, making you argue his side for him.

"The war against the Saxons," said the centurion.

"Uter or I would be lying on the ground dead. Maybe both of us," said Gorlois. "He has a gift. People like him. Hades and Tartarus, I used to like him. He knows how to fight a war. We've forgotten that. We need that."

"Then come back. My commander and the others will make sure he leaves your wife alone."

Anna could see that her father was thinking about it, trying to find a way to agree. "One day I would find myself and my men accidentally cut off somewhere and massacred, while Uter wins a great victory and goes to console my wife."

"He wouldn't do that."

"You wouldn't do that. But him? It's better if I just take myself— and her—out of the equation."

The centurion frowned, never losing his rigid bearing. "He'll order us to pursue you."

"Then he's violating his oath to everyone."

"I'm telling you what he'll do. And some of the tribes will come along with him. They don't care who they plunder."

Anna found herself shivering. Her father was nodding sadly, with that bull-like stubbornness she knew meant he would not turn aside. Something horrible was going to happen. And neither of these men would do anything to stop it.

"What would you do? If it were your wife?" her father said.

"I would have killed him on the spot. That's honour," said the centurion. "But you have a reputation for being wiser than the rest of us."

"Maybe that's my downfall," said Gorlois. "Go back to your commander. If he's as good a man as you, he won't come after me. Maybe no one will follow Uter except his own men, and he'll come to his senses."

The centurion frowned. He saluted again, and headed back down to his horse.

Anna's father sat down. She could see how weary he was. Anna had a tremendous urge to run to him and kiss him and make him laugh. But she was cold with dread, and she couldn't take a step in his direction.

When she could move again, she ran back to the carts. Her father got the men back on the march before the centurion had even disappeared into the distance.

Chapter Two

DIN TAGELL

That night they burned their supply carts and kept marching until they couldn't march anymore. They marched for three long days and nights before the Wall of Din Tagell appeared on the horizon.

As the sun slid into the sea, and the exhausted men marched through the gates, Anna's father took her up on the wall. "Why is this a good place to have a fortress?" It was one of those grown-up questions he liked to ask her. She had always liked those questions. But today it didn't seem like fun anymore. It was serious.

They were on a headland, its hundred-foot cliffs jutting far out into the sea, attached to the mainland by a thin rocky ridge. That was the "Neck." The Wall of Din Tagell ran across the neck. Din Tagell meant "Neck Fort" in British.

Farmers were swarming in from their pastures and fields, driving their cattle and sheep onto the Neck and into the fortress. Beyond the green fields, somewhere in those woods, an army was closing in on them.

"He won't be able to get past the Wall," Anna said. None of them used Uter's name anymore.

"Good girl." Gorlois nodded. "But what if he comes by sea?"

Anna looked toward the cliffs. The Irish barbarians lived across the sea. But they hadn't raided Din Tagell for as long as she had been alive. There was only a small beach at the foot of the cliff, and the steps cut into the side of the cliff were only wide enough for one man. "You can only come up the steps if you're friendly," she said.

Her father nodded approvingly. "But we can't hide behind our wall forever," he said. "He could lay siege. If you hide in a bottle, someone is going to put a cork in it."

Anna nodded, nervous.

"So we're going out to attack."

"What?" she said.

"You and your mother will be safe. I'll leave some men on the Wall, but I'll have to take most of the soldiers. We'll hide in the woods and hit him when he's not looking."

Anna was terrified. She'd heard stories about Uter. A Saxon had given Uter his sons as hostages to seal a truce. Uter brought up those boys like his own foster sons. But when the Saxon broke the truce, Uter burned the boys alive and sent them, half-dead, back to their father's village. They were a long time dying, those boys. Uter had burned so many villages that year that his men began calling him *penn dragon*, which meant "Head Dragon" in British.

"Please don't leave us," Anna begged.

Anna's father chuckled in that reassuring way he had. He gestured back at the settlement. "How are the crows doing?"

Anna looked back. The hilltop was dotted with sleek black birds. Far away, she heard them cawing. The war goddess Bellona Morigenos had given the crows to Din Tagell. So long as they stayed, Din Tagell was under her protection.

Anna tasted blood. She realized she had bitten her lip.

"Stop that," he said, with an edge to his voice. "If my own daughter is scared, everyone else is going to be terrified."

Anna's father was solid and deep like the bones of the land. He never said anything just to make you feel better. She wanted very much to be brave for him. She forced herself to feel strong.

The next morning Gorlois marshalled his force of seven hundred soldiers. Anna thought he was going to make an oration. But all he said was, "Let's move out," and the soldiers began to march out through the gate.

Anna ran up to her father and threw her arms around him. She wanted to ask him again not to go but she forced herself not to. She wanted him to pick her up and spin her around like he used to when she was smaller. But she just held him tight for a moment.

Then her mother was standing beside her. Ever since the war camp, Ygraine had been strangely quiet—as if she was ashamed of something. But it hadn't been her fault Uter had kissed her. Had it?

Her father took her mother's hand. They didn't say anything for a long moment. With a sudden urgency, Ygraine pulled Gorlois close to her and kissed him. It was a long hard kiss.

"Let me go to him," Ygraine said. "Men shouldn't die over me. You shouldn't die because of me."

"I would rather die than give you up," said Gorlois. He kissed her back, and Ygraine melted into his arms.

Gorlois pulled away first. "I'll be back soon," he promised. Then he spun on his heel and strode off after his men, not once looking back.

AS the sun began to slide down toward the sea, three women came up to Anna's mother. Anna didn't recognize them, but they must have come from the outlying villages. They knelt. It was strange for anyone from the district to kneel to one of her parents. It was the sort of formal thing that official couriers did. Anna left off feeding bread crumbs to the crows and came over to eavesdrop.

The oldest woman was tiny and white-haired. She wore a yellow dress. "My lady," she said, in British, "the old sacrifice to Morigenos..." Her voice drifted off, as if she expected Ygraine to know what she was talking about. But Anna's mother only nodded. "Such as we did when I was a girl. Well, the men are at war, and they need all the help they can get, don't they?"

"Sacrifice?" her mother said, and frowned, perplexed. "Well, the governor has never objected to the old rituals. But if you need to borrow men from the Wall, you have to talk to Bretel."

"We don't need the men," said the second woman, chuckling. She was fat and motherly. "It has nothing to do with men."

"My lady," said the youngest woman, "you'll be the one leading the ritual."

"What? I don't know any rituals for Bellona Morigenos," said Anna's mother. "My people are from Brittany."

"You're the wife of the man who rules Din Tagell," said the white-haired woman.

"I'm not a priestess!"

"Morigenos isn't one of your oh-so-proper Roman goddesses as needs her own special priestess!" laughed the fat woman.

Ygraine frowned. "I don't know how the governor would feel about me leading a ritual," she said. Anna's father didn't like magic. He never talked about it, and Anna had noticed that other people stopped talking about it too, if he was near.

But Anna's father wasn't here, and this was important. She ran up to the women.

"You have to," she told her mother. "Bellona protects the Wall!"

The old woman smiled at Anna and nodded. "She knows. Never has Morigenos let an enemy come across the Wall."

Her mother thought about it. Then she nodded. "If it will make people feel safer."

ꝢꞪꞓ crow was woven out of wicker, five feet from tip to tip of its outstretched wings, rubbed all over with black soot, then oiled with rapeseed oil to make it shine.

Dozens of the women of Din Tagell gathered in a circle near the cliff's edge. The sun was low over the water. Anna even thought she recognized some of the women she'd seen praying at the priest's cross. Wasn't that the weaver's wife? The women talked in excited whispers. They'd been full of nervous energy ever since the men had left. Now they finally had somewhere to put it.

"Remind me why no men?" Anna's mother asked the white-haired woman, in British.

"We're invoking the goddess."

Ygraine frowned, uncertain.

"The goddess comes into us. She's not going to come into a circle with a bunch of men in it, is she?"

"I guess it was like that back home," said Ygraine.

The sun touched the sea at the horizon. The white-haired woman carried a brazier into the centre of the circle. She struck sparks off a flint, and the tinder in the brazier caught, and flames began to lick upward. A young blonde woman walked around the circle, dropping grains of salt on the ground from a bowl. Anna felt the evening breeze blow in off the sea. As the young woman walked past her, Anna shivered. The woman was murmuring softly in British, but Anna couldn't make out the words. But she felt cleaner somehow. It felt like when you sweated in the sauna and then washed yourself in the hot and cold baths.

Again the young woman walked around, and then a third time. Anna was filled with a sense of purpose, though she didn't know what was supposed to happen. She had never been to such a ritual. She had watched the Christians pray. She had gone to the harvest festivals. She had seen officials pay homage at the altar of Bellona Morigenos, though her father always found an excuse to stay away from those rituals.

This was different. The air seemed alive with intent.

As the sun vanished beneath the sea, the grey-haired woman picked up a small bell. In the pink glow of the bright clouds overhead, she walked around the circle, ringing it. The bell seemed to pull at Anna, though it was nothing, just a little brass bell like you might put on a lamb. Somehow the noises from the village dropped away, until there was only the bell and the wind and the waves crashing on the cliffs below.

When the grey-haired woman put her bell down, the light had faded from the clouds. She walked into the centre of the circle, plunged a torch into the brazier, and came away with flame. Then she walked the flame out of the circle of women and walked around the circle. As the sky darkened, the torch became the only light except for the faint glow of campfires far off in the village. Anna felt strange. She was on the familiar grass of Din Tagell, but it felt different and new.

"The circle is cast," the old woman croaked, in a voice that could have been a crow's. "We stand between the worlds."

Anna could feel it. They were standing exactly where they had been all along. But now they were also standing somewhere else, some other, uncanny place that Anna couldn't see, but could sense.

The three women began to chant. Some of the women in the circle took up the chant; the others hummed along. It was British, but strange. Anna didn't know all the words. The ones she did know didn't make sense; they hinted at and dodged around meanings. Sometimes one of the three women sang out and the other two responded. Sometimes they chanted as one. Sometimes the three of them sang at the same time, and the sounds created an alarming discord. Yet the dissonance made some kind of sense, though Anna couldn't say what it was.

The words rolled and swayed, and somehow they began to seem familiar, as if she had heard them before, and still she didn't know what they meant. But she began to feel as if each word was on the tip of her tongue before the others said it.

Then the women stopped. Anna felt something stirring, almost ready to be awakened. She looked around at the women of Din Tagell. Did they feel it too? They looked anxious, like they were worried whether the ritual would save Din Tagell or not.

The young blonde woman handed Anna's mother an unlit torch and gestured her forward. The three women took turns whispering words to Ygraine, and her mother repeated them out loud. At first she spoke awkwardly, tripping over the strange words, like someone reading a badly scrawled manuscript. But slowly the words began to come more easily. They were old and dark, that was all Anna could grasp. But there was the cawing of crows in them, and men slain on the battlefield, and crows feasting.

The words thrilled Anna. She could feel something in the air. Something? Someone. Someone she couldn't see.

The white-haired woman gestured, and the torch Ygraine carried burst into flame. Anna's mother seemed only a little surprised; she strode over to the wickerwork crow and plunged the torch into it. The crow blazed up, flames leaping into the sky.

For a moment Anna felt someone's presence. Someone old—beyond old—and enormously powerful. Someone female, and ageless, was in that other circle—the uncanny, invisible one. She was ready to cross into the circle of grass and dirt that Anna was standing in, but she needed someone ready to accept her inside herself.

Anna shivered. Was it all her imagination? But she'd never imagined anything like this.

The white-haired woman kept murmuring. And then Ygraine's voice rang out. In clear, ordinary British, she said that *She* accepted the sacrifice. She would bring destruction to the enemies of Din Tagell, if the people stayed faithful to her.

And then the crow suddenly collapsed, its wickerwork burned through. The women in the circle gasped. They clasped hands and began to circle leftward, like the sun's shadow around a sundial. They started singing in British. They broke the circle at one point, and one side began spiralling inward. The women were soon spiralling close around Anna and her mother.

But nothing had changed. Whoever was in that other circle—the one who seemed so close, as if She was just across a veil—had not crossed over.

"You didn't do it, Mama!" Anna said.

"I did exactly what they told me to!" her mother said, under her breath.

"You said the words but…" Anna knew there was supposed to be more than words. Something was supposed to have happened.

And it still could. There was still something in the air. Someone waiting to be summoned. Still waiting to be asked. "It's not too late. You can still…"

"I can't. I couldn't. I…" Her mother shook her head.

The ritual moved on. The dancers turned the spiral outward with much laughter and joy and confusion. The moment passed.

Her mother had almost done something. She had started something; Anna could feel it. She had almost stirred something old and powerful. But she had not awakened it.

"I'm sorry," Ygraine murmured, maybe to Anna, maybe to herself. "I just couldn't."

The women of Din Tagell finished dancing their spiral outward. They were happy: they had done something to help. It pushed away the fear.

Now the three wise women were reciting words that Anna was too upset to hear. They walked around the circle in the other direction, moonwise, the direction in which the moon slips backward across the sky from night to night. The old woman doused her torch and scattered the embers of the brazier onto the ground; and the three of them gave thanks, in British, to Morigenos for accepting their sacrifice and for Her promise to destroy their enemies.

And then the ritual was over, and the women of Din Tagell broke up into happy clumps.

"That was different," she heard one of the women saying to another as they headed back to their houses. "Was that how it was done in the old days?"

"At least it was something to do," said the other, and the two of them walked away into the shadows of the houses.

Anna wanted to stay in the circle. There was still something there, something she could feel, but she did not quite know the shape of it. She ran up to the old wise woman, who was standing beside the smouldering crow. "Something almost happened, didn't it?"

The old woman stared at her, surprised. "Did you feel it?"

"Someone very old was here," Anna said. "You brought Her here...and the words...and all of us."

"Yes."

"But she didn't wake up."

"No," said the wise woman.

"Because my mother wouldn't let her in?"

Anna's mother came up to them.

The old wise woman turned to Ygraine and said, "That was good, but if we could do it again, it would accomplish more."

"We have to try again, Mama," said Anna. "This time for real."

Ygraine shook her head. She seemed upset. Shaken.

"Let me talk to your mother alone," said the old woman. She seemed troubled.

So Anna left them and walked along the perimeter of the circle the women had made. Din Tagell felt different, but it was hard to say in what way it was different.

It felt as if it were swaying slightly. As if Din Tagell were floating ever so gently in the waves. As if the land were straining to rise. As if it were a great stone on the back of a great beast struggling to rise up from under the sea.

She remembered the story an old fisherman had told her. Once Din Tagell had been a great mountain towering over rolling green downs that stretched as far as the eye could see.

"Where did the land go?" she'd asked. "It sank, didn't it?"

"The giants who lived here, their king fought his son over a woman." The fisherman had squinted out at the sea, as if he could almost see them. "Maybe he sank the land with his magic. Or maybe he used up all the magic that held the land above the water." She'd giggled. "Don't you laugh! Look at the land!" he'd said. Miles and miles of undulating green downs that looked as if they could go on forever suddenly dropped off into the sea, just as if the land had broken off and sunk beneath the waves.

Anna knelt. She put her hand to the ground. She felt the steadiness of the rock beneath the turf, beneath the soil.

There *was* something alive in the earth here. The headland did feel like a leviathan trying to rise from the depths of the sea. It was silly.

SO STOP THINKING THEN.

What?

STOP THINKING. THINKING IS NOT THE WAY TO ALL ANSWERS.

What?

But the voice—was it even a voice?—was gone.

She watched the stars wheel over the sea. A chill breeze was kicking up off the ocean, but even in her light dress she wasn't cold. The stones of Din Tagell warmed her with a heat that came from deep beneath the earth.

MUCH later Anna went to bed. Her mother was already asleep, the straw under her blankets rustling as she tossed back and forth. Anna climbed into her mother's arms. Ygraine wrapped herself around Anna like a cloak. She smelled of saffron.

SOMETHING woke Anna in the early hours of the morning. Her mother was still sleeping. She could always sleep soundly when there was nothing to do but worry. Plump Eithne, Anna's old nurse, was curled up in her alcove. Eithne, of course, slept through anything. Her father said that was because Eithne was a slave. She didn't get to make her own decisions, so she never worried.

Eithne's people were Irish sea raiders. A small band of them had tried to sneak up the steps from Din Tagell's beach. Her father had taken prisoners and forced them to tell him where they had come from. Then he raided their village across the sea, taking a dozen captives, including Eithne. If Uter killed her father, Anna realized, Eithne would still be a slave. So why not sleep?

Anna felt vaguely resentful about that. She reached out and touched the cold tiles. She felt queasy. The island felt like it was rocking. Things that were supposed to be solid were rolling and shifting.

Was it the magic of the ritual the women had done? No. It was something else. Something uncanny was snaking through the air. Something ugly. Something was wrong. If she could only figure out what.

But Anna was only eleven, and she could not understand what it was she sensed. So she fell into dreams.

Chapter Three

ANNA'S DREAM

In her dream Anna was her father, riding at the head of a column of men. Her soldiers walked softly behind. She could feel how excited the young men were. They had never tasted battle. But the old men were silent.

Bretel rode alongside. "I hope the Enchanter's not mixed up in this," he said to her.

"The Enchanter is not my enemy," Anna answered, and she was sure it was true. Merlin came and went mysteriously, and never took anyone's side. Men called him the Enchanter because they were afraid that if they invoked his name, he would know they were speaking of him, and he might do something to them.

The road underfoot was as black as the forest. Torches would betray their approach, so they were following the faint path of starlight overhead. They had muddied their shields, armour and faces, so they wouldn't glint if the moon came out of the clouds.

Anna knew she was dreaming. She could even feel her mother's breathing on her cheek. Dimly she could hear the distant surf. But the dream felt just as real as the straw she was sleeping on. She was in the forest, and she was in Din Tagell. She was between two worlds.

In the dream, Anna and her men crept up the side of the old hill-fort toward the bright orange glow behind its walls. Her scouts had seen Uter's men make camp there. It was a good place to camp: high ground empty of trees, hidden in the forest. Uter would not be expecting an attack there. Anna's men would catch them by surprise.

But when they got there, the place was empty. The orange glow was from a dozen torches stuck into the ground. Two foxes were fighting over a scrap of meat in the flickering light, but they ran off.

The men looked around the empty campsite, confused. Bretel stirred a fire pit; embers glowed. "We must be close," she told him.

"Doesn't feel right," he said. But they had to pursue. She had to fight Uter; it was the only way to protect Ygraine.

They followed Uter's trail into the shadows. The torchlight still danced in their eyes; the forest seemed impenetrably black now. But nothing could stop them. Each man was the leg of a giant centipede, marching forward in the darkness.

Suddenly Bretel clutched at an arrow in his throat. He gurgled, his windpipe filling with blood. The scouts sagged off their horses. The bushes ahead of them were alive with dark shapes. Men tried to fight them, swinging into the tangled shadows with their axes and hammers. Cynric, her second cousin, was struck by a battle-axe. Anna's two foster brothers, terrified, broke and ran, but arrows cut them down.

Her men quickly recovered their senses. Once the shock of the attack was gone, it was just man to man in the dark. There were not as many ambushers as she'd thought. "We outnumber them!" she shouted. The young men whooped. The attackers faltered, backing into the woods.

Then a chilling ululation echoed through the trees. Behind her, the dim bushes became men too. Branches became arms, leaves became blades. It was an ambush within an ambush. Her men began screaming that they were trapped. They stopped fighting like soldiers and started flailing wildly.

She had to stop the panic.

Anna recognized the man at the head of the enemy's troops. It was not Uter. It was Ectorius, a stout man with a beard. She knew him: a good soldier, but a follower, not a leader. She screamed, "Show me Uter! Let me fight him!" She lunged forward, striking down bigger men, her sword leaping and slashing and punching through armour.

She reached Ectorius and shield-smashed him down to his knees. "Where's Uter?" she screamed. Ectorius cringed, not even trying to strike back.

Then there was a wrenching pain. She could see a bloody spear point. It was coming out of her breastplate. Someone, she thought dully, had stabbed her in the back. She wondered who had done it. The air was still thick with noise and pain. Ragged shouts of men, steel ringing, horses wildly neighing. She saw blades swinging in the moonlight, men spinning and falling.

Then the sounds began, oddly, to fade. The cries of anguish died away. Now she could make out the twang of the bowstrings. You never hear that in battle, do you? She heard a horse wheezing over his dying rider. The horse's heart hammered.

The trees were creaking softly in the breeze. It was uncanny; she could still see blades swinging in the moonlight, see men spin and strike and fall, but she couldn't hear them. All she could hear was the talons of an owl shifting its feet high in the oaks, hear it loosen its wings and jump into the air, gliding across the grove. All she could hear was a mouse sifting through dry leaves for food. The owl's wings beat once, its wings rushed through the air, and the mouse's back snapped. The mouse screamed as it died.

She could hear water rushing. She somehow knew, the way you know in dreams, that she was hearing the forest itself, the rush of sap flowing through the veins of the trees.

A dark sound rang out, low and terrible. It was a deepness beyond hearing, but she heard it, heard the rip and curl of stone surging upon the skin of the world.

She was scared now, gasping for breath, falling into this abyss of sound so low she could only feel it. She struggled to leave the dream, or at least, in her dream, to move, but she was stone.

She was on her back, looking up at the wheeling stars. The spear point had disappeared from her chest. A face popped into view. It was a familiar face. He had smiled at Anna, made her feel special, back at the hill-fort. But the moonlight was dim like a dying ember, and his face was oak-hard now.

The oak-hard man turned and looked at a dark little man who stood behind him. Why did he seem familiar? She had never seen him before, but she knew him. The dark little man raised an odd-looking curved sword—not a sword, a sickle. He raised it, and brought it down hard. But Anna felt no pain.

The oak-hard man reached down, and his hand came up bloody. The dark little man nodded. What was his name? You didn't say it if you could avoid it. You said, "the Enchanter."

So he is here after all, she thought.

The Enchanter was on nobody's side. He came and went as he would. Some doubted he really was a man. Why was he here?

The stars went out all at once.

Then she was not scared anymore. The earth had taken even her fear.

"ANNA?"

Whose name is that?

"Anna?"

YOURS IF YOU WANT IT.

"She's not breathing! She's not breathing!"

DON'T YOU WANT TO GO BACK?

"Breathe! Please! Please! Anna, wake up! Gentle Sulis, give her back to me!"

She was nameless. That meant she could be anything: the wind rippling through the darkness, or a wave rising and falling with the sea. She could learn secrets. Something secret had been done here, beneath the surface of the world, something that had changed the shape of reality. If she stayed, she would know what it was. And she could put it back to rights.

But someone was screaming and she had to return, like a cork has to rise out of the water. The screams went on and on, terrifying her, until Anna finally realized that she was the one screaming.

"I'm sorry," said Anna, shivering. "I'm sorry." Ygraine scooped her up into her arms. She held Anna tight and crooned soft words in her ear, as if Anna were still a little girl. She stroked Anna's hair. Anna forced herself to breathe. In and out. In and out. In and out. Her stomach unclenched and she finally relaxed.

Anna tried to remember the dream, but she couldn't see it anymore. There was only a black swirl of confusion. It was all wrong. "It's all wrong, Mama."

"What?"

She reached for the dream. But the dream wasn't there anymore. All she could say was, "Where is my father?"

"He's outside the walls, sweetheart, leading our men against Uter."

"He's dead," Anna said. "They killed him."

"You had a bad dream." Her mother pulled her close, but Anna pushed her away. Ygraine stroked her cheek, trying to calm her.

"I saw him." Anna shuddered. "The Enchanter."

"Tomorrow your father will come home and everything will be all right."

Maybe it was a bad dream. A horrible dream. "Mama, will you seal the house against bad dreams?"

"Oh, darling. Aren't you too old for that?"

"Please, Mama?"

Her mother could do magic. Maybe she had just been pretending when the women had burned the wicker crow. But when her mother cast a circle in the sleeping chamber, the bad dreams really stopped.

Anna sat up on the bed. Her mother opened a small oaken chest. She took out a silver chalice and a scroll. Then a limestone head with three faces carved on it: a maiden, a woman heavy with child, and a withered old grandmother. Ygraine held up a spearhead made of black glass. It was chipped all along its edges and so smooth along its flat side that you could see your face in it, strangely distorted.

Her mother aimed the spearhead at the front door and scribed an imaginary line all along the base of the round walls of the house. The circle was cast. It would keep the spell from blowing away like smoke. She carved shapes in the air with the black glass blade at the four directions of the sun: the north where it slept, the east where it rose, the south where it peaked, and the west where it set.

Anna felt the room become taut, like a drum. There was a tension in the air like before a thunderstorm. Something flowed into the circle, spiralling inward. Her mother's face seemed to transform. She was becoming older, and somehow younger too. A young woman with old eyes.

Anna rocked back and forth, her arms tight around her knees. There was more power this time, more than her mother had ever summoned before, as if it was powered by the bad dream Anna couldn't remember anymore. The colours in the room were coming alive. By now her mother had to know something real was happening. She could see her mother's face flush red, see the bones beneath her skin. Her own heart raced as if she were running. Anna felt the power flowing into the house, but some of it was coming out of her mother too, and from Anna herself. It fed on them like fire fed on wood. But when the spell was unleashed, she would be safe; no bad dreams could reach her.

But there was a tumult outside. Shouting, cheering, in Latin and British. "The governor! The governor!"

Her mother stopped moving. Spells must not be halted halfway. Anna shuddered. Her mother shook her head, coming out of her daze. Someone shouted, "We sent them running!"

Harsh words rang out. "Where's my wife?" There was a strange, savage ring to the words.

Her mother took a step toward the door.

"But the circle!" Anna said.

"The spell is going to have to wait, my love. Your father's home."

"Ygraine!" bellowed her father's voice, nearer this time.

"You can't stop in the middle of the spell," Anna cried out.

But the door tore open, and a man stood there with a wild expression. It took her a moment to recognize her father's eyes and nose.

"Papa!" she said. "Don't come in. We were—" and she stopped herself. Her mother's spells were a secret between them.

"Don't come in?" he bellowed. "Don't come in?" He caught himself, and became gentler. "Isn't my own daughter pleased to see me?"

Then he stepped inside and broke the circle.

Anna gasped. Her mother swayed and Gorlois caught her in his arms. Anna couldn't breathe. She felt sick. Something had been ripped out of her. Her father lifted her mother up and kissed her. Ygraine seemed limp in his arms.

Anna heard loud voices outside. "Where?" "How?" "But where are the soldiers?"

The soldiers weren't back yet. She could hear Bretel saying, "They're making their way back."

Then Anna watched as Gorlois pulled away from her mother to look at her pale face. Ygraine's eyes were unfocused. She was still between the worlds. Gorlois picked her up and laid her gently back onto the bed.

Anna's mother turned toward her. Her lips formed the word go. Anna watched her mother's fingers flex, barely wrinkling the woolen blanket.

Anna struggled, forcing herself to move. She could do it if she argued with her body, if she insisted. First she fell onto the floor. Then she scuttled to the door. As she left the house, she caught a glimpse of Gorlois kissing her mother. It seemed unnatural.

Outside, the air was chill. The sky was dark. The moon had sunk into the sea, following the sun. Anna realized her cloak was still inside, but she didn't dare go back in to get it. She sat down on the ground, her arms around her knees, too weak to get up again.

Bretel was watching her. His eyes seemed even wiser and sadder than they always did. In the starlight, Jordan stood by his side, her father's foster son, the sea wind blowing tufts of his hair. Jordan asked, "Why are you crying?" But he didn't move to comfort her. Why didn't he? He was usually like a big brother to her.

"Why aren't you happy?" she tried to shoot back, but it came out as a whisper.

Bretel said nothing. He just watched her. She shivered, and she wasn't sure why.

Jordan said, "Ah, well. That would be…because we lost some good men." He didn't seem too sure of what he meant to say.

"Men are punished for the sins of their leaders," said Bretel quietly.

That was an odd thing to say. "What's a sin?" It was something the Christians talked about. But Bretel wasn't Christian.

"Now there's a question. Why don't you ask him something easy?" said Jordan. "Like what will happen to us after we're dead?" Jordan looked at Bretel, and shivered. "You probably know, don't you?"

Anna had no strength to stand. Why wasn't Jordan helping her up? This was all wrong. Jordan was never sarcastic. And Bretel was never mysterious.

And then she knew with profound nausea that the old man who looked like Bretel wasn't Bretel. And the young man who looked like Jordan wasn't Jordan.

Bretel looked deep into her eyes. He frowned. As if he knew she knew.

"Who are you, really?" Anna asked him.

"That's a ridiculous question, girl," Jordan answered. Far below, the sea boomed against the cliffs. Girl? Jordan never called her *girl*.

But the man who wasn't Bretel was still looking into her eyes. He was sad. "I'm sorry," he said. And he meant it. But it was a threat too.

Then Anna screamed, as high and piercing a scream as she could manage, clenching her fists as she sat there on the ground. But no one came. Not even Eithne, who was always there to rescue her.

A different cry ripped out of her parents' house. A rough groan, almost triumphant. She had never heard a sound like that before.

With horror, she remembered her dream. And she stared at the man with Bretel's face. "My father is dead," she said, and she knew it was true. "Who is with my mother?"

"Sleep," said the man with Bretel's face, looking deep into her eyes.

She did not want to sleep. She desperately did not want to sleep. She fought it. But his words insinuated themselves into her veins. "Sleep now," he said with sad eyes, his voice whispering like the wind.

Anna opened her mouth, but no sound came out. She was exhausted. If not for the broken spell, the spell that man had smashed when he came in, she could have fought back. But she was hollow, and the world was tilted.

"Sleep now," said the man with Bretel's face, almost mournfully. "And when you wake up in the morning, run. Run far away. And never come back." He reached out and brushed his fingers across her eyelids. His voice was soft like the earth, and she slept.

Chapter Four

THE SILENT PART

A dull grey light was seeping into the eating hall through the cracks in the wattle and daub walls. Anna had slept long and hard, without dreaming. She wondered why. Her father had come home. He had won a great victory. Hadn't he? Why didn't she feel joy and relief? There had been a secret. She'd learned a terrible secret. Now it was gone, the way dreams go. But it had been a secret, not a dream. Something was terribly wrong.

Anna wanted to run. To run far away. She couldn't say why. She forced herself to calm down.

She disentangled herself from Eithne's thick arms, Eithne who could sleep through a battle among the giants. Anna couldn't find her cloak anywhere. She stepped out of the great hall into the chill morning.

She shivered, and it wasn't just the cold, or the cold grey sky. The air was dank with fog and hearth smoke. It wasn't dawn yet. Roosters ruffled their wings and began to strut nervously around their hens, but they seemed unsure whether to crow yet or not.

Anna watched the lone guard on the wall pull his furs tightly around his neck. It was Dafydd. He was thirteen.

Where was her father? Where were the soldiers?

The world was not right. She needed to run. But where?

A tall wolfhound got to his feet, his ears up, sniffing. It was Dart, the dog all the other dogs looked up to. He sniffed again. The other dogs got up, also sniffing. They seemed uncomfortable.

She realized how terribly cold she was, cold and weak. She felt sick, empty. Had she been sick in the night?

She began to cry, and she could not for the life of her remember why.

THE dawn crept up without warmth. Anna drifted restlessly across the peninsula, listening in on conversations. People were confused. Why would the governor slink back like a thief in the night, alone? And then leave again? And where were the men? Some of the women talked about slaughtering lambs for a victory feast, but that hadn't felt right, so they hadn't done it.

Something was missing from the peninsula. What was it?

Anna watched the shepherd's boy guide his sheep in search of the last patches of grass; he was scared to take them out beyond the walls. They wandered too close to the cliff, and one of them stumbled over the edge, bleating all the way down. The boy cursed his dog for not stopping her. The brewer's wife began cursing at everyone suddenly for no reason. The potter's wife ruined a fancy cookpot she had almost finished, and burst into tears.

The peasant women went out to gather hay from the fields. It was still wet with the morning dew, but they wanted to see their men when the soldiers returned.

Anna didn't want to be inside the walls either. That much she was sure of. She went out with the women.

She looked at the forest. She could run there and hide. But then what?

Anna couldn't figure out why she was so scared.

She stared at the ground. There was a strange beetle in the meadow. She poked at it with a stick, trying to remember. It crawled onto the skeleton of a large bird, with black feathers scattered around it.

A crow.

The crows were gone.

That was what was missing.

Then someone shouted. Anna could see them half a mile away, galloping out of the east: three horsemen, riding in toward the wall. The sun had broken through the clouds; it glinted off their armour. Anna's heart leapt, and she shouted, and the women yelled, and the old men on the wall cheered.

But as the riders got closer, it became clear that something was wrong. There were three horses, but one rider was slumped in the saddle, his spear sagging, her father's raven flag flapping raggedly from it. And the other rider held the reins of a third horse. It had no rider. Something bounced awkwardly, roped to the saddle, something long and bony, brown like wet leather, stained with the dark red of clotted blood.

Something the size of a man.

Anna and the women ran to the gate and followed the horses inside the wall.

The riders were boys, still beardless. They looked weak, bone-weary, shamefaced. As they slid off their horses, two women threw themselves out of the crowd and embraced them, weeping. The other women brushed them aside in order to unknot the cords that held the bloody body to the horse.

Anna's father fell out of the cloak he was wrapped in. His face was pale. His eyes were open but blank.

Anna wanted to breathe, but she couldn't. She ran to him and held his face in her hands, hoping it wasn't true, that he wasn't dead, that it was someone else.

She wanted to scream. But she couldn't. She was silent. This was impossible. She had seen her father alive.

As the women fell to their knees, weeping, Anna stood quietly, staring at her father's pale blood-streaked body. The taller rider, a boy, long-shanked and spindly, pushed himself awkwardly loose from his mother. He started to speak, his voice hoarse, then stopped. His cheeks were flame red with shame. He took a cup of cold water someone offered him, downed it, and gathered his thoughts.

But the other one, the short one, pale with shame, spoke first.

"Uter abandoned his camp on top of the fairy fort," he said. Anna knew his name, Lovernios. Blood was seeping out of the cloth wrapped around Lovernios' upper arm. It flowed crimson over dark, crusted dry blood. "He made it look like he'd just left camp, like he couldn't wait to get out of Trigos. They left behind a dead man...oh God...and torches. Simon"—Lovernios jerked his head at the long-shanked boy—"was trying to see if Uter left behind anything worth taking."

Simon's mother shot him a look. Simon wouldn't look at her. She pulled away from him.

Lovernios went on. "It was an ambush, oh Hades..." He had to gather his strength to speak. "Gruffydd fell off his horse on top of me. I fell under him and I stayed there because I was afraid..." He stopped, choking on his own words. Anna felt only chill. Lovernios had played dead and had survived.

"And the other men?" asked an old man in the crowd.

"Nobody else lived."

The crowd was dead silent.

Simon found his voice. "I hid in the woods until they went." He wouldn't meet anyone's eyes.

The old women were cleaning the dirt and blood off Gorlois' face with the corners of their clothes. One of the oldest cradled his head in her lap. "I was his nurse," she was babbling softly. "Thirty years ago I was, until he was sent out in fosterage." Her hair was white, her hands crabbed. She was sobbing faintly. The other women didn't make a noise.

"The Enchanter was there," said Lovernios.

All the women quieted down. An old woman near Anna muttered, "Then there never was any hope."

"He said to conse...consecr...to give the field to the Queen of Shadows. So Uter's men left all our weapons and all our men lying there."

"Some of the Picts wanted to take their heads," said Simon. "Uter was going to let them. But the Enchanter said no."

Where was Anna's mother? How could she have slept through the shouting? Anna looked at Eithne. Eithne stared back, pale, frightened, her jowls rippling. She was scared to bring the news to Ygraine. The other women were lost in their own grief, or making themselves busy, or running to their children to tell them.

Anna ran to the house. The embers of the fire were still warm. Her mother was still sleeping peacefully, a soft smile on her face. Her pale skin was flushed. Of course. Her husband had come home safe in the night, victorious. Anna went over and sat on the bed. The world was upside down. Grown-ups give children bad news. Then you cry in their arms.

Anna leaned over and touched her mother on the cheek. Her mother stretched and looked at her. Then her face clouded. "What is it?" asked her mother. "What's wrong?"

But Anna couldn't say, she couldn't get the words out. Then her mother heard the wails and keening of the women outside, and she was out of bed, grabbing her cloak around her, heading for the door.

"Don't!" Anna screamed, but her mother was out the door running, already moaning as she ran toward the crowd.

And then her mother saw, and started screaming, her hands tearing at her clothes, ripping at her breasts, leaving bloody scratches across her cheeks, until the women pulled her back and held her hands tight, and Ygraine fell to the ground sobbing.

Anna could make out just a few words, "...but he swore..." over and over. The women held Ygraine and comforted her.

Then suddenly her mother stood up. Fiercely, she looked over Lovernios and Simon. "Only you two have come back?" she demanded. Simon looked down, unable to meet her eyes. She asked again, "He didn't take any prisoners?"

The boys shook their heads.

"No one had time to surrender, my lady," offered Simon, who had cowered and watched.

"It was too quick," said Lovernios, who had fallen and hidden.

Her mother was as pale as ever, but there was a fragile power in her eyes. "How far away are they?"

"After the ambush, they made camp, right in the fairy fort. They all got drunk. The moon was up, so we could see everything. The crows. There were more than I ever saw. You should've seen how fat they were. They could barely fly."

So that's where the crows had gone. To feast on the battle dead.

"They're still hung over," said long-boned Lovernios, his voice weak with shame. "That's how we found each other and stole the horses."

Ygraine closed her eyes. "He's giving me time to get used to the idea," she said. "It's his idea of gallantry."

Anna stared at her.

Suddenly her mother looked at Simon and Lovernios. They were shivering. "You haven't eaten, have you?"

"Not since the middle of last night, no, milady," said Simon. "The moon was just up, and she's a half moon waning, so that's the middle of the—"

"The moon was just up?" Her mother looked confused. "It had just risen?"

"She was just about risen when we got to the fairy fort—tops of the trees, but no light in the forest itself. He couldn't've timed it better."

"Liar!" Eithne cried, outraged. "The governor came here an hour after the moon came up. He came with Bretel and Jordan. He said he'd won a great victory, and he didn't leave till dawn."

Ygraine looked pale as death. She moved her lips. No sound came out. She tried again. "I'm sorry to keep asking. The ambush was just after the moon rose. Not just at dawn?"

"It was the middle of the night," said Lovernios softly.

Ygraine nodded. "And when did my lord the governor fall?"

"Almost right away. Somebody got him with a spear in the back. Seemed like it took him forever to fall."

Eithne snapped, "Then who came to milady in the middle of the—," but the look on Ygraine's face silenced her.

And Anna understood. It came rushing back, like water breaking through a dam. The man with her father's face, whom she barely recognized. The man with Bretel's face who wasn't Bretel. He had made Anna sleep. She knew, somehow, that he was the man with the sickle in her dream. He was the Enchanter. So the man with her father's face must have been Uter.

Everyone around Anna was sobbing. But the silent part of Anna could only put things together, one by one. The Enchanter had changed Uter's face so that Uter could sleep with her mother. He had used her father's blood to give Uter her father's face.

There was a long silence as the other women absorbed what had happened. Some whispered to each other, but most kept quiet.

Finally Anna's mother said quietly, almost formally, "When Uter is well rested, he'll come. Make everything ready." Her words felt distant to Anna. "If we meet him with the gentleness due a conqueror, maybe he'll show us all mercy." The women stood there, still in shock. "Go. Make ready."

The women ran off.

And Anna knew. She took her mother's hand.

"Oh, Anna," her mother said, trying to comfort her.

But she didn't want comfort. "We need to go, Mama," she told her mother. "We can't stay here."

And her mother stared at her. "You're right. You can't be here."

Anna stared back at her. *She* couldn't be here? Wasn't her mother coming? But Ygraine turned to Eithne. "Get Anna's things together." To Simon and Lovernios she said, "Would you like to do something brave?" Anna could almost see Simon's relief. "There's a skiff in the cove under the Neck. Eithne will tell you how to rig and steer it. Where's the Greek?" She called to Eithne. "Find the Greek. Tell him to pack." She turned back to Simon. "Eithne knows how to pilot a boat, and she speaks Irish."

Then she explained to Anna, "The Queen of the Déisi is kin to us."

"When do we come back?" asked Simon. He glanced at his mother. She was staring at the ground, biting her lip, making strange little noises Anna couldn't make out.

"Stay in Ireland," said Ygraine. "Protect my daughter."

"How long?"

"Until Uter's dead."

"You're sending me away?" asked Anna. "But—"

"If I go with you, he'll follow. I'm sorry."

Leave her mother? How could she?

"What does a tomcat do to a litter of kittens?" her mother blurted out.

The poor barn cat. She had had kittens by the white cat. She had licked them all clean, and nursed them. But a wildcat tom had come to Din Tagell that night, clawing his way up the cliff's edge. He was twice as big as the mother cat, and he had killed every one of her kittens.

That's why Anna had to run. She had to run far away.

Lovernios tried to stand up, but couldn't. "I don't think…" he said, but he was having trouble speaking. "I can't…" Anna and her mother looked at him sharply. "I can't," he said.

Lovernios rolled up his tunic. There was a mass of bloody bandages underneath. "It doesn't hurt much, but…" He pulled the bandages away. They were dripping blood.

Everyone gasped. It was a gut wound. You could live all day with a gut wound, but there was no surviving it. Everyone stared.

Lovernios' mother screamed and embraced her boy. She began to cry.

"I'm sorry, mama. I'm sorry," he said.

But she was weeping, holding him, all her shame washed away. "You came back," she said. "At least you came back."

YGRAIÞE slid the pewter brooch pin through the black cloak, and smoothed Anna's hair down, although the sea breeze blew it back up immediately. She pinned a gold brooch inside the cloak. "Don't show that to strangers."

Anna wanted to cry. But she couldn't. Her mother was on the verge of breaking, and Anna's tears would break her.

Her mother was so beautiful.

Great beauty should have great power, Anna thought, *not grief. If I grow up beautiful, they'll be scared of me like they're scared of Uter, and they'll never take what's mine.*

It was a strange thought, and it came from a place deep within her. And she was so very angry. Her anger was bigger than the man with Bretel's face. It was bigger than Uter. It was as big as Bellona, their goddess, with a scourge in her hand, the Kindly Ones following at her heels, leashed in like hounds. Maybe Bellona was useless as a protector. Maybe she was only good as an avenger. But that was enough.

Anna felt a lightless, volcanic heat deep within her. Perhaps it was Bellona herself. Perhaps Bellona was part of her, Anna thought. Her silent part. Her father had said once, "When you don't have any firewood, vengeance will get you through a cold night." It was a strange thing for him to say. But maybe it was true.

"Uter knows you," her mother was saying. "And you have your father's face. Don't ever tell anyone who you are. Do you understand? He'd pay money to bring you here. And he would kill you."

"Who will take care of me?" Anna asked. For some reason she didn't feel scared, only numb.

"Ciarnat. She's queen of the Déisi. They're a great clan in Munster. It's in the south of Ireland. Your uncle Owain married her sister. She's kin. They take kinship very seriously in Ireland."

Ygraine tried to smile for Anna's sake. But it only made her cry. Anna waited until her mother stopped.

"You'll have to forget your name. Don't tell anyone except Ciarnat that you're Anna of Din Tagell, daughter of Ygraine, daughter of Ceinwen of Brittany."

"I won't be me anymore?"

"You need a new name."

A new name? Anna looked around at Din Tagell. She was losing her home, and her mother; she had already lost her father. But even her name?

"You'll be reborn from the sea," said her mother. "When your boat lands in Ireland, you won't be Anna anymore." And she whispered a new name in Anna's ear. "It means 'born from the sea,'" she said.

AS women loaded the skiff with supplies, Anna's mother kept saying odd things like, "When you meet the queen, you may kiss her, but not her ring. We're allies and cousins, but she's not your lord." Then she would fall silent, fussing with Anna's cloak, her hands flying, until she thought of another odd bit of advice to give Anna.

Anna wrapped the cloak tightly around herself. It was her father's good cloak, the one he had left at home. A foot's span had been cut from the bottom so it would fit, and another foot of it sewn up, so she would never outgrow it. She could sleep inside it if she had to.

Her mother was trying to be reassuring, but she was saying things that Anna could barely absorb. "Remember, they're barbarians, the Irish. They don't know how to read or write, and they're always at each other's throats, and no one loves his neighbour. But they have honour."

Anna guessed her mother was trying to make her feel better about being sent away. But she wanted to go. This place was tainted. Her mother belonged to a murderer, or would soon, and she wasn't even running from him. Why wasn't her mother getting on the boat with her? The thought only made her sick, when she needed to be strong. She pushed it away.

"There's a sweet breeze," her mother said. "You'll make good time." Then she hugged Anna tightly for a long time. Anna breathed in her mother's scent. "Don't forget me," Ygraine said. "Don't forget this place."

"I'm going to take it back," Anna said. "I'm going to come back and rescue you. As soon as I can."

"Don't even try. Please." Her mother was choking up. "Make a good life there. Be happy. You don't owe Din Tagell anything."

"I'm going to come back and kill Uter. And rescue you!"

Eithne took her hand and led her down the rock-hewn stairway, down a hundred steps. When Anna looked back, her mother had gone.

Ϯℏℇ skiff was no more than twenty feet long, made of oak, with a square sail. The Greek and Simon had stowed food in it: salt pork, pots of ale, hunting spears, a bow and arrows.

Eithne tied the last knot of the rigging. A smile covered her face. It looked strange on her. Eithne had always been grumpy, steadfast but never happy. Now she was beaming.

Of course she was. Eithne was returning to her island after twenty years of slavery in a land where no one spoke her language.

The Greek and Simon pushed the skiff into the surf. It nearly overturned, but they righted it and climbed in, soaking wet, as the sail billowed. They paddled furiously until they were out of the breakers. The water was choppy and the skiff felt terribly small, but Eithne didn't seem frightened.

Anna looked out at the vast expanse of the sea. Then she turned back and watched the headland disappear into the distance. The rays of the late morning sun washed the peninsula in a rich golden light. She could barely make out the houses. Smoke rose from their high thatched roofs. She imagined Anna of Din Tagell floating up in that smoke. She watched her old self cling to the headland for a moment until the sea breeze picked up again, swept that girl ashore, her old name and shadow scattering across Britannia.

"I'm going to kill him," she said, and she was surprised at the growl that came out of her throat. She stood up in the boat and shouted back at the cliffs. "I will return and kill Uter Pendragon! I swear to Bellona Morigenos!"

Now, as the boat pulled away from Din Tagell and everything she had ever known, she mouthed her new name, the one that meant "sea-born" in British. It was a darker, redder name than the name the wind had taken. It contained vengeance and power. It wouldn't be so easily silenced. The sea breeze caught the name she spoke and hurled it, too, toward Britannia.

"Morgan," she said, and then she shouted it: "Morgan!"

Chapter Five

A SEA CHANGE

They sailed north across the wide Severn Sea. The night sky was clear. Eithne showed Simon how to point the skiff toward the North Star when the boat yawed and rolled as the waves slapped its side. The Greek moaned. He hadn't spoken to anyone since he'd got on the boat. Morgan stared straight ahead. She didn't want to eat, because her stomach was matching every movement of the boat, but Eithne insisted that she eat something and there was no arguing with Eithne once she got an idea in her head.

Her father would have wanted her to eat. She took a piece of bread. But it was barely down her throat before it came back up again. She was too sick even to cry.

Eithne laughed. She had been different from the moment they'd got on the boat. She could not stop smiling, and looking west toward Ireland. "You'll get over it," she said, in Irish. She had always talked in Irish to Morgan when they were alone, ever since Morgan was a baby, but now she refused to speak British at all.

Morgan felt helplessly sick. It had started only a few hundred yards from the land, and it hadn't stopped since, even though her stomach was long empty. She hated that her father had been killed and all she could think about was throwing up. She summoned up his face in her mind. She clamped down on her stomach, the way you clamp down on a cut to stop it from bleeding. But she kept wanting to throw up.

WHEN Morgan woke they were sailing through a vast flock of pelicans, thousands of them floating on the water, hundreds more reeling above their heads. One of them dove at the water and came up with a fish. The pelican threw its head back and the fish disappeared into its gullet. All around were blue-black dolphins too, leaping out of the water, their white bellies flashing in the sun. It was glorious.

Then she remembered why she was in the boat. She started to cry. It was dreadful to feel this way. There was nothing she could do to save her father now, nor even her mother. She had never felt this helpless.

It wasn't fair. Her father would never have let her go out to sea in a small boat, but now that she was here she was miserable, though it should have been an adventure. She saw a blast of fog a hundred feet away: a whale. Its vast head rose out of the water, then splashed back down. Then its tail flopped out of the water, and then that, too, sank out of sight. It was marvelous, something out of a fairy tale.

It was all ashes in her mouth.

Morgan realized that she was hungry. She decided to risk eating a piece of bread, and to her surprise she was not sick anymore. The rolling and yawing of the boat seemed the most natural thing in the world. If she could get used to that, maybe she could get used to the catastrophe. Maybe.

She decided to stop crying, and to her surprise, she found that she could.

Ϯᕼᗩ Ϲ afternoon the mountains of Isca rose from the ocean, higher and higher, until they could make out a river delta. There they pulled the boat up on the land and slept.

In the morning they followed a small fleet of fishing boats out into the Irish Sea. There was a mild breeze out of the west, which meant they had to sail back and forth, a technique that Eithne called *tacking*. Slowly they tacked away from Britannia until they could see nothing but ocean. They sailed all day.

Eithne kept looking at the horizon to the west. She would cry out that she saw land, and everyone would look, but it would turn out to be a cloud, or a whale, or seagulls. Never land.

The sky began to darken to the north. The wind began to pick up. The seabirds flew off. The waves became choppy. The skiff leaned hard into the rising wind, and Eithne told Simon to bring in the sail. It began to drizzle, and then rain—cold rain that stung. Morgan rolled herself up in her cape, but it grew wet, heavy and cold. They were swallowed up in a grey curtain of rain.

The sky darkened. The waves disappeared into blackness a hundred yards away. Then fifty. Then the air and sea closed in so that Morgan could barely make out the others' frightened faces.

Then they heard it, a low booming noise ahead of them. It got closer and closer. The sky was black now, their vague dim hands and faces the only thing Morgan could see. The booming got louder and louder, but they couldn't see a thing. Then Eithne screamed, "It's surf!" It was the sea battering the land ahead of them, smashing against the coast. Eithne screamed something else no one could hear, and then she sank the steering oar deep into the water and forced the boat hard over to the left. For a moment the skiff ran before the north wind.

"We'll run off course!" screamed the Greek.

"Those are cliffs!" Eithne screamed back. The waves were easier to handle now, and the boat no longer rolled; instead it chased the waves. "Trim that sail!" she screamed at Simon.

The wind shifted with a freak gust, and the steering oar ripped out of Eithne's hands. Morgan jumped to grab it, but the Greek yanked her back into the boat as the ship heeled over. The oar was gone in the blackness. The boat began to slide sideways through the waves, the wind pushing them, rudderless, toward the invisible coast.

Simon began to scream prayers Morgan couldn't understand, something about trespasses and bread. The Greek leaped on him, cursing him for disrespecting Neptune, as the boat skidded across the water toward the invisible cliffs. The skiff would be crushed against the rocks, and they would all drown.

Morgan was suddenly angry. The sea had no right to her. She belonged to Din Tagell, to the land; if she was going to die, it would be there.

She grabbed the side of the boat and howled into the wind. She screamed that the sea couldn't have her. She couldn't even hear her own voice.

Then she saw them: flashes of white shooting out of the waves and splashing back in. Morgan grabbed Eithne's hand. A dozen dolphins were leaping out of the water in what seemed to be an endless line. But they were heading in a different direction than the boat.

Were they showing the way?

She had to turn the boat. Morgan grabbed a spear and stuck its butt end into the water. It didn't do much, but the Greek saw what she was doing, broke off a plank from a seat and jammed it in the water too. Slowly the boat began to slew around in the direction the dolphins were going.

The booming got louder and louder. Soon Anna could see an even blacker darkness looming over them, higher and higher. Cliffs. She was sure the boat would crash against them any second now.

A great wave surged up under them, and she felt the skiff rise into the air. She was sure the boat would keel over, but they slid down the wave's face, and the foam broke behind them and pushed them forward.

Then they were past the surf. There was blackness all around them, but the booming was behind them. The boat sailed onward until it scraped to a stop, knocking them all to their knees. Gasping for breath, Eithne untied the rope that had been holding the sail up, and the sail crumpled onto the boat.

The Greek, Eithne, Simon and Morgan pulled the boat up the beach until they could feel grass under their feet. They rolled it over and crawled underneath it, exhausted. Morgan listened to the rain drum on the wooden skin of the boat for only few seconds before she fell fast asleep.

Chapter Six

EXILE

They sailed along the coast for days, watching the cliffs rise and subside like waves. The cliffs were topped with forests, but they saw nothing that looked like a settlement. There were no other boats anywhere.

They sailed past a beach where fishermen were standing in the surf, pulling in nets. Nearby, their women were gutting fish and spreading them out to dry on rocks.

"Us Irish don't much like to fish from boats," Eithne said with a snort.

They sailed toward the fishermen, but the fishermen, scared, ran up onto the rocks. Eithne shouted to them, asking where they could find the Déisi lands, but the fishermen seemed to have no idea, shrugging and pointing in various directions.

While they sailed, Eithne told old Irish stories. When Morgan had been a little girl, Eithne's tales had seemed like wonderful fairy stories, full of gods and heroes, tricks and broken taboos and terrible magic spells, made more wonderful by being in Irish, a language only she and Morgan knew. Now they seemed alarming, full of violence and savagery. Eithne seemed taller and stronger than when she had been a slave. She even seemed a little scary.

FINALLY, they came to the mouth of a river that poured out between two hills. There were the skeletons of two boats rotting on the sand. Eithne smiled at the moss-green frames. "I know this place. Neighbours of ours live here. If we go up this river a bit, I can get us some directions." She pushed the new steering oar they had made to replace the one they'd lost, and the skiff headed into the river.

"How far?" asked Morgan.

"Oh, right around that bend, so it's hidden from the coast." Eithne seemed thrilled, watching the greenery go by with an intense look. Morgan watched it too. It seemed so empty compared to Britain. But if the Irish were sea raiders, then maybe no one lived in sight of the coast.

And then Morgan remembered: the Irish were always at each other's throats. They didn't help with directions. "Aren't you afraid of your neighbours?" she asked Eithne.

The Greek was listening now.

"What do you know about my neighbours?" asked Eithne. "We were great friends with our neighbours!"

But when Morgan looked into her eyes, Eithne averted her face. Morgan could tell she was lying.

The Greek whipped the shortsword out of his belt. "It's your village, isn't it?" He was red-faced and angry now.

"What are you talking about?"

"You're leading us right to your village, and when we get there, we'll find ourselves all slaves, with you for our mistress. Won't we?"

"I'd never do that to you!" Eithne said.

Simon entered the fray. "In that case, you won't mind if we head in another direction." Then he turned the steering oar and the boat sailed away from the river mouth.

Eithne slumped down. "I just wanted to go home."

A shiver ran down Morgan's spine. She could never trust Eithne again. No one spoke.

At evening they rounded a headland. A small boat like theirs appeared on the horizon, but it turned tail and ran before they could get close. "They think we're pirates or raiders," said Eithne, still bitter.

"Let's follow them," said Morgan.

"They'll go and get their friends."

"I'm not afraid," said Morgan.

"You should be," said Eithne. "You were right. Here, your neighbour is not your friend. Only the enemy of your neighbour is your friend."

THEY were sailing westward now, the sun bright against the coastline at noon. Finally they came across two small boats a few hundred yards out from the shore. The fishermen, for once, didn't try to flee.

As they approached, Morgan saw that twin brothers were working a net between the two boats, rowing hard and stretching the net into a big circle. They were hauling in fish, but whenever they got a crab they threw it back into the water. They ignored the strangers completely until Morgan threw them a gold coin. The coin glittered in the air. It missed the boat and plunged into the water, but one of the brothers dived after it. After what seemed like an eternity to Morgan, he came up holding the coin between his thumb and forefinger.

"What's this?" he said.

"It's a Roman sesterce," said Morgan.

Eithne turned to Morgan. "There's no money in Ireland," she said. "It's gold," she told the fisherman.

The fisherman climbed back into his boat. He seemed worried. "Are you a queen of the fairy folk, that hands out gold to poor fishermen? Will you steal my children in the night?"

Morgan laughed and shook her head. "Take us to the land of the Déisi. Then I'll give your brother one as well."

The brothers led them into the mouth of a river they called the Black Water, though it was perfectly clear. One brother pointed up the river. "The Déisi are two days' journey inland," he said. "When the river bends to the west, leave it and go east." But they refused to go up the river, claiming it was against their religion. Morgan reluctantly tossed a coin to the other brother, and the two fishermen sailed away as fast as they could. Eithne mournfully watched them go.

"My mother said you'd be free," said Morgan. "I swear once we get to the Déisi lands, you will be."

"You probably mean it," said Eithne quietly. "But it may not be up to you."

They sailed up the river until it took a turn to the west. Then they pulled the boat ashore and covered it with branches.

The countryside was empty. There was nothing like a road, only a path; the grass wasn't even worn through. "Why didn't the Romans ever conquer Ireland?" grumbled the Greek. "I'll tell you why. Nothing to conquer." They walked a whole day and passed only a merchant travelling on a cart with four servants, all heavily armed. Morgan wondered what sort of a wilderness her mother had exiled her to, all woods and green meadows. This must be a terrible place, if there were no people to farm the meadows. They must kill each other constantly.

THE next morning Eithne was gone. No one was surprised. There was no point in trying to track her down. Morgan hoped she would reach the boat safely.

The three of them kept heading east on the path of worn grass. About noon Morgan surprised a boy hiding in a thicket. He was about her age. He had a knife and a bundle of thin branches. "Don't be scared," she said, trying out her Irish.

"Are you People of the Goddess Danu?" asked the boy.

We must look strange, Morgan thought.

"We came from Britain to visit our ally, queen Ciarnat," she said. It was the one thing she could say with perfect confidence in Irish.

"Oh!" said the boy, his jaw dropping. "She rules there. In her fortress." He waved his hand in the direction the path was heading. "It's huge and grand, my lady," he said. "Full of fierce warriors."

"Good," said Morgan.

"You must be fine folk," he said, looking at their cloaks and sandals, and eyeing the sword the Greek had on his belt. "You'll come to Inishannon in a few hours. There's nothing like it in all Ireland."

THE "grand fortress" of Inishannon turned out to be a settlement of two dozen round thatched houses hiding behind a fence of eight-foot sharpened stakes, the fence sitting on a four-foot earth wall. The entire fortress was not more than three hundred feet in diameter, with no outlying farmsteads. It must not be safe to live outside the fence.

Morgan tried to look at the place with her father's eye. A serious attacker could set the fence on fire. There was no wall walk from which you could hurl spears down at your enemies. There weren't even any towers.

The Greek looked at Morgan mournfully from under his bushy eyebrows. He wasn't impressed either.

TⱧЄ gates of the great stronghold were open and the three of them walked inside. Boys ran hollering to a large house at the far end of the enclosure.

Ciarnat came out in grand style. She was a short pudgy woman in her late twenties, wearing a blue silk tunic, a yellow wool cloak and a gleaming neck-ring made of three cords of gold braided together, each cord as thick as a finger. When she stood in front of Morgan, Morgan could see small creatures baring their teeth at each end of the neck-ring. They might have been dogs or dragons. Ciarnat wore gold thumb-rings, golden bracelets in the shapes of coiled snakes and silver rings with precious stones.

Morgan whispered in her ear a speech she had practiced with Eithne: "I am the daughter of Ygraine, wife of Gorlois, governor of Din Tagell, and sister to Owain, husband of your sister."

"Why are you whispering?" whispered Ciarnat, almost as loud as talking.

"Can I tell you inside?" asked Morgan.

"Ooooh, I like secrets," said Ciarnat, grinning. Morgan liked her already.

CiⱯRⱧⱯT took Morgan inside her house. She made Simon and the Greek wait outside even though Morgan explained that they were not her slaves. Ciarnat was loud and boisterous. "The daughter of Gorlois of Trigos! My sister married your mother's brother! What does that make us? Cousins? Too complicated. Call me Auntie," she hooted. "You must be hungry." She went to the door. "Wine!" she shouted to no one in particular. "Meat!"

In a minute an old man came in bearing a pitcher of watered-down wine which made Morgan's head spin. Ciarnat began boasting about her hundreds of cattle, and her chariots, and how fat her pigs were, and how brave her warriors. Morgan had no idea why she was boasting to an eleven-year-old girl who was throwing herself on her mercy, but maybe Ciarnat didn't get much chance to boast to strangers. Ciarnat wound up her recital by crying out, "I am richer than the gods!" That made Morgan shudder. The gods punished pride. But then she thought of the Roman baths at Aquae Sulis, and the rows of three-storey stone buildings, and the great Colosseum there that seated ten times as many people as Ciarnat ruled, and she decided that any god would laugh his head off before he could possibly be offended by her ridiculous boasting.

Morgan told Ciarnat of the disaster at Din Tagell. Ciarnat made her tell it over and over until she had all the details. Each time, she looked sad and angry at the right places. At the end, she swore she would raise Morgan as her foster daughter. That way no one would have to ask what Morgan was doing at Inishannon.

"How many warriors do you have?" asked Morgan.

"Five hundred of the best fighters in Ireland!" said Ciarnat fiercely.

Morgan tried to think how many men it would take to force Uter out of Din Tagell. Once all his allies went home, how many men would he have there? She frowned.

"Not enough?" asked Ciarnat, grinning.

"Uter has two thousand, I think."

At that Ciarnat looked worried for a moment. "You don't think he'll come here after you? We're two days in from the coast!"

"No! No, of course not. Why would he come here? I was just hoping…" Morgan stopped to think. What about boats? How would you even sail five hundred men to Britannia? That would take a hundred small boats. You could do it with five merchant ships, but where would you get those in Ireland?

"Oh, wait. You weren't thinking…" Ciarnat burst into laughter. "Oh, I see."

Then Ciarnat's laughter dropped, and her face took on an immense sympathy. Morgan realized her lip was quivering and she was fighting to hold in tears. Ciarnat said, "I, ah…yes. When I become…if the Déisi should conquer all of the south of Ireland… if we become a great and powerful people…then I'll lead them to Din Tagell and avenge you. I will. But look around you. I have brave warriors. You have disciplined soldiers. I have heard stories of the Romans. You want to know a proverb of ours?"

Unhappily, Morgan nodded.

"'Me against my brother. My brother and me against my cousin. My family against my clan. My clan against all Ireland.' That's us Irish."

An old man came in with a roasted suckling pig on a platter, which Ciarnat hacked up with her knife and ate most of. Soon they moved to the eating hall for another feast. Warriors boasted about what they had done on a cattle raid, and what they would do in the next raid. The bard told stories of heroic day-long combats between great warriors, full of feats of arms and witty repartee. Everyone drank buckets of ale, except Ciarnat, who treated herself to wine. Eventually they all fell asleep.

The next day was the same, and the next, and the next. Morgan felt out of place. There was nothing for her to do. No one had ever even seen a book, and when the Greek picked up Morgan's lessons in writing again, Ciarnat put an immediate stop to them. Writing was an invention of the dread Christians about whom she had heard horrible stories.

That left Morgan with nothing to do. She wasn't interested in learning to weave and knit like the other girls, but that made them hate her, so they wouldn't play with her. She was bored.

Gráinne, a tall blonde girl, gathered a basket full of meadow flowers. As a prank, Morgan fed them to Ciarnat's chariot ponies. Ciarnat laughed, but Gráinne and three other warriors' daughters got Morgan alone behind the barn and tore her hair and ripped and muddied her dress, and Ciarnat laughed at that too.

After that, Morgan didn't have much to do with Gráinne and the other girls. She tried to get the boys to play her favourite game, which always involved a fort, an invader named Uter and a well-organized sortie that destroyed the attacker. Morgan loved her game because she could really throw herself at the boys playing Uter. But after she gave them a few black eyes, they refused to play anymore.

They called her "the stranger," and they wondered out loud if she, with her too-wide mouth and her too-long nose, was really born of human parents, or if she was really one of the Fay, the People of the Goddess Danu, from whom the Irish had taken their island.

After that, Morgan was almost entirely alone except for the Greek. Simon was training as a warrior, and teaching the older boys Roman fighting tricks. When she tried to speak to him in Latin, Simon answered in Irish.

Then she got the idea to talk to Ciarnat's warriors. They were always interested in stories, and she knew how real battles went, ones with soldiers, and she told them stories her father had told when he was talking with Jordan or Bretel.

But she did not tell them about the ambush in the trees, though that was the only battle she had ever seen with her own eyes, because she would not have been able to stop from crying. She did not tell them that her father had fled with all his army from Uter so he would not have to fight him, because they would have considered him a coward. She did not tell them that she had sworn to avenge him, because they would have laughed.

There was one warrior, Eochaid, handsome and young, who seemed to like her. She told him about Britain, and how wealthy people were there, and how much braver Irish warriors were than British ones, and how easy it was to sail from Ireland to Britain if you had good weather, because the wind was always blowing out of the west.

"You want me to invade Britain for you, don't you?" he laughed.

She nodded.

"I'll need about a thousand more of me, even to fight a little battle."

"Don't the Irish raid Britannia all the time?" she asked.

"We don't attack fortresses."

"My nurse...her people attacked Din Tagell."

"Oh, they did, did they? And what happened?"

Well, Morgan's father had killed half of the raiders, sailed to their home village and burned it to the ground, and taken their women as slaves.

"When will you have a thousand men?" she asked.

"When I'm a *very* great king," he said, still laughing.

"When I grow up, I'll be your wife, and I will make you a very great king."

"You're different," he said, with a smile that made her like him very much. And so, for a little while, she had a friend.

But when night fell and Anna was in bed, she was alone. She had no home. She couldn't stop thinking about Uter sleeping in her mother's bed. She imagined returning to Britain at the head of an army, to take revenge on Uter and reclaim her home. But she was in a land where an acclaimed chief ruled over a few dozen huts, a land whose warriors spent their time boasting instead of marching.

She thought about the Enchanter. She thought of how he had made her eyes lie to her. *That* was real power. But how could she get that kind of power?

Chapter 7

THE CATTLE RAID OF INNISHANNON

Soon it was summer, and Morgan turned twelve. The Irish fought battles every summer. There was nothing they liked better. From what Morgan could make out, their idea of a happy afterlife was nothing but fighting. While they were still alive, summer was the only time they could do it. After Beltane in the spring, there was planting, and between Lugos' day, six weeks after midsummer, and Samain in late fall, there was harvesting, and in winter it was too miserably soggy and cold to go wandering around the countryside. Also, it was too difficult to torch your enemy's roofs. Straw wouldn't burn in the rain.

So when the weather was clear and fine, and the roads dry, the Éoganachta sent a challenge to Ciarnat, and she accepted it. Everyone was excited. It was like the days before a festival.

THE two armies spread out on a field not far from Ciarnat's stronghold that, thoughtfully, had been left unplanted. The charioteers drew up their chariots in front of the men on foot.

There was a low hill where Ciarnat had her slaves set up her folding chair and the open pavilion that kept the sun off her. Her poet and her druid settled down on the grass to watch with her, as if they were watching chariot races.

Morgan noticed suddenly that the trees all around the field were dotted with crows, thousands of them, like pointy black fruit dotting the branches. Fat crows and even bigger ravens were spiralling down from the air, more of them landing in the trees every minute. Somehow they knew they would be feasting soon.

"Will we win?" Morgan asked.

"What do you think?" Eochaid grinned fearsomely.

She looked at the enemy, lined up in ragged rows just like the Déisi. It was hard to tell which side had more warriors.

"If the Morrígan fights on our side, we'll win. Otherwise we lose." The Déisi worshipped Bellona Morigenos too, but they called her the Morrígan, or War Crow, or just Crow. Morgan remembered the great wicker crow the midwives had burned for Morigenos. Her father had lost anyway. But her mother hadn't completed the ritual; she hadn't let the goddess in.

Why hadn't she? Didn't it matter enough to her?

"Either way, we'll be covered with glory," Eochaid said.

"Is that the same as being covered with blood?" Morgan asked.

Eochaid chuckled. "Usually."

"Why didn't we ambush them on the road?"

"Where's the glory in that? It'd look like we were scared of losing."

"But then they'd be dead, and we'd win," she said, frustrated.

Eochaid looked confused. He smoothed out some creases in his tunic and cloak. "You don't think I'm afraid of dying in battle, do you?"

"It isn't better to lose, is it?"

"Well, no, but no one writes poems about you if you ambush your enemy. They only make up poems about face-to-face fights."

Morgan frowned. Who cared about poems? If you were dead, you couldn't hear the poems.

Once the armies had lined up on the field, they turned their backs to each other. Morgan was stunned. They spent a good hour on their hair, shaping it into the most fantastic styles, using rancid butter to hold it in place. They didn't seem to be putting on any armour. They had on their best clothes, the most beautiful multicoloured cloaks and tunics, with golden brooches and fine pendants. All they had for protection were their bronze shields.

When they'd done their hair, Ciarnat's chief poet led the warriors in great blood-curdling cheers, and told them how brave their ancestors were, and how they would surely defeat the Eóganachta, and how no warrior truly lives if no one tells stories about him. As far as Morgan could tell from the low hilltop, the other side's bards were leading their warriors in pretty much the same cheers.

Then Ciarnat's chief druid spoke. He told the warriors about the Morrígan, how She would select the best warriors who died that day by eating them on the battlefield, and they would live on in a glorious afterlife of continual feasting and fighting. The warriors cheered.

Morgan thought of her father, how he had led men into battle with just, "Let's go." He'd hated war, hadn't he? But he had marched to join all of Britannia against the Saxons.

But then he had fled, and Uter had brought war against him. And Uter had brought the Enchanter.

Morgan shivered. She said a little prayer to Bellona Morigenos, in case she could hear.

Let Ciarnat be victorious. Let her defeat and occupy Glennamain. Let her become an empress with thousands of warriors. Let her have a hunger for conquest so great it takes her across the Irish Sea to fight Uter.

The armies turned to face each other. Each army was a glorious, multi-coloured mob, the warriors' capes and trousers billowing in the breeze. They shouted, and banged their shields and spears together, and shouted some more.

Then someone flashed a sword downward, and with a wild high-pitched scream, the two mobs hurled themselves at each other. Javelins flew up from both lines, arced through the air and plunged into the other line. Some men fell, transfixed, but the two mobs rushed forward. The opposing lines smashed into each other, and for a brief moment she could see two distinct sides fighting.

Then the lines dissolved, and all she could see was a crowd of men dressed in their finest clothes hacking at each other.

Who was winning? Ciarnat seemed unworried, drinking wine by the cupful. "Fine day for a battle, isn't it?" Ciarnat said. "Light breeze. Not too cold, not too hot."

Morgan nodded, but she only had eyes for the men falling here and there on the green grass only a hundred and fifty yards away. The green grass was stained with blood now. She could hear dreadful screams that were sometimes cut horribly short. She lost track of time. It felt like the fighting had gone on for hours. But then she realized the sun had not moved; shadows were still straight down. There was an intensity to the very moment, as if a hot wind were rising up and swirling around the battlefield in waves. Sweat dripped down Morgan's neck. She wiped her wet hands off on her tunic.

The battle moved toward their hill. When Romans fought you could tell whose eagle standards were advancing and whose were retreating, but here…

Morgan looked at Ciarnat. "Are we winning?" she asked.

Ciarnat focused on the battle. It seemed to be crawling up the side of their hill, getting louder. Ciarnat stood up. She was frowning. She jumped up on her chair to get a better view of her men. She shouted to her poet, "Where are my lords? I can't see them!" Morgan didn't recognize any of the warriors heading up the hill, and there were far too few with their backs to her, fending off the advancing men. How had this happened so fast?

Ciarnat cursed, and yelled, "Chariot!"

Behind her, Ciarnat's charioteer was fighting for his life. A single lanky young warrior of the Eóganachta was jabbing at him with a lance. Ciarnat hurled a javelin at the warrior. It slammed into the young warrior's head, knocked him down and transfixed him to the ground. He quivered like a slaughtered chicken. Ciarnat jumped into the chariot, grabbed the whip from her charioteer and snapped it at the ponies. They bolted, already frightened, galloping down the side of the hill. Morgan ran after her, calling to her, but Ciarnat never looked back.

Morgan looked around. She saw two men run at Eochaid with their long spears out. He ducked behind his shield, but they came around either side of him. One grabbed him, the other stabbed him and he fell. Ahead of her, the druid, an old man, dropped to his knees, gasping for breath, surrendering, for who would kill a druid? Ciarnat's poet, a middle-aged fat man, ran past her. No one was supposed to kill poets either, but he was Ciarnat's brother.

Morgan ran for the stronghold. She was a hundred yards from the walls of Inishannon when she remembered how little she thought of them. But behind her were the chariots. There were no woods for a mile around Inishannon. Nowhere to hide.

There were a handful of Déisi warriors sprinting from the battlefield. Some were cut down by the charioteers, some were opening a lead. One swept Morgan off her feet, threw her over his shoulder and carried her into the stronghold.

The gates were shut barely ahead of the chariots. A tall woman ran to slam the heavy wooden bar home. Morgan backed away from the gates. The woman was shouting orders, and people were jamming planks up against the gate to reinforce it.

There were not many people inside the settlement. The slaves had fled. Morgan knew the planks wouldn't stop the Eóganachta for long. She looked for somewhere to hide.

Spears began to fly over the fence. Then fire showed through the slits. People were screaming.

There was a barn with a rotten floor. She'd hidden underneath it back when the girls still played hide-and-seek with her. They'd never found her there.

Morgan slipped into the darkness of the barn, dug into the dried ash and elm leaves kept there for winter fodder, and slipped through the small hole she had made in the rotten floorboards. It was muddy underneath, with spider webs. Small creatures skittered around. On another day, it might have been fun.

She heard a muffled, rending crash, and men shouting. That would be the gate coming down, she thought. She could hear women screaming. But at least she was safe in the cold darkness.

After a few minutes, the screaming died down. Now she could hear sobbing, with only an occasional scream. She thought she could hear Gráinne weeping, not far away. She was sorry for Gráinne and the others. She was sorry for everyone.

After a while she heard singing. The wailing went on, but now men were singing. The sound of the singing closed around the barn she was hiding under.

A low roaring began to penetrate the quiet of the space she'd crawled into. She smelled smoke. She could feel heat wafting in under the house.

They were burning Inishannon.

Someone yanked open the door above her and tossed a burning torch into the leaves.

Morgan thought for three heartbeats. There was no way out of the crawl space, except through the hole. The leaves would go up in flames, and she'd choke to death in the smoke.

Morgan screamed.

A man shouted, "Danu's Tits! There's a girl in here!" Morgan put her hand through the rotten hole, and the man grabbed her and pulled her up. He was a warrior, covered in blood. The leaves were already burning. He grinned at her. "You're not stupid, are you?"

Chapter Eight

THE LAKE VILLAGE

Inishannon burned all afternoon. It took the Eóganachta that long to round up all the cattle and sheep, while a few warriors guarded the women and children in a corral. Morgan saw a warrior leading the Greek, his hands bound with rope. The Greek wouldn't meet her eyes.

The warriors tied the hands of the women together, one after another, making a long chain of captives. Gráinne looked at her. Morgan thought she was going to gloat. But she only whispered, "Do you have anyone who'd pay your ransom?" Morgan shook her head.

There was only one man who'd pay her ransom. Uter Pendragon. He would pay for her just to kill her.

She wondered dully if someone would tell them. She wondered if she would be sailed back to Din Tagell as a captive, to be put to death there, or if Uter would ask them to send only her head back. She prayed that if she was found out, she would die here, alone. She couldn't stand to see her mother in Uter's arms.

Ciarnat was nowhere to be seen. Morgan guessed she had been killed. Simon was probably dead too, on the battlefield. Only the Greek knew her secret. She hoped he would keep it.

The women and children, tied by their wrists in a long human chain, had to follow behind a cart piled high with the heads of the Déisi men. More heads were tied to the wagon by their own hair. The gory heads swung and stared back at Morgan. Sometimes one of them would slip off, and the Eóganachta men would stop the cart and tie it back on, arguing over who had tied the bad knot. Morgan had talked to some of those heads, back when they were living men.

The women Morgan was tied to had been married to those heads. But they seemed to accept their new status as captives. When the cart slowed down, leaving slack in the rope tying them together, they cleaned the soot from each other's faces with spit and combed their hair with their fingers. Whenever a rich warrior passed by in a grand chariot, they tried to catch his eye. Morgan realized that they were hoping to attract an important and wealthy master.

I am a slave, Morgan realized dully. She'd sunk as low as she could go. A Roman citizen could not be made a slave. But she was no longer a Roman citizen. She was a slave in Ireland.

But no, she wasn't a slave. She was a war captive. She was the daughter of Gorlois and Ygraine, and the enemy of Uter the Dragon. She had to hold onto that, or she really would be a slave.

There would be another raid. Someone would raid the Eóganachta, maybe even one day the Déisi, and she would escape into the woods. And then...what? She couldn't see the road that would take her from here back to the Wall of Din Tagell. So she let the dust of the road mix with the soot on her face, and hid in the shadows of the women ahead of her, trying to avoid being noticed.

They came down through gentle hills, and the settlement of the Eóganachta rose from a low hill where the two forks of a river joined. Morgan could see a man wading through the near fork; it couldn't be very deep. On the far side, what she could see of the river was narrow and swift, with steep muddy banks.

Her father would have thought it was a good place for a fort.

Morgan and the other captives were led into a corral and untied. A few cows moved off to a corner, mooing nervously. The warriors closed the gate, not so much to keep them inside by force—for it was only a cow fence of woven willow branches—but to warn them not to stray.

They waited outside in the chill night, guarded only by a few boys carrying spears. In the great hall, the warriors drank and sang and boasted. Morgan could hear every word through the open door. The slaughter of the Déisi warriors in a chaotic battle was already becoming a collection of single combats, with great feats of arms on both sides, and witty repartee.

Morgan lay down. She wanted to sleep, but she was too exhausted and hungry. And she hurt all over. Her feet were covered in blisters, some of them broken and bleeding. Her wrists were raw from the rope.

Now the women and girls allowed themselves to weep, and Morgan understood why they hadn't cried before: they hadn't wanted to cry in front of their captors. That was good, to keep your pride.

The women wept on and on in the darkness. Their moans rose and fell. Morgan shoved her hands over her ears, pushing her earlobes into them to block the sound. But their moans seeped through.

They would all be slaves. She thought of Eithne, who had lived from moment to moment, without pride, all those years.

Morgan had to stop listening to the weeping.

The night before her father was killed, she had dreamt of the battle, but the sound of the fighting had gone away, in her dream. What was the way of it? Could she do that intentionally? She tried to remember how it had happened in her dream.

Morgan tried to go under their weeping. She tried to find the underneath of their sorrow, the dark beneath the wailing.

And the moaning faded away. She could hear the women breathing. She heard a faint rattling: maybe one of the boy sentries outside the corral, his teeth chattering in the chill night air.

She could feel power here. She was floating above ancient rock, great stones buried long ago by a different people than the Irish. The hill was a burial mound, earth heaped high over a cave. There were bones that had been here two thousand years. They were still alive, their spirits were caught here in some web she could not see.

Protect me.

OH?

Please?

BE LIKE US.

I can't be bones. I'm a girl.

The bones seemed to ponder that for an infinite while.

THEN BE SILENT FOR A WHILE, AND ONE DAY YOU WILL BE LIKE US.

She wondered if it meant she would be safe like the bones, or only dead like them. But at least the voices were quiet now, and in the quiet around her, she slept.

IN the morning the chief of the Eóganachta had the women slaves brought out to where his warriors were assembled. "Cú Meda, this is really your victory," said the chief, loud enough for Morgan to hear, "for it was your prophecy that yesterday was a good day for a battle."

A stout man came out of the ranks. He wore a druid's robes. His face was blotchy red. Morgan guessed that *Cú Meda* meant something like "mead dog"; maybe he drank too much honey wine. Mead Dog the druid glared at the women. They shrank back from him, even the ones who had been trying to attract the attention of the best warriors. He stalked back and forth, looking them all over. For a moment he stopped and stared at Morgan.

She froze, like a fawn in the sight of a wolf, and looked down at the earth. She kept silent, and in her mind she called to the earth to make her unnoticed, the way the earth is, and she hoped he would pass her by.

He shook his head for a moment, confused.

Then he pointed at someone else, a tall, beautiful redheaded woman, the widow of one of the Déisi's greatest warriors. "She'll do." With a strange sort of pride, the woman followed her new master away.

Then came the lords of the Eóganachta. The grandest came first, the ones in the finest silk tunics. The bard jumped in with short poems, and the warriors gave him small chunks of gold.

As the day went on, the common warriors picked their new slaves. Morgan felt a quiet settle on her. They were not going to pick her. They would not even notice her.

While the free men were still lining up, a woman walked brusquely through the mob of them. She was dressed in an old green cloak. There were a few blades of loose grass in her hair. She wore a necklace of small bones; Morgan hoped they were from animals. The woman was muttering under her breath. Her eyes darted here and there.

She must be a wise woman, Morgan thought.

Her mother had always humoured the wise women of Din Tagell. You let them have their ways. The men stepped away from the strange woman. She walked right past them, and past the chief too. He shrugged with a resigned grin, the way you do when your dog makes off with a fish.

Something about her made Morgan nervous too, so she stepped back behind the older women. She struggled with the quiet that surrounded her, wrapped it around her like a cloak.

But the wise woman stepped into the corral. She walked through the other women, brushing them aside. Morgan didn't look at her, hoping she'd pick someone else. The wise woman pulled Morgan's chin up with a calloused finger and looked her in the eye. "Don't think you can hide from me," she whispered hoarsely, "with your big nose and your big mouth and your long fairy face. Oh, you've got the fairy blood in you, don't you. Well you can just stop that." And she slapped Morgan in the face, not hard, but hard enough to smart, and she laughed as she did it.

She gestured with her finger, and Morgan knew she had to follow the woman out of the corral.

The wise woman said, "Call me Buanann." But she smirked as she said it, so Morgan wondered if that was her real name.

ᛒᚢᚐᚅᚐᚅᚅ lived in an Eóganachta village called Carrigadroid, about fifteen miles up the eastern fork of the river. They walked there behind some of the free warriors and their new female slaves. Morgan noticed that Buanann stopped muttering once they got out of earshot of the people of Glennamain. She combed the grass out of her hair. She stood up taller, and seemed younger.

Morgan wondered if Buanann's craziness was an act.

Buanann didn't bother to put a rope on Morgan, though their journey brought them through dark woodlands she could easily have darted into and vanished in.

Morgan tensed, ready to bolt.

"Wolves live in those woods," chuckled Buanann, reading Morgan's mind. "I bet you don't know what there is to eat in a forest. You'll never survive alone there."

So Morgan didn't run into the woods.

AS day was fading, they came to a *crannog*, a village built all on small, squarish islands made of mud in a shallow lake. Morgan could see fields spread out on the lakeshore, and cows and sheep grazing the nearby hills, but all the villagers' houses were on the islands. There were empty corrals on some of the islands; it looked like they had enough room to store all their cattle and sheep if they had to.

Morgan looked at the place with her father's eyes. To get to the village, you had to walk down a hundred-foot walkway made of planks, that went from the shore all the way to about ten feet from the village's gates. The planks were loose; Morgan realized they could be pulled up easily if the village was in danger. There was a drawbridge too, at the end of the walkway.

This was almost as safe as Din Tagell, in its primitive way. An enemy could block the walkway, but all along the many islands, Morgan could see small boats lying upside down against the rain. The lake was broad and wide. You could never cut the village off from help, unless you had dozens of boats yourself, and you would have to carry your boats all the way to the lake.

It would be hard to run away from, too.

Buanann led Morgan to her own islet. There was a boardwalk that connected it to the blacksmith's island, which connected to three other islands. They were on the outskirts of the village.

Buanann had an herb garden on her island, but she told Morgan, "You'll help me gather herbs from the forest." She chuckled again. "Some you gather by moonlight, and some in the rain, and some standing on one foot, and some by moonlight in the rain on one foot, which takes some doing." Buanann was not as young and agile as she had once been, she told Morgan, and so Morgan would climb trees with a silver sickle to cut down mistletoe. "That's why I picked a girl. The mistletoe grows on the far outer branches sometimes, and a man or a boy would break the branch and fall to his death." She cackled. "Then I'd have to get a new slave."

ON matters of high wisdom, the people of the lake village deferred to the druids. The lake village had no druid of its own, but Cú Meda came by regularly, with two lesser druids, to make rulings and offer sacrifices to the gods. Cú Meda ruled on how many cattle one man ought to pay the family of another man he'd killed in a drunken fight, and the village chief, Dúngal, made the man pay.

On matters of low wisdom, the people asked Buanann. She treated fevers and set broken bones, sewed wounds shut with catgut, and made poultices to heal sores.

But the people of the village did not seem to like Buanann. They never talked to her unless they needed her. The women glared at her, and the men would not look her in the eye.

IT wasn't long before a man came to Buanann one night. Morgan heard them talking in low tones outside the house. He came inside and Buanann took him into her arms. Morgan curled up on her bed of straw and tried to be invisible.

SHE woke up long before dawn. Buanann and the man were talking in low tones. He left the house. Buanann followed him to the edge of her island, but stopped there. In the sharp shadows of the moonlight, the man walked as quietly as he could on the creaky boardwalk. He slipped onto the blacksmith's island, and then down another boardwalk, and was gone.

Buanann was crying quietly.

Suddenly she turned and spotted Morgan watching her from within the house. She strode over and slapped Morgan's face.

But then Buanann curled herself up in her cloak and pretended to go to sleep.

Morgan felt the sting on her cheek. It had been meant only to put her in her place.

And the shame wasn't hers. It was Buanann's. In the shadows of the house, Morgan could hear her crying softly, curled up in her cloak.

Why would Buanann give herself to a man who had a wife, who by day pretended he had nothing to do with her?

MORGAN began to learn the craft of a wise woman. Morgan stood by when Buanann delivered babies, ready to run for herbs or water or anything else. Buanann talked to herself while she worked, reminding herself what to do next, and so Morgan learned as much of that craft as can be learned from watching and listening, which is much.

Buanann knew her craft by song. She knew hundreds of songs about herbs and gods, and she sang them in front of Morgan. Sometimes, when she couldn't remember, she made Morgan sing them back. She told Morgan offhandedly that she was not *teaching* Morgan. But Buanann would explain things to her too, things she had learned from the druids. She talked about how a dead man or woman's soul migrated into the body of a newborn baby. She talked about the gods of Ireland, bright and crafty Lugos, fertile Ceridwen, the fierce and wise Dagda, and the terrifying Morrígan, who was called not only Crow, but also Terror, and Panic, and Queen of Shadows. Buanann told Morgan all about the four peoples that had invaded Ireland, one after another, until in the end the Men, the "sons of Mil," defeated the People of the Goddess Danu, who were called the Sidhe, or the Good Folk. The sons of Mil had exiled the people of the goddess underground, where they lived today.

Morgan began to piece together why Buanann was so alone. She had nearly died bearing her only son, Gabrán, for she had only been fifteen, and small. She had never given her husband another child, so he left her and took another woman to bed. Her husband's new woman gave him three sons and five daughters, and taught Gabrán to despise his mother.

Because she was no longer good as a wife, Buanann had gone away for druid's training. A druid must know all the laws of Ireland and of his own people, and the generations of kings of all the great tribes, and all the incantations for all the rituals of the year, and of the nineteen-year cycle that brings the moon and sun together. He or she must know it all, without fault, from memory.

But Buanann's memory was not good enough to become one of them, and they sent her back, neither wife nor druid.

Buanann had no man, except that sometimes the man from the village would sneak over to her in the middle of the night, with mead and soft words, and leave before dawn. And that made it worse, because the village women suspected she was sleeping with their husbands too, and hated her for it.

Sometimes Morgan caught herself sympathizing with Buanann. She was weak, and sad, and alone. Morgan was only a slave. But she had vengeance to keep her strong, and brave, and to keep her company in the night.

MORGAN had a better memory than Buanann. Soon she knew Buanann's songs better than Buanann did. The wise woman was not all that old. She was just forgetful. Sometimes she would sing the songs and mix up the verses without even realizing it. The first time Morgan reminded Buanann how a song went, she got a beating, so she learned to sing the song near Buanann, so Buanann was able to remember it without being shown up by her slave.

It was not all lore and midwifery. There were rituals Buanann did when Morgan helped her gather herbs. Some of the rituals seemed aimless to Morgan. Maybe Buanann had forgotten something important. But other rituals communed with something in the tree, something in the meadow, drawing its healing power out and into the leaf, or cutting, or root, or cup of water they were taking back to the village.

When Morgan was thirteen, she helped Buanann prepare a charm of binding to protect a young man from harm in battle. In a quiet grove of trees near the lakeshore, Morgan swung the small hand axe to get the heartwood of a rowan tree sapling. Buanann chanted, taking great care with the ancient words of the charm, for the young man had been kind to her. Morgan could feel something in the grove stir as though from a dreamy sleep. It stretched its back and yawned, and its claws came out of their sheaths.

But Buanann stumbled over the words, and got upset when Morgan whispered them to her, and Morgan could feel the thing circle its own tail a few times, softly relax and curl back up into a dreaming ball without ever really waking up.

Morgan suddenly thought of her mother, how she had called to someone across the Veil, in the ritual with the wicker crow. But she had not let that someone cross the Veil into her. She had been scared, or unwilling.

Morgan was willing.

That night Morgan held the rowan heartwood in her hand—Buanann had carved it into the shape of an elaborate, multi-layered knot—and tried to awaken it for herself. In the wood she could feel the faintest wisp of something. The ritual had bound some of the power of the grove into the wood.

She thought of returning to the place where they had cut the rowan wood, but how could she, alone, at night? The drawbridge was drawn up. She could steal a boat, but there were spikes hidden in the water all around the village's walls.

She sat quietly, listening to her own breathing.

She had never, out of nowhere, tried to reach the place where such power seemed to abide. It had come to her only when she needed it.

She thought of the circle her mother had always cast. But Buanann was a light sleeper. There would be no going around in a circle, waving a knife around.

But was the magic in the gesture? Or was the gesture only supposed to focus her mind?

In her mind only, Morgan drew a circle in the straw on the floor around her. She let the breeze sweep through it, cleansing it. That felt right. That was the way. She felt the fire in her own veins, the heat of her body and the dim warmth from the chunk of dry peat slowly smoking in the fire pit. That purified the circle too. Then there was the water that surrounded the island, which gathered in any hole you might dig; the mist that clung to the lake surface and crept into the house. That washed the circle clean.

Air, fire, water.

And there was earth, in the silences in between. She did not need to call it. It was always there, pure and deep.

She thought she might be between the worlds.

She reached out, into the heartwood knot she held in her hands. There was a knot inside the grain itself, tied by Buanann's words and desire. It was a sloppy knot, badly tied. But it bound something into the wood, something that slept. It was as if she could run her hands along it, stroke it.

Buanann's breathing changed. Morgan knew she wasn't asleep anymore. Buanann was pretending. That was odd.

Morgan was suddenly scared. Buanann had caught her. Frightened, she withdrew as fast as she could. She pulled the circle into herself and sent it into the earth. Something still lingered of the spell, something in the air. But she was safe.

She lay back on the straw on the floor where she slept, on the other side of the room from Buanann's bed. Her skin tingled. Her cheeks were flushed. She was sweating.

THE next day Buanann was oddly quiet, never saying much to Morgan. Morgan accidentally broke a bowl full of ointment. Buanann picked it up and mended the bowl as best she could, salvaging as much ointment as possible. She never even raised her voice at Morgan that day.

From then on Buanann stopped repeating spell songs to Morgan. But sometimes she would ask Morgan's opinion about odd things, like what plants to use in a salve, as if Morgan could possibly know more than Buanann. She would ask Morgan what she thought about the druids' legends. "Do you really think we live more than once?"

Morgan didn't have an answer. This life was hard enough to figure out.

Morgan didn't reach out to the secret places if Buanann was in sight, and she was almost always in sight. But Morgan still began to notice more about the *underneath* of the world. She began to feel more of what Buanann was doing when she sealed a house as a woman went into labour. She felt the bursting energy of the baby, and the strain of the woman trying to give birth. It was as intense as the feeling she'd had on the battlefield, before the people of Glennamain lost their battle.

Buanann was more and more alone in the village. Maybe because she was less and less willing to humiliate herself. Now she expected anyone who needed her skills to come to her; she would not seek them out.

One evening Morgan saw a young man come to Buanann. He was more a boy than a man, and maybe a virgin. She had seen him eyeing Buanann for weeks. Maybe he thought the stories that the wives told were true, that she would give herself to any man.

He was headed across the boardwalk to the blacksmith's island. There was a knot of women he would have to pass in order to get to Buanann's house—women who loved nothing better than to mock Buanann behind her back.

Morgan guessed that Buanann wouldn't turn the boy away. She had been sad and lonely, and she'd had nothing to say to Morgan for days.

This time Morgan didn't want the wives to mock Buanann. It was none of their business. She wanted to make the boy pass unnoticed. It was what she had tried to do in the corral at Glennamain. She thought it might be a simple thing to call upon the earth, to ask for a sort of silence.

She had no time to build a spell. But she suddenly realized with what tremendous force she wanted this silence. And for some reason, there it was for the grasping. She drew it into her.

The boy walked right past the women. The women went on talking without ever noticing him.

BÙAŊAŊŊ was pensive all day. Finally she called Morgan to her. "There's luck, and there's more than luck," she said.

Morgan knew she'd been caught, but she'd long ago learned that it was best to let Buanann speak.

"When you're a child…a creek…a path through the meadow… that's all accidental, isn't it?" said Buanann. "You don't think about why it cuts one way and then another. It's just there. It's always been."

Morgan nodded.

"One day you stick your hand in a creek and you see how the currents change."

Morgan nodded.

"Those women. They didn't say a thing about that boy."

Morgan nodded.

"They could have somehow all not seen him…"

Morgan nodded.

"Don't give me that! It's ridiculous! Accidents! I'll clop you one on the head, and you can call *that* an accident!"

Morgan looked down. No good deed goes unpunished.

Buanann looked at her for a while. For a moment she almost looked like she was about to thank Morgan. It was as much as Morgan usually got, the expression of almost thanking. You don't thank your ox for pulling the plow.

But Buanann broke into a smile. "I'll teach you to do that the right way."

And so Buanann taught Morgan a small cantrip that would direct someone's eye away from what you did not want them to see. It was done by creating a distraction, and holding the target's eye on it. "I don't know what it was you did. But it was dangerous and foolish, and you're never to do it again."

But anyone can make a distraction, thought Morgan. You didn't need magic to throw a stone into the lake, and make everyone turn to hear the plunk. What Buanann wanted to do was clunky, and useless if people were on guard against it. What Morgan had tried to do was subtler than a distraction, but stronger.

But Morgan realized what she had done wrong back at the corral, and what she had done wrong here. The warriors' eyes had passed right over her then, not seeing her, but Buanann had noticed her—and so had Cú Meda—because it was obvious to them that she was trying not to be seen. You not only had to hide the thing that you wanted to conceal; you had to hide the spell too.

Morgan began to put together a small, invisible bag of craft. She made sure to do cantrips in front of Buanann that were childishly done. She learned to make a fire flare up, or stutter and fail, or catch a mouse that was hiding, or call a raven to perch on the post. But she also did cantrips that were well made. They were slight, chancy gossamer things. She could make someone forget what they were about to say, or stub their toe in the crack between two planks. At first she did them out of sight. Then when they were perfect, she did them in Buanann's presence, but unknown to her. They were secret, and they were hers alone.

 THE spindle of the year whirled round and round, through death and birth, harvesting and planting, and in between there was always the fallow time, when the land was cold and wet, and voices from underneath welled up to just below the frost. The Horned God hunted, Ceridwen stirred her cauldron, the Morrígan ate the dead on distant battlefields. When the moon was new, the druids sacrificed sheep and cattle, and once even a slave captured in battle, because that year the crops were bad. In summer Morgan watched the men leave the lake village to go on cattle raids. Sometimes they brought back cattle and slaves, sometimes they brought back their kinsmen's corpses, sometimes they didn't come back. It was a chancy thing.

She dug for roots in the woods, and harvested mistletoe, and weeded Buanann's garden. She made a point never to dig the last bit of root out, so that the weeds would come back. She liked to imagine that one night the villagers would go to sleep, and stay asleep for ten years. And when they woke up, their islands would have all sunk into the lake. The weeds would have overgrown their fields, and the wolves would have left nothing of their cattle but bones rotting in the rain.

Morgan never stopped thinking about leaving the lake village. Once she dreamt of a carpet that could fly through the air and take her back to Din Tagell. But when she got there, the place was empty, the huts rotted away, the villa overgrown with moss. She woke up in a sweat, terrified that it was true, that Uter had died before she'd got home.

But what good would it do to leave the lake village? Here she was a captive; but even a free Irishman didn't leave his own lands. Only a druid or a poet or a tinker or a messenger could travel from one tribe's lands to another without being murdered.

And then there was the open sea. And then there was Britannia. Perhaps Uter ruled all of Britain by now. She had nothing to bring back, no army, no power, no weapon. There was no going back, not yet.

And the lake village was giving her something. As Buanann's memory slipped away, the wise woman became fearful. There were no more than a few streaks of grey in her hair, but she was forgetting things, like how to stop your heart and appear dead, and she would ask Morgan to remind her. And sometimes Morgan would remind her of things, and Buanann would not realize that she had never taught them to Morgan, nor ever known them.

Buanann never talked of releasing Morgan from her slavery. Another slave might have hoped that if she could only give Buanann enough of the feelings the village would not give her—comfort, trust, loyalty—then Buanann might release her.

But being a slave taught Morgan silence, and silence has its own power. She could feel the tides that flow through the land. She could feel the bel-fires at Beltane in the spring, and feel how the

Veil between Seen and Unseen was thin in the fallow time between the last harvest at Samhain and the returning of the winter sun at Imbolc. She could sometimes hear the dead whispering, if she stretched her mind toward them. She could tell that Cú Meda could truly manipulate the strands of power in the moon rituals, but that when he performed a sacrifice to Epona, the horse goddess, he was only putting on a show for the people.

Morgan wondered about her mother. Had her mother ever felt the world around her like this? Her mother could do small magic. She must have felt the tides of the land, felt the Veil, felt the cold Moon in her hands. For a moment she had almost summoned someone at the ritual for Morigenos. She must have felt something. But she had turned away.

And now her mother was a sort of slave too, if she was still alive. She had surrendered to Uter. She was Uter's property now.

To avenge that, to avenge her father, Morgan could wait. Morgan owned nothing, not even herself. So she had nothing to lose.

What would she have become in Ciarnat's village? Would she have married an Irish warrior, and borne him children? Would she have forgotten Din Tagell? Slavery kept her hot, like embers underneath ashes. Slavery reminded her who she was.

Chapter Nine

THE OUTLANDER

Morgan had just turned fifteen when the outlander came. It was after the winter solstice, and the weather was bitterly cold. The grass was covered with frost every dawn, and sometimes there was a faint sheen of ice on the lake by the shore. A chill wind blew out of the north. It tugged at Buanann's roof, and the timbers creaked. Inside the house, smoke from the chunk of peat in the fire pit swirled around and around. The swallows refused to leave their nest in the thatch.

Morgan was running out of time. She had been in Ireland for four years. A man like Uter didn't live forever. He might already be dead.

Why would that be bad? Morgan asked herself.

If Uter was dead she could reveal who she was. Her mother would ransom her and she could come home.

But when Morgan tried to imagine returning to Din Tagell after Uter's death, it felt all wrong. She wanted vengeance.

She was running out of time. The boys of the village had begun to look at her in that way, and some of the men too. So far her cantrips had kept her out of trouble. It helped that she wasn't beautiful. Her mouth was too wide and her nose was too large. She was much taller than other girls her age, and skinny from eating nothing but scraps. But her breasts were filling out. The cantrips wouldn't work forever; she wasn't the Enchanter. Sooner or later a man would approach her, and she would have to give in.

She could change the cantrips and choose one of them. Some of the Déisi girls had attracted the men they wanted and become their concubines. They were still slaves, but they nagged their men like real wives. And they ate as well as any wife.

But Morgan didn't want a man for comfort, or lust. She wanted a man for war, a man who could command warriors. She could choose one of the village boys and make him notice her. But none of them was worth attracting.

One day when Morgan was feeding mushrooms to the chariot ponies of Dúngal, the headman, to cure them of colic, she saw a stranger heading up the walkway across the lake. A dozen villagers were trailing behind him, and more were running in from the fields to see who he was. He wasn't carrying a messenger's baton or a tinker's tools. He had no entourage, so he wasn't a poet; and he did not seem to be a druid, because he didn't wear any whorls made of silver, or tiny axe heads, or labyrinths, the way the druids did. The front of his head was shaved, as if he were balding, but in back, his hair hung in the long single braid that warriors wore. He had a weather-beaten face, the face of a shepherd who spent even the worst winter days out in the fields with his flock. He was muscular, and his legs were incredibly hairy.

Morgan had never seen a stranger like this man come to the village. There had been the usual thirsty poets, and the tinkers who made the rounds of the southern Irish tribes fixing pots, and the occasional druid apprentice on his way to Glennamain to bring a message to Cú Meda.

Morgan had no idea what had been going on in the world since she had come to the lake village. Tinkers told funny and fanciful stories, but they never had actual news. Druids wouldn't talk to you. Poets would tell you only what you wanted to hear, hoping for food or mead. But this stranger was none of those things. Maybe he knew what was happening in Britannia. Maybe he knew about Uter, and the Saxon wars.

Morgan squeezed into the gathering crowd. There was a light drizzle, and Dúngal's lords showed the outlander into the great eating hall. The hall filled with over sixty men and women, slaves and serfs, some sitting down at the grand table and others crowding around. Morgan edged into the back, unnoticed.

"I came from Dun Ailinne," the outlander said. Morgan had heard of the stronghold; it was somewhere to the north.

"Through the lands of the Osraige?" asked Dúngal.

"I came through there," said the outlander carefully.

"How did you get along with them?" asked Dúngal. The Osraige were the Eóganachta's neighbours, and therefore enemies.

The outlander didn't answer at first. Morgan watched as the men tensed up. A few of them had dropped their hands down to their holstered knives or swords.

"They let you pass through unharmed?" asked Dúngal.

"To tell you the truth," said the outlander, "I don't think they liked me very much."

"Well that's all right, then!" said Dúngal, with a laugh, and the men relaxed. Dúngal called for food and ale. Under the iron law of hospitality, that meant he now had to let the outlander live.

The outlander said he was a storyteller. Morgan was disappointed. She'd had her fill of tinkers' tales and druids' myths. But it turned out that the outlander had only one story to tell. It was set in the mysterious Roman Empire, at the far eastern end, where the Roman Sea ended.

The people of the lake village didn't ordinarily care for stories about distant lands they knew nothing of. But it was after midwinter, with the wheat harvest long ago stored in pits, the extra cattle slaughtered, and nothing to do but mend things. And his story was new, even if it was alarmingly short on battles. So they listened.

The outlander was a small man, and his hands moved quickly, shaping the air when he spoke. His face was large and wide, so that she could see his expression from a distance. He laughed easily, and used different voices to tell his story. But the most important thing about him was that he seemed completely at ease with himself. He seemed to have a secret that made him happy just to be alive.

But the outlander's story was odd. There were no battles and hardly any bloodshed. No one did anything for the sake of honour. There weren't even monsters, just one evil god who tried to distract the hero from a righteous path. The hero died at the end, which was always good in a story, but he failed to take any of his enemies with him, or even go down fighting. In fact the hero forgave his enemies.

Forgave them! That part left the warriors bewildered. Some of them suggested different, better endings, involving lots of bloodshed. But the outlander claimed that this wasn't a made-up story, that this story had actually happened. Most of the warriors left the eating hall, taking their slaves and serfs with them. But many of the women stayed. Even Buanann came in just as the warriors were leaving.

The warriors missed the most interesting part. The hero came back from the dead on the third day. He was really a god in disguise—a god of death and rebirth—and by worshipping him, the poor and the weak and the sick could get after death what they hadn't got in this world. In fact the outlander said that only through believing in the hero of his story could anyone go to the good afterlife. The lame would walk again, and slaves would be free. That got laughter from the remaining men; then they ordered all the slaves out of the hall immediately. But the women still stayed, especially after the outlander told them that his god listened to the prayers of men and women equally. He told them he had renamed himself Salvatus, which meant "saved" in Latin, because only his god could save anyone from the bad afterlife.

Morgan kicked herself for not recognizing the story earlier. The outlander had told it as if it were a legend. He never said he was a Christian. The Eóganachta hated Christians as much as Ciarnat's people did.

Now her mind was awhirl. A missionary! A missionary would be able to read Latin! A missionary would have news of Britannia!

And with that hope, she felt a sudden rush of fear. She had lived so long without any reason to hope. She had looked for hope in Buanann's little spells. The rest had been survival. Could the outlander help her? But he wasn't here to free slaves, he'd said so. Anything he did would turn the entire settlement against him and his message. Why would he help her?

At least he could give her news of the outside world. She had to find a way to talk to him alone.

The outlander stayed up all night telling his story in the dining hall. Many of the slaves snuck back in after their masters had fallen asleep. As the day began to break, Morgan had to go back to Buanann's house.

Bᵁᴬᴺᴬᴺᴺ was poking at the peat in the fire pit. She barely looked up. She seemed exhausted. Maybe she hadn't slept. Buanann sometimes lay for hours, her eyes open, breathing shallowly and restlessly.

"The druids," Buanann said. "Tomorrow the moon is full. They'll be here." So she wasn't angry with Morgan for staying out all night.

"How do you think they're going to feel about the outlander?" asked Buanann. "His god is the only thing the druids are afraid of."

"Why?" asked Morgan.

"Because if you believe in his God, you don't need druids. Christians write things down. We heard a lot about the Christians when I was training to be a druid."

"What's wrong with that?" Morgan asked.

"Suppose everything the druids knew was on one of those sheepskins with the markings on them," Buanann answered. "A person could learn to read it, couldn't they? And then you could argue with them. I don't mean *you*, obviously. But Dúngal, or one of his lords. Suppose they could read what the law was, instead of having to ask the druids?"

Only the druids knew the laws. You couldn't prove one of them wrong. A druid could say that something was a time-honoured tradition, unbroken since men had come to Ireland. Or he could say it was only a local custom. They could accuse someone of violating the sacred law, and have the blasphemer put to death. Or they could quote laws that said the man was guilty of only a misunderstanding. If the laws were written down, the druids would lose their power.

"They'll kill him," said Buanann.

"But Dúngal likes Salvatus," said Morgan.

"They'll fix that pretty quick."

Buanann was quiet for a moment, then she eyed Morgan meaningfully. "Don't you have any tasks you need to do?"

Morgan ran back to the dining hall. There were only a few women and slaves still there to hear Salvatus talk. His voice was hoarse.

"My mistress the healer wants to speak to you alone," Morgan said to him.

"But we were still talking with him, Morgan," said one of the slaves, an old man named Suibhne who was owned by the tanner.

"You'd better get back to your house," Morgan told him. "It's practically dawn."

"It is that," said Suibhne sadly.

Salvatus nodded. "Don't worry. I'll be right back." And he followed Morgan to Buanann's house.

SALVATUS wouldn't listen to reason. Somehow, that didn't surprise Morgan. "I'm not afraid of druids," he told Buanann. "I've faced them before. God has always protected me."

"Not these druids," said Buanann.

"I'm not afraid," said Salvatus easily.

"They'll kill you," said Buanann.

"Then I'll go to heaven," said Salvatus softly, and he was so sure of himself that Morgan almost found herself convinced. "Is that all you wanted to tell me?"

"If they kill you, then no one here will have anything more to do with your god," said Buanann.

"Are you so sure of that?" he said.

Morgan knew that the Christians put great stock in being martyred for their god.

"You have to challenge the druids before they can denounce you," said Buanann. "Challenge them to a contest of magic. Otherwise they'll put a knife in your back."

"Magic is the devil's business."

"Either your god's magic is more powerful than theirs, or you're an idiot for going around preaching for him."

"God will bless you for your advice," he said.

"Well, I tried to warn you. Don't tell anyone I talked to you," Buanann said. "They already hate me enough."

"Is that why you're trying to help me?" asked Salvatus.

"I'm wondering why myself."

As Morgan ushered Salvatus out of the house, she wondered if he would take Buanann's advice.

But challenge the druids? That was crazy. He needed to leave.

No. She needed him to leave and take her. He was a man who travelled, who would be in touch with Britannia.

Maybe he could buy her. Maybe he needed a slave.

Then she had a better idea.

MORGAN took Salvatus behind the house. There were no fishing boats out on the lake this early, so no one would see them talking.

"Are you in touch with the church in Britannia?" Morgan asked, in Latin. It wasn't good Latin. After four years in Ireland, the words felt strange in her mouth.

He stared at her. "Are you of the faith?" The outlander spoke Latin with a heavy Irish accent. Morgan's Latin was better than his.

"I am a slave, but my soul is free," she said. It wasn't a lie.

He embraced her, whispering, "Sister!"

She had to know: "Who is High King in Britannia?"

"I'm not sure," he said, and her heart sank. If there was no High King, then Uter must be dead. "We talk about Gaul, and Rome, much more than we talk about British politics."

"But who leads the British in battle against the heathens?"

"Why, Uter Pendragon. He is a mighty hammer for the Lord."

She laughed with honest relief. "May he go with God," she said. Then she made her face serious. "You have to leave. Buanann's right. The druids will murder you."

"What would that say for my faith in God, if I ran away like a thief?"

"If you throw a seed of wheat on a stone, it will sprout after the rain. But then it will die when the sun comes out," she said. "This village is a stone."

"You know your gospels," he said.

Morgan had no idea what he was talking about. "I'm worried," she said.

"For yourself?" Salvatus asked. "If they find you out?"

Yes! That was it. Surely he'd help her escape now.

"They nearly caught me praying last week," Morgan lied.

Salvatus nodded thoughtfully. "We are gathering a community of Christians about three days' walk from here. Only Christians—no pagans at all—with no tribe but the faithful, and no chieftain but the Lord. We would take you in as a sister in Christ."

Her heart leaped. It was more than she'd hoped for. "If I escaped?"

"Yes. If you're not truly a slave, but only a captive of war, you have the right to free yourself." That was the Irish law. "And if you are of the faithful, we will deliver you from your enemies."

"Brother!" She threw herself into his arms.

What am I doing? I'm no more Christian than the fish in the lake!

"You know the river at the north end of the lake?" the outlander asked. "Follow it upstream for two days until you come to a settlement on an oxbow lake. Then walk straight west half a day through the notch in the mountains. From there you'll be able to look down on a lake with yew trees on the shore, and a settlement."

Morgan gasped. Her mind was whirling.

I have a place to run to, a place not three days' journey from here.

But then she realized something terrible. "I can't run away while you're still here. Dúngal would call you a thief." She couldn't for the life of her say why she wanted to protect this man. But she didn't want him to be shamed before the druids.

"Mmm, that *would* be bad for the Faith, wouldn't it?" He chuckled.

"If you leave today, I'll follow you in a few days."

"I have only just begun my work, sister," said Salvatus firmly.

Morgan looked in the outlander's eyes. He had the same arrogant humility she saw in herself. She had no more chance of persuading him to save his own life than he would have of persuading her to give up her dream of killing Uter.

So Morgan led the missionary through the dim pre-dawn back to the dining hall. They kissed each other's cheeks like sister and brother, and she went back to Buanann's house.

Chapter Ten

THE TRIPLE DEATH

Cú Meda arrived with his two junior druids, by chariot, the morning of the full moon. Everyone ran to see what would happen.

Dúngal the headman embraced the druid. He immediately pointed out Salvatus at the edge of the crowd, and announced with wonder, "He's a Christian!" Cú Meda stared at Salvatus' outlandish half-shaved head. But before Cú Meda could process this, Dúngal said, "He says his god is stronger than ours. Can you believe that? I told him it wasn't true, of course, but I'm not as smart as you are. You won't mind demonstrating the power of our patron god Lugos by defeating him in a challenge, will you?"

That was clever. Cú Meda must be outraged that Dúngal had allowed a Christian to utter blasphemies in his village. But he had been challenged. All the villagers were looking at him. A man who backs out of a fair challenge is no man at all. Morgan was enjoying this. She suspected Dúngal was too, though he was smiling blandly at Cú Meda.

Cú Meda looked around. His neck veins bulged out even more than they usually did. Morgan imagined he was trying to think of an excuse to torture the outlander to death on the spot. But all he said was, "I accept."

Now he was honour-bound to fight fair.

"There will be two parts to the challenge," said Dúngal grandly. "The first is a disputation. Let our beloved druids show how the outsider's religion makes no sense. Let the outsider try to pick holes in the majesty of our traditions." He was laying it on thick, Morgan thought. "Then let there be a challenge of miracles. Whose god can change the face of the world? The god who gives us prosperity and victory? Or this new god who died in a distant land, long ago." Cú Meda snorted as Dúngal went on: "Then we will all judge whose god is greater." He meant the free men, of course. Each free man would swear an oath for one side or the other, and, as in any trial in Ireland, he would add his honour price to the side he swore for. Dúngal's own voice would be forty-nine times the voice of the lowest free man. Whichever side had the most honour would win.

"When shall the challenge begin?" asked Cú Meda. "Tomorrow?" No doubt he was already scheming for something to happen in the night.

"Why tomorrow?" asked Salvatus, coming out of the crowd. "Why not now? Surely you know as much today as you will know tomorrow. My truth won't change either. Why don't we begin now?" Cú Meda glared at Salvatus. "Unless you're nervous."

Cú Meda looked like he was about to burst open. "Let the challenge begin immediately," he said, with all the dignity he could muster.

SALVATUS began by asking questions. Morgan guessed they were ones he had asked the druids before, and never got a decent answer.

"In many Irish legends, a god will fall in battle, only to be alive again in a later story. Can gods die? How are they reborn?"

In the crowd of listeners, Morgan heard a man mutter to his brother, "I asked them that, and they told me to shut my yap."

Salvatus continued, "The soul never dies, but is reincarnated into a newborn infant at the moment of death. But what if more children are born than there are dying people? Where do the extra souls come from? Do the gods keep a bucket of spare souls handy just in case?"

That got a big laugh.

Salvatus pulled out two sprigs of mistletoe and defied the druids to tell which one had been harvested according to the rites and which had not. And, if they couldn't tell which was harvested properly or not, what was the difference?

To Morgan's surprise, Cú Meda and his junior druids had cunning and clever arguments to answer each of these puzzlers. At least, they seemed awfully pleased with themselves, and they said complex and weighty things. But Morgan had no idea what they were saying. Looking around the crowd, she could see the villagers didn't either. The druids had never educated their people on their doctrines, so when they referred to them, the people were left bewildered. Dúngal kept a befuddled expression on his face that was awfully close to insolent. The druids were rebutting Salvatus' questions point by point, and losing the crowd.

But it was worse than that. Apparently Salvatus had heard their rebuttals before too. He explained the druids' answers better than the druids could. Then he tore more holes in their answers.

Finally he asked, "Who made the world? And why?"

The druids couldn't even fathom that question. The Irish gods were not creators; they had merely conquered the land of Ireland from previous gods, who had conquered it from even earlier gods. Why? The question boggled their minds.

Dúngal intervened. "Who do *you* think made the world?"

Salvatus said there was one god, who had made the whole world in seven days. Cú Meda tried to laugh that off. "And who made him?" But Salvatus had obviously spent years preaching to everybody from chiefs to village idiots. He answered, and then circled his answer back to the son of his one god, who had been crucified by Roman soldiers. If you believed in him, your sins would wash away. Otherwise, you would burn forever in the bowels of the earth.

It was a hard story to shake. Every time the druids tried to poke a hole in it, they gave him another chance to tell his story.

After an hour of this, the people were tired but fascinated. The youngest druid stopped asking mocking questions and started to ask questions whose answers he really wanted to know. Cú Meda must have noticed, because he cut the young druid short. "It is time for the midday meal," he said. "But this village is tainted. We cannot eat or sleep in your village until it has been resanctified."

The druids walked out of the lake village to eat in the fields.

At first Morgan had counted that a victory for Salvatus. He had made the druids retreat. But then she felt the shiver run through the crowd. In all their excitement, no one had thought that they might be declared outcasts. Morgan heard one man tell his brother, "Dagda's Sack! I've got a lawsuit against that bastard at Glennamain, the one that sold me a dozen head of barren sheep? Cú Meda's supposed to rule on it!"

After the midday meal, they moved on to the challenge of miracles. Here Salvatus announced flatly that he was stumped. "I'm no saint. I can't work miracles."

The crowd murmured. Morgan was surprised. The Christian priests at Din Tagell said their god changed wine into blood. Had Salvatus got himself in too deep? And worse: if he couldn't help himself, how could he help her?

"I'm just a sinner," Salvatus went on. "I can't do magic. When it rains, I get wet. When it gets hot, I sweat." The crowd was grumbling now. It sounded like he was backing out of the contest, when he had been doing so well, and after he'd exposed them all to the retribution of the druids. "But the druids can't do miracles either. Oh, I know, they send you into battle, and if you win, they say their god won the battle, and if you lose, they say you made the wrong sacrifice. Some miracles."

The crowd was really unhappy now. "I've seen Cú Meda turn his staff into a snake!" said a man in the crowd, and others nodded.

"You don't think he really does it, do you?" Salvatus smiled, like you might smile at a five-year-old who's been fooled by sleight of hand. "It's all fakery! You can see right through it, if you open your eyes."

The druids had never heard anything like this. The youngest druid slammed his walking staff into the ground, intoning in a grand voice, "If you think my serpent is fakery, you are not long for this world!" The staff split in two, and the vine that twined around it became a serpent, a yellow and black creature that spread a hood below its face and hissed. The crowd gasped. The cobra slithered across the green grass and reared its head up at Salvatus. Morgan gasped, scared for him.

Salvatus laughed and grabbed the cobra, saying, "Illusions. See?" And he snapped it over his knee, and handed the two gnarled pieces of wood back to the young druid. The druid yanked his hand back, and the pieces fell to the ground.

Morgan stared at the broken stick. The snake had not been an illusion. She had felt it come out of the stick. But it was sticks now.

The second oldest druid, a tall man with a beaked nose, made an incantation in a strange, foreign language.

A nearby apple tree caught fire. The crowd gasped. The flames raced across the bare winter branches until, in moments, the entire tree was ablaze. "Behold the fire of Lugos!" yelled the beak-nosed druid.

Salvatus walked calmly over to the tree, climbed into the inferno of flames, and sat on a branch. The fire burned. Salvatus prayed, his hands together. He did not catch on fire. The fire guttered and went out.

Morgan had felt the heat of the fire; she'd heard the flames crackle. But the crowd pressed forward. They touched the branches. "It's cold!" said a man.

"Illusions, brothers and sisters," said Salvatus. "The druids have been deceiving you. Don't be deceived."

But there had been a fire. Morgan had felt the druid call to it. She had felt the fire answer his call, surging up from wherever the element of fire lived.

Morgan bent down and picked up a twig that had fallen from the tree as Salvatus climbed into it. It was charred. She closed her hand over it.

Everyone was looking at Cú Meda. His eyes were filled with hatred and fury. He was waving his arms and calling out strange words.

As they all watched, a breeze began to whisper through the lake village, circling the settlement. Faster and faster it spun, and the old druid's voice became louder. The wind plucked at her dress and blew her hair in her face. Cú Meda was smiling now, smiling darkly, still incanting ancient and strange words, and the wind spun more, and spray began to whip up from the surface of the lake. The wind seemed to surrender to his voice, and soon it roared in a vast circle around the lake village.

The people were frightened. The druid laughed, and it seemed that his laugh came from all around them. He said he cared nothing for their village, for it was a village of fools and blasphemers. They had unleashed the whirlwind against themselves, and they would pay for it.

Morgan felt a deep chill in her bones. She could not feel the wind within her. She could only feel it outside of her. All she could feel was…a darkness.

Cú Meda had not called on the wind. He had invoked a darkness, and the darkness was sucking the wind into it. He had called on a place where the sky was black and the sun was pale and far, and shadows were utterly black. It was sucking the air out of the lake village.

Morgan stood there, terrified, and she knew the villagers were terrified too.

Salvatus began to sing. He sang with a high soft voice, though his speaking voice was low and gravelly. Morgan was surprised. His voice pierced the wind's roar. She could hear him perfectly, singing of a night of a million stars, but one brighter than all the others. He sang of shepherds in the fields on a quiet night, a sacred night. He sang of a child born in a stable among the animals. He sang of peace.

The song tugged at her like a child's hand, and Morgan knew she wanted that peace more than anything.

The heart went out of the gale, like a stag struck by a hunter's lance, its knees crumpling. The wind fell away like a maple seed fluttering out of a tree. The breeze faded like night when the sun's rays first tickle the clouds. By the time his song was done, the only wind in the lake village was coming out of the mouth of Cú Meda. The darkness was gone.

The red-faced druid dropped to his knees, exhausted.

The other two druids picked Cú Meda up. He seemed incapable of speech. They started to help him out of the crowd. He began muttering curses at everybody, but there was no magic in him anymore, no power, only sickly fury. Everyone watched the druids help him walk away.

It had been a spell. Morgan knew it. It had been a spell more powerful than she'd have thought a single man could make—any man except the Enchanter. Cú Meda had opened a door she wasn't sure he could have closed. But Salvatus had shut it with a song.

The people milled around, buzzing. Everyone was congratulating Salvatus, even those who had avoided him before. Morgan was thrilled. She felt, inexplicably, as if she shared his victory.

Salvatus had done something far beyond the little cantrips she had learned from Buanann. And it was so simple. Not easy, but simple. Cú Meda's spell had been arcane, crafted by decades of learning. She did not have decades. But Salvatus' power came from nothing more than faith.

Could *she* learn to do that?

Cú Meda didn't come out of his tent for the rest of the day. He still had a few supporters, and they said that it was not fair to judge the contest while the man was sick. Álmath shouted at them, "There's no adjudication to have, is there? Why is he hiding in the sick-house, if he didn't lose?" Men took her side, and a few took the side of the druids, and soon they were bringing spears out of their houses.

Dúngal quieted everyone down. "It's been a long day. There's no hurry. Let's feast, and give thanks to all the gods." He had two gigantic sows brought from his own corral and slaughtered on the spot, and placed on spits and roasted. There was a feast for all the free men, and the slaves were grateful for the marrow bones and the guts. Salvatus gathered his crowd around him and talked into the late hours, while Cú Meda's friends went to bed early.

Morgan had hope now. With miracles like these, Salvatus could convert the whole village to Christianity. Then who would stop him from taking her away from this village? She would be free again.

THERE was a lot of yelling in the middle of the night. Morgan rushed out to see what was going on, along with everyone else. A mob of Dúngal's lords was dragging Salvatus out of the shed he had been staying in. He was naked. Moments later, Dúngal's daughter Fand came out too, naked, clutching a blanket around her. It was hard to see how the two could have been sleeping inside the shed, for there was barely room for a dog to curl up inside it.

Salvatus opened his mouth to protest, but one of the lords punched him in the throat so that he could barely whisper, and they threw him on the ground and beat him, and bound his hands so he couldn't weave a spell.

It all happened so fast. Dúngal's lords dragged the struggling outlander in front of Dúngal, and swore they had seen Salvatus and Fand sleeping together, naked. The lords were loud; they wanted the crowd to gather, to see what a fraud Salvatus was. The other lords said nothing; they'd seen what Salvatus had done with Fand, or thought they had.

And so Salvatus was instantly convicted. Cú Meda pronounced a terrible judgment upon him. "You are a blasphemer. You dared to violate the daughter of our chief, Dúngal. You violated the hospitality of our village. For any one of these crimes you deserve death. Do you have anything to say?"

Salvatus struggled to make a speech, but they had a rope around his throat so that he could barely breathe.

"Then you will be executed according to the law," intoned Cú Meda.

Salvatus looked around at the villagers. He could see in their faces, Morgan knew, that there would be no rescue. No one would stand up for him, not against Dúngal's lords, not after that scene.

He should have been a shocked and broken man.

But he straightened up and smiled. It was eerie. He looked up at the sky, where his god lived, and whispered something. As if he welcomed what was coming. As if the druids had given him the greatest gift in the world. He kept moving his lips until one of the lords hit him in the mouth to stop him from cursing them all.

Morgan and the mob followed as the lords lowered the drawbridge and frog-walked Salvatus over the boardwalk. They marched him by torchlight along the old peat-diggers' path to the bog. His back was straight, his eyes alive, like a man walking to meet his lover.

Buanann was out in front of the crowd, baying for Salvatus' blood. For a moment Morgan wondered if Buanann had betrayed Salvatus, if there had been a deal between her and the druids. But probably Buanann was only trying to protect herself.

At the edge of the bog, Dúngal's lords shoved the outlander over to the druids, who stood him above a hole where slaves had been digging peat lately. The hole had filled with murky water. They strung a garotte around his neck, and Cú Meda twisted it tight until Salvatus was choking. Before he could choke to death, the druids struck him with axes, in the skull, the back of the neck and the throat. He plunged into the hole. As he lay there, choking and bleeding in the ugly yellow water, they pinned him down until he drowned.

It was the triple death.

Everyone in the village stood watching, transfixed. It had all happened so suddenly, no one had had time to wonder how Salvatus could have got the energy to enjoy a woman when he had barely slept in three days, or why he would have been stupid enough to pick the headman's daughter, or why Fand, who lived in desperate fear of her father, would have betrayed him.

It had been a set-up, Morgan realized. Fand must have come to Salvatus in the dark, on her father's orders, so that his lords could find her there. Dúngal must have decided it was too dangerous to be the chief of a Christian village, or worse, a half-Christian one. He was much smarter than he let on.

Ͳꞓꞓ entire village was listening to the druids make loud and angry pronouncements about treachery and false gods and thieves disguised as prophets. Suddenly Morgan realized she was outside the village, in darkness, and no one was paying her any attention.

Salvatus had saved her after all.

The thought of Buanann made her hesitate. Buanann was almost a friend to her. Buanann might teach her more magic.

No. That was fear talking. If she did not run now, when would she run?

She backed into the darkness. When she could no longer make out the faces of the villagers in the darkness, she turned and ran.

ЅҺЄ had forgotten how dark the night could be when the sky was cloudy and the moon was down. She had no idea where she was, except that twice she had blindly run back to the lake. Running—that was hardly the word for what she was doing. She could barely see in front of her. The land was black. The trees were invisible; their branches tore at her in the dark. Their roots tripped her. The sky was charcoal black. There was no way to choose a direction.

She could hear dogs yelping. She had forgotten about the dogs. They had her scent. She had caught a glimpse or two of torches. At least that gave her a direction to stumble away from.

Rich men sometimes killed their runaway slaves, to avenge the insult. Poor men maimed their slaves for running. But Buanann needed her to climb trees. Didn't she?

Morgan stumbled blindly onward, no longer caring if branches ripped at her skin. The yelping dogs were closer. The more scared she was, the easier they could track her scent. She could definitely see torches now.

She put her foot in a hole and went down hard. She got up, but her ankle was in agony. She managed a few more strides. Then she realized the trees were parting, and she could see the dim sky. In a clearing she stood a chance. She took a few more steps. The land sloped downward. She put her foot on a bare rock.

She was at the lakeshore again. It was stupid to keep running. She turned to face the dogs and their men.

Chapter Eleven

THE COLLAR

Morgan dreamt.

She was watching her son playing.

Her son? Who was she, in this dream?

He was five or six years old, she guessed, and he was fighting with another boy. They each had a charred stick for a sword, and a child-sized shield. Her son fought hard and fast. He took risks, sometimes reckless ones, but the other boy kept retreating from the rain of blows, until he tripped on a root and fell down, and her son had the charred stick at his throat.

Her son was brave and fair, and he had her features.

The wind brushed her hair into her face. She smelled the salt in the air, and looked down from the cliff to the breakers far below. She loved Din Tagell.

Her husband came over to the boys. He was showing them how to hold their shields. He turned and looked at her with love in his eyes.

It was Uter. The boy was Uter's son. She had been dreaming she was Ygraine.

MORGAN woke up.

She was no longer a slave. She was a captive again. Now she had an iron collar around her neck. It was heavy, but not tight; it was made for a full-grown man. But it made it hard for her to sleep. She would roll over, and the chain attached above her head to the post would catch on her face, and she would wake up.

She marvelled that such a little thing as a chain could keep someone from straying. If she had an axe, she could break the chain with a few blows. If she had a clamshell, and enough time, she could dig through the dirt floor of the barn all the way to the bottom of the post, and slip the chain out from underneath. Given a stone, and time, she could wear her way through the chain. But all she had was her ragged woolen dress. She could dig till her fingernails bled, but it would take much longer than she had.

Mosquitoes buzzed around her in the shadows of the barn. That was the worst thing about the lake village. From Beltane to Lughnasahd, they swarmed in humming clouds you could actually see.

There had been almost no mosquitoes at Din Tagell, she remembered vaguely. There was almost always a stiff breeze coming off the sea, and the nearest lake had been miles away.

Morgan was furious at herself. For years she had waited for a sign. She had made herself stronger, but she had done nothing.

She had been a sheep. A sheep wouldn't jump a low fence made out of willow branches, a flimsy thing it could easily kick through. A sheep likes a fence: inside, she is safe from wolves, and the village dogs guard her lamb from the foxes.

The lake village had been safer than the wild woods. Morgan had been fed, like a sheep, and she had told herself that she was biding her time.

Uter wouldn't have waited. He would have slit the sentry's throat at the drawbridge, stolen Dúngal's chariot and ridden off into the east before he had even turned twelve. And if he'd died trying, he would have died laughing.

Her father would have…what? She couldn't imagine her father as a slave. But he would have thought it through, and then tried to live with the situation as best he could. Maybe he would have found a way to make himself indispensable to Dúngal.

Morgan had done neither. She had been a prisoner of comfort. And then she had run without thinking it through.

She had too much of her mother in her, she told herself. Her mother had run from Uter. Then she had stayed to be his slave. Surely she was still at Din Tagell, bearing children to Uter. Morgan tried to push the thought out of her mind, but it wouldn't leave.

Footsteps approached. A woman and a man. She tensed. The door opened. The light outside was blinding. She could make out a woman—that would be Buanann—and a big man.

Buanann came straight up to Morgan. "They asked if you're a Christian," she said.

What would they do to her if she were a Christian? Give her the triple death, too?

"I told them you're a slave, and slaves will run when no one's looking," said Buanann.

Morgan nodded.

"So you won't be able to gather herbs in the forest anymore."

"Not because you're not permitted," said the man, and from his rough voice she could tell it was Gabrán. "We're going to cut off one of your feet." He seemed pleased with himself.

Buanann sighed. "I told them a chain would do. But Cú Meda said that if the only punishment for running away is chains, then any slave will run away, because to be a slave is already to be in chains."

Morgan was surprised that Buanann was quoting Cú Meda. She wondered if the druid had come to terms with the wise woman now that he felt vulnerable.

If they cut off her foot she would never be able to run away. If she could not climb trees, they would set her tasks on the island itself. And if Buanann was no longer outcast by the druids, then Buanann might no longer need a helper.

Morgan needed time.

If I say I am a Christian, they will have to give me the triple death, Morgan thought. *But not right away. Not right after Salvatus.*

They would take their time. They would spend at least a day making speeches.

She had no other chance. This time she was not a wild beast running. She was a warrior, letting her guard down in the hope that her opponent would make a mistake.

"I am a Christian," she said. "My saviour is the Lord Jesus—"

Gabrán kicked her in the face, and she found herself on the ground. She started to get up, stupidly, and he kicked her again, very hard in the gut. She crumpled in pain. Then he leaped on her, striking her with all his force. He was a strong man, and with each punch a shock of pain ripped through her. She curled up in a ball, trying to hide from the punches, but Gabrán kept hitting her, grunting from the effort.

As she screamed in pain, she hoped she had made the right decision.

Gabrán punched Morgan in the back, in the kidneys.

"That's enough, Gabrán," said Buanann.

"She's a Christian," said Gabrán.

"Then they will give her the triple death."

Gabrán stepped back. Morgan lay there, in agony. Buanann came down to her. Pulled her face back. Stared at her.

Morgan realized that Buanann was looking at her with a hurt expression, as if she had been betrayed. "Why?" Buanann asked. "You were like a daughter to me."

Morgan said nothing.

Buanann spat in her face, then got up.

With her eyes barely open, Morgan could make out the mother and son leaving the barn.

Morgan lay back. Her ribs ached. Her jaw was sore. It was hard to move.

She was ridiculously proud of herself. *I bet they weren't expecting that!*

She had defeated their plan to cut off her foot by cunningly making them want to kill her three times over. Morgan began to laugh. It hurt to laugh. But it made her feel better too.

Father would be so proud.

She began to weep. She wept quietly so that no one would hear her, and she cried until the sunlight vanished outside.

IT was almost dark. Morgan waited, listening to the rain drip in through the turf roof of the barn. The ponies and cows slept standing, their hot breath warming the barn. Every part of Morgan's body ached.

In the three years she had lived in the lake village, she had done small magics—a wound healed here, a curse of impotence there, a divination to find out who had stolen a brooch. Morgan had learned to feign death, to go unnoticed and a dozen other small things. But she had never done a great magic, like Cú Meda had done, or Salvatus, or the Enchanter. She had never dared summon the great power she knew lay beneath the earth.

It was dark. It was time to raise that power, if she could.

She didn't know what she could do with it. Maybe it would tell her.

MORGAN could only walk around the circle once before the chain began to wrap itself around the post. But she could use that. Her world was no larger than the limits of her chain. She scratched a line in the dirt floor with her foot. Then, with her mind, she reached out and continued the circle a second time, and a third.

She needed salt and water to purify the circle she had drawn.

That was easy. She could taste her tears. She wiped at her tears with her fingers, and flung the drops to the four corners of the room. Morgan was alone inside her circle.

The circle was a door. With her need, her desperation, she opened it.

She realized how much she had been holding back. All her spells had been careful, limited. She had worked to hide them, to weave them through the world so that Buanann wouldn't notice them. But she was alone, and she did not have to hide anything now.

She touched the earth, and the silent power of earth surged into her.

She breathed in. She let her lungs fill with air, and the speed and intelligence of air swirled through her.

She needed fire. But she had desperation, and a hunger to live. She *was* fire. Her skin and her blood were hot. The passion of fire filled her. She caught fire like dry oak, and blazed inside.

She swirled her spit around in her mouth. She was made of water, and water was around her on all sides. She let water fill her with its flowing force.

She was brimming with will and need. She needed to leave here. She needed to break her bonds.

The world lurched and spun. Morgan was between the worlds. The circle was cast.

But something else was there, rising out of the depths. It clawed at her and it dragged her down, as a drowning man pushes another under the water to get to the air. She gasped, and pain lanced through her body. She struggled, but as she struggled, she was sinking into that other world, as the thing beneath the circle tried to rise into her world.

Something wanted to fill her body. Something angry, and hungry like her. Morgan thought of her mother, how she had not wanted to let the Morrígan inside her at the ritual of the wicker crow, and she suddenly knew what her mother had been afraid of.

And with anger, she thought she could let the something take her. Her body would not die. Gabrán and Cú Meda and Dúngal would return to meet a demon, she thought. It would be a form of vengeance…

…that was not the vengeance she wanted. She brushed these thoughts aside. She would not let the thing take her. She would take power from it, that was all.

The rocking and lurching slowed, and steadied. She was lying on the dirt floor. But she had power in her now.

She thought of the collar around her neck. She sent the fire within her into it, and the air, and the water, and the earth. She thought it old, as old as the giant stones beneath Glennamain. Then, before the power could take her again, she let go.

SHE woke up exhausted. Had time passed? Had she done anything? The collar was still on her neck. It felt as heavy as it ever had. It also felt rough. Flakes of rust came off on her fingers.

She grabbed the collar with both of her hands, and twisted it. Its rusted halves fell away like rotten bark.

Chapter Twelve

ESCAPE

Morgan was exhausted, too tired even for the old familiar cantrip that made people look away. But it was dark, and she could hear rain outside. She found a knife among the other tools in the barn, and slid open the wooden latch on the outside. She took a sack of wheat, and stooped over so that her hair was in her face. She walked out into the night. If anyone heard her from inside their house, and looked out, they would wonder what sort of idiot let a slave carry a grain bag in the rain. But they wouldn't want to go outside to find out.

The world was muddy and dark. She didn't feel cold at all. She was made of earth and air and fire and water, and she could call the fire out of her, as though she were dry oak burning with a hot, strong, lasting blaze. She could barely feel the rain on her arms.

The pier was on the island with Dúngal's house. His two boats were lying upside down, the drizzle thudding on their leather skin. She threw the grain bag into the chill water. It sank out of sight. She slipped into the lake.

She guessed the water was frigid, but her body was still filled with uncanny heat. She could barely feel the cold trying to stab into her.

Morgan ducked her head and swam away from the lake village.

She swam as quietly as she knew how, kicking with her feet, her hands in front of her to feel for the spikes she knew were in the water. In less than a minute, she guessed, she was already out of sight.

She kept swimming. She was bruised and exhausted. A soggy hand grabbed at her, but she realized it was only a mat of slimy water weeds.

After a few minutes she could hear running water. It was the river that fed the lake. She pulled herself up onto the bank, shivering, and gave thanks.

She could not rest. She started walking along the riverbank, away from the lake, upstream. It was her only landmark in the rainy dark; it must lead away from the lake village. At least the pursuit, if there was any, couldn't start until dawn. They would have to guess which way she had gone, and any footprints she might have left, and any scent, would be washed out in the rain.

Maybe they would decide she had drowned herself to avoid the triple death. She hoped so.

ĐẢẎ broke on Morgan's right, in shades of grey. So she was heading north. Good. Now she could feel the bruises all over her body. She had to let the fire of the spell fade. Soon she was too cold and numb to hurt much.

After a few hours, the rain stopped. She drove herself onward. According to Salvatus, the Christians were to the north. To the south was death.

The countryside was wild and empty. There was no road. Where the soil was rich, the trees grew tall, all the way down to the river's steep bank, and she had to wade through the shallows. Where the soil was poor, there were only grasses and rocks. Her feet were calloused from years of going barefoot, but her callouses had softened from her long swim, so she had blisters. She was hungry, and everything hurt.

In one place there was a peat bog, and as she walked over the squishy yellow peat, she thought of how Salvatus had welcomed his death. As his god had.

There were gods all around her. Spirits, at least. Unnamed powers in ancient places. They called to her to stop and rest. She was not sure where she was. The sky was overcast and bright, but it was also somehow night, and there were stars.

No. There weren't stars where she was. That part wasn't true. The stars were in that other place, where she had summoned the power to break her collar. She realized she had not completely let go of the spell. She was still partly between the worlds.

Morgan thought that if she stepped back into her own world, she might die.

She had to focus. She was hungry, and her mind was wandering. She had to keep to the riverbank. Always upstream.

The riverbank widened into a meadow. The grass felt so soft and inviting under her feet. She wanted to touch it with her hands. It felt good on her face. She would lie here for only a few moments.

MORGAN felt a chill and woke up. A wolf was looking at her from only twenty feet away. It was a beautiful creature, its tail swishing back and forth. She picked herself up off the grass and waved the knife she had stolen. The wolf just watched her. It didn't seem anxious to attack her.

She must have slept for a couple of hours. At least she was no longer seeing a night sky in the middle of the day.

She started walking again. The wolf followed her. She almost welcomed the company. At any rate, it kept her moving.

Morgan kept walking north along the river's edge. The wolf kept its distance. Sometimes it would see something in the river's shallows and abandon her. But it was too late in the season for there to be salmon. It would catch up to her with its easy loping gait. She guessed it was wondering if she was weak and might fall down.

It occurred to her that if she feigned unconsciousness, the wolf would come over and sniff her, and she could slice its throat open and drink its blood.

The wolf cocked its head, almost as if it could read her thoughts. It shook the rain off its back, vaguely insulted. Then it broke off and started loping away to the east. She envied how easily it moved, almost floating over the ground. In a minute it was gone.

IT was long past the season for berries. Morgan knew a dozen kinds of nuts that you could eat, but the only nuts she found were acorns, and those you had to soak in lye first. She didn't have any lye, though she could have made it from ashes, if she had ashes and a cauldron. She also knew fifty roots you could make a soup out of, if you had a fire and a cauldron. She knew two hundred and fifty medicinal herbs, but none of them would cure hunger.

Here and there she found leafy green weeds that filled her stomach, but they gave her no energy.

As the sun was falling into the hills, she came to a place that seemed, somehow, right...and she realized she was looking at a low, round hill no taller than a man, a pimple on the surface of the earth. No, not a hill. It had a rectangular opening framed with giant stones, and it had a ceiling made of another giant stone.

It was a barrow grave. Ancient people had made it. Time had emptied it.

If it was good enough for the ancient dead to sleep in, it was good enough for her, she thought, and she curled up inside of it like a fox, the knife in her hand, and for some reason she dreamt of nothing but horses all night long.

In the morning the spell was gone. Morgan felt normal again. She was starving, but her mind was clear.

She started walking. A chill dry wind blew down out of the northeast. She was shivering. Her bruises ached. She hadn't eaten in two days.

A path appeared, running alongside the river, and she wondered if she dared take it. A barefoot girl in a ragged woolen dress, walking from nowhere to nowhere. What else could she be but a runaway slave?

Suppose she said that thieves had attacked her party and killed her men, and she had barely escaped from them? But wasn't that exactly what a runaway would say?

It was all her fault. If she hadn't run away, if she had gone back to the lake village after they killed Salvatus, she could be picking herbs in the woods right now, wearing a warm cloak.

I'm going to die, she thought.

Why couldn't she have made the most of the lake village? When Buanann died, she would have become the wise woman.

She began to weep. She fell to the ground, her knees squishing on the soft grass. She had been strong for five years, strong and alone. Now she found herself missing the people who had spurned her. That was horrible.

She thought of Eithne. Had she made it home to her own people, or had she been captured, or murdered? Morgan's mother had loved Eithne, Morgan was sure of that. Morgan hoped she had shown Eithne love, too. God knows she missed Eithne now. She wondered how her mother would have welcomed Eithne back if Eithne had run away. She tried to imagine Buanann forgiving her...

Stop that! she told herself.

She had to remember who she really was: the heir to Din Tagell, to the hundred of Trigos, in the lands of the Cornovii, in Britannia. Another life had been put on her, like a garment that doesn't fit right. So what if it had kept her warm? She had to strip it off, like a snake rubs its old skin off to grow.

These were not her people. They had destroyed and subjugated her mother's allies. They had degraded her into slavery. She hated them for their barbarity, their wars, their boasting drunkenness, for their elaborate laws that only added up to the strong taking from the weak. She hated them for their dirt paths and their pathetic strongholds. She hated them for burning peat in their fire pits, making their houses smoky all the time. She hated them for not knowing how to read, or even wanting to.

She wanted to go home. Whatever she had done wrong to the cosmos, she had paid for it. She wanted to go home and sit in front of a stone fireplace filled with burning oak and pine. She wanted to read about Caesar's victories against the Gauls, and how Fabius had defeated Hannibal and his elephants. She wanted to hear her father reading out loud the letters his friends had sent him from Isca and Durnovaria, from Hispania and even Rome.

Uter had stolen that from her. Uter had brought war against her father. He had broken his oath; he had betrayed Gorlois' trust. He had brought the Enchanter with him, and her father never had a chance.

Usually that thought roused her. But she was too exhausted, shivering and starving, alone in a wasteland where crows perched on dead trees, calling to each other.

She could just lie back and die. She could just die, and all the suffering would be over. The crows would like that. They would feast. On the eyes first, unless she lay face down.

She stopped crying and began to laugh. Why be mean to the crows? Didn't they deserve a couple of nice fresh eyes?

She forced herself to keep walking.

AS she followed the path, it became clearer. There were even patches of bare dirt. She was near somewhere people lived. As the sun came down, she could make out a high circular fence. It was small, not even a village, just a family's settlement. But the setting sun glinted off a body of water beyond it. The oxbow lake!

Morgan thought about avoiding the settlement. Why would they help her?

But she was so very hungry. Maybe she could steal some food. Maybe a blanket too, or even a cloak.

Then she saw crows circling above the settlement. Lots of them. Crows?

She knew she should wait until the sun sank below the horizon before she dared go any closer. But there were so many crows circling. And as she crept closer, she could see more crows perched on the settlement's fence.

There was no smoke coming out of the settlement. Nothing from cook fires. Nothing for warmth.

In this weather?

When she came around to the gates, they were off their hinges. There was a half-dozen men lying dead, with gaping wounds, helter-skelter. The crows were perched on them, pecking away.

She shivered.

Morgan noticed a cloak on one of the dead men. She pulled it off him with some difficulty, for he was rigid with death. She wrapped it around herself.

A small man had boots; she took those too.

She remembered hearing talk in the lake village of the Múscraige people to the north, who had been raiding villages farther and farther south. If they had attacked this settlement this morning, and if they took a direct route instead of following the curves of the river, they could be at the lake village as early as tomorrow... She hoped that was where they were going. It would mean the lake villagers had much bigger problems than one escaped slave.

She smelled burned meat. There was a haunch still hanging over the campfire, on a spit. The attackers hadn't bothered to eat it, but they had left it hanging over the fire. It was charred, but on top there were parts that were only hard and dry. It was food.

Chewing the bits of charred dry beef, she went looking through the settlement. The raiders had not been thorough. There was a basket of crabapples, and she ate all of them. She even found strips of smoke-dried salmon, and those were excellent.

Morgan realized why the raiders hadn't burned the settlement. The people of the lake village might see the smoke.

She could warn them by lighting the thatch roof on fire. The Eóganachta had done nothing wrong, by their own traditions, in enslaving her. They enslaved all the peoples around them, and from time to time, their villages were raided for slaves; that was why they had built their village on a lake. They had treated her no worse than the other slaves, and no better than they would have expected to be treated themselves. Her father had enslaved Eithne, and others, after all. She had no claim against her captors. Salvatus would have found it in his heart to light the settlement on fire as a beacon, even though the Eóganachta had put him to death.

She found water in a pitcher, and doused the embers in the fire pit, so they couldn't possibly throw a spark and light the roof thatch on fire. It was satisfying. There would be no beacons for the Eóganachta. She wished she could give the Múscraige thunderbolts to wield against them.

Morgan pulled the bodies out into the centre of the settlement for the crows to eat. These men had died in battle. They would want the goddess Morrígan to come down as a crow and eat them, so She could take them to the warriors' afterlife. Then Morgan walked out of the settlement and found a small patch of woods a hundred paces away. She made her bed out of a half dozen bloody cloaks, and slept better than she had in years.

Chapter Thirteen

THE YEW TREES

Morgan came over the ridge, and there at the centre of the misty valley below her, by the shore of a lake, were a dozen round houses. Peat smoke sifted out through the high-peaked thatch roofs. There were muddy corrals for a few cattle and pigs, and around all of it, a twelve-foot fence of woven brushwood.

It was right where Salvatus had said it was. She had worried all morning that she had misunderstood his instructions. She was tired, her feet raw and swollen inside the too-big boots, and she had wondered what she would do if she was lost, or if there was no settlement, or if it had been burned by raiders. But there it was.

She wanted to run down there in joy. But she needed strength for that, and she was exhausted. So she sat down and watched the settlement until she could no longer stand the anticipation.

And then she walked steadily down to the gate.

As she came down the hill, the settlement disappeared behind its fence, but she could smell the peat fires. Closer to the lakeshore, she found herself walking among yew trees. Imleach Iubair, "the lakeshore of the yew trees," that was what Salvatus had called the place. Then she came to a split-rail fence, and the woods opened into a pasture where cows were grazing. Nearby, a woman goaded an ox past tree stumps as a man guided his plow. The stumps looked solid: they must have cleared the land only a few years ago.

As soon as she got within a hundred yards of the settlement's fence, two huge shaggy creatures charged out of the open gate and ran right at her, their bodies covered in grey-brown fur, like unwashed sheep, but with huge floppy ears and no horns. Their teeth flashed as they hurled themselves at her, barking furiously, but they were too shaggy to be frightening. A young man ran out after them, frantically calling them off of her, "Stop! Sit! Lie down!" but they raced toward her, tongues lolling, and knocked her onto the grass. They were happy. They were pawing her, licking her face madly, as if they'd always known her. They were gigantic puppies, each as big as she was.

She realized she was smiling. Smiling like an idiot. It felt strange. She couldn't remember the last time she'd smiled. She hoped it wouldn't create a bad impression, because as the two eighty-pound creatures rolled off her to squirm in ecstasy on the grass on either side of her, she just couldn't stop.

As Morgan stood up, the people outside the settlement streamed toward her. It was strange. They smiled at her, and waved, and walked with her toward the gate.

At the lake village, a lone fifteen-year-old girl appearing out of the woods, wrapped in a bloodstained cloak, wearing a man's boots that were too big for her, would have been a sensation. Everyone would have peppered her with questions. But these men and women just walked with her, with welcoming smiles on their faces.

Three women came out of the gate. They seemed to be in charge, but they were dressed the same as everyone else, in simple,

139

walnut-brown woolen robes. One was a short fat woman. One was tall and mannish. One was strikingly beautiful, with long blonde hair worn loose. All of them seemed to be in their thirties.

The mannish woman had a calm stateliness about her. "Welcome to Imleach," she said.

"Thank you, I—" said Morgan, and she was about to explain herself, to explain what a lone girl was doing coming out of the woods, with dried blood on her blue cloak. Morgan had rehearsed a dozen responses to the questions the Christians would ask her. But the woman hadn't asked her anything. Morgan found an amazed smile spreading across her face.

The mannish woman responded with a quiet smile herself. "We're about to sit down to supper. My name is Béfind," she said.

MORGAN found herself in a clump of people bubbling into the eating hall. Everyone smiled and nodded at her, like they already knew and liked her. Did strangers come to them all the time? Did they welcome them all like this?

She had a feeling she wasn't in Ireland anymore. These men and women seemed mysteriously content, like they all had a happy secret they shared. And they treated each other as equals. Including her. That was bizarre. Morgan had been a governor's daughter, watching her father hold court from his couch. Each guest had had his place, according to how honoured he was. She'd had her place among the slaves in the lake village, eating rags of bread after the dinner was over. The people of Imleach neither made way for her as an honoured guest, nor pushed past her to get inside.

Béfind gestured for Morgan to sit by her. But even Béfind was sitting in no particular place, near the far end. A wiry man was handing out loaves of bread. People were passing them around, breaking off hunks, juggling the fresh hot loaves a little. Morgan took a hunk and passed her loaf to Béfind. She started to eat. But nobody else was eating.

The hubbub died down. Nobody said anything. This must be when they would ask her who she was. Was she a Christian seeking out the community, or a lost traveller, or a runaway slave foolish enough to admit it?

But no, a pair of lanky older boys brought in a stewpot and heaved it up on the table in front of Béfind. Morgan could smell the beef and turnips and greens. What were they waiting for? Was *she* supposed to make a gesture? Morgan reached her knife toward the stewpot, but the girl at her left pulled her hand back.

"You must be starving," she murmured, and smiled brightly. She was about Morgan's age. "I'm Luan." Luan nodded her head toward Béfind. Morgan guessed Béfind was supposed to eat first.

"We're hungry, and we can smell the stew," said Béfind. "And after dinner, we'll be full. But hunger always comes back."

Morgan looked around the table. Everybody was listening raptly. Morgan felt a cramp in her stomach. She hoped whatever Béfind had to say wouldn't take long.

"This world is nothing but hunger. But in the next world, there will be no hunger for those who have faith in God. So let us give thanks, for the food for our bodies, and the food for our souls."

Then they began to pray, the forty or so Christians around her: *Benedic, Domine, nos et haec tua dona, quae de tua largitate sumus sumpturi.* "Bless us, Lord, and these your gifts…"

Morgan looked around the table, trying to keep her mind off the food. The Christians were younger than she had imagined. A convocation of druids would have been dozens of white-haired men presiding over hundreds of grey-haired men and women. The friendly girl at Morgan's left, Luan, couldn't be more than sixteen. There was a youngish man who seemed to be with two boys, maybe five and seven years old, who were scrambling around underneath the table. Except for two old women past childbearing, and one truly old, toothless man, there was barely a greybeard there.

She wondered what sort of families they had all abandoned. Each of them had left their tribe, to carve out a new home on this wild lakeshore.

Holy Michael Archangel, defend us…

The Christian prayers were different too. They were just talking. The druids always put on a show, with chanting and furious gestures. Luan was just talking quietly, like you'd talk to someone who loved you, the way Morgan had used to talk to her father at bedtime.

Luan looked up and saw Morgan watching her. She smiled at Morgan as if they were already best friends, and shared a secret. That was strange. Morgan remembered smiles like that. Her mother and father and she had shared smiles like that, long ago. But Luan didn't even know who Morgan was.

"Let's eat," said Béfind, and they all started stabbing meat out of the stewpot with their knives, and Morgan tucked into her first proper meal in eight years.

IT was only once they were well into the bread, the stew and the beer that Béfind finally turned to Morgan. "Your cloak was bloodstained. Are you all right?"

"It's not my cloak," said Morgan. "There was a settlement, half a day from here, to the west."

Morgan noticed the conversations around her dying out.

"I know the place," said Béfind.

"They're all dead," said Morgan. "Raiders. From the north. I think they were headed toward the Eóganachta."

Everyone nodded. Some shivered. They had dodged a blow.

"I was cold," she went on, "so I took a cloak and the boots."

Béfind turned to Morgan and finally asked the question Morgan had been dreading. "Where did you come from?" Suddenly everyone was listening intently.

Luan was gazing at her, still smiling. It unnerved Morgan. These people were Christians, and so they did not follow all the barbarian customs of Ireland. They would not care about the laws of insult and honour and vengeance. But they were still Irish. They would never hide a runaway slave. So she could hardly tell them the truth, or even let them guess it.

But she'd had three days of nothing but walking and thinking about what to tell them, and the thinking had taken her mind off her aching knees.

Morgan had learned a lot about lying in eight years of slavery. The obvious lie she could tell was that she had been travelling, and raiders had killed her companions while she had got away. But that was the story that any runaway slave would tell. They would see through any story she told.

And that, Morgan knew, was the secret to a good lie. To give them a story they would see through, but make them see an even better story behind it. If they thought they'd guessed the real story, they would believe it more than anything she could tell them directly.

So she began. "I'm the daughter of a chief. My people are the Corco Duibne." She could see them nodding. The Corco Duibne were a mystery. From the lake village it was ten days' hard walking to the southwest to get to them, through bogs and a dense forest. Not even tinkers or poets visited them.

"A storyteller came to our village," she went on. "He called himself Salvatus."

"Salvatus?" gasped Luan.

"He helped us found this place," said Béfind.

"He wasn't handsome, but he had a…" Morgan let herself blush, "…a *presence*, so that when he was there, you felt…" and she let herself pause, embarrassed, "…you wanted to *be there* with him. You felt…*safe* with him."

She wasn't saying it, but she hoped they would guess that she had been in love with him. So she pretended to hide her feelings, as the girl she was pretending to be would have. "It must have been the power of the Lord within him," she said. Her audience nodded and whispered approvingly. "And he baptized me. With his own hands, and his, his…" this, with a big blush, "his holy spirit."

They—Béfind and Luan and the others—were all looking at her with intense interest. She looked down at the table and didn't meet anyone's eyes. She realized she really was blushing, not just faking it as she'd practiced.

"My father, the chief, wouldn't listen to him. There was a contest of miracles." And she told them about the snake and the stick, and the burning tree and the whirlwind that Salvatus had quenched. That part she didn't have to fake.

"Amen," the people murmured. Luan was smiling with pure delight.

"I swore I'd go with him, spreading the word of life. My father grew wroth," she said, using an odd word, like the Corco Duibne might. "We were praying alone together. But they caught us, and they said that we were…" She managed to blush. "And the druids said that he had violated me, and violated our hospitality, and blasphemed against the devils they call gods. But we hadn't," she choked, and had to gather her composure. "They gave him the triple death."

They knew what that was, didn't they? Weren't they horrified? But they were nodding, entranced, the way warriors do when they hear the story of a battle. Béfind had a serene smile, the kind you have at the end of a perfect day. Luan seemed almost radiant. Suddenly she knew how much Salvatus had wanted to end his life story that way.

"You should have seen him," she said. "He never begged for his life. He only prayed."

She was angry. That was real. The druids had killed a great man because they were small, and his greatness had frightened them.

"And you?" asked Béfind.

Morgan snapped back to her lie. "They wanted to kill me for the insult I had done my father. But I…but my father took pity on me. And they only beat me"—she showed them the yellowing bruises Gabrán had given her—"and sent me away from the lands of my people. And so I came here."

She looked around with as wide-eyed a look of innocence as she could manage, trying to make sense of the company. Some of them were weeping. Luan was embracing her like a long lost sister. Two men came over from down the table and embraced her too.

Morgan snuck a look at Béfind. Béfind nodded at her wisely. "Surely Salvatus is looking down now at all of us," said Béfind, "and praying for us. I believe he is a saint, and God has guided you to us so that his story will not be lost."

They believed her? She hadn't expected them to *believe* her.

Someone tapped Morgan on her shoulder: Luan, smiling brightly. "Welcome to Imleach, sister," said Luan, and embraced her again.

Morgan smiled to herself. The part of her story she thought they'd have the most trouble swallowing was that she was the daughter of a chief. And *that* part was true.

She didn't have to talk anymore. Béfind gave thanks to God for Morgan's survival, and, "more importantly," for Morgan's conversion to Christ. Then she gave thanks to God for a lot of other things after that. Morgan was exhausted, and full. She had eaten as much as she possibly could. Though it was midday, the ale was making her sleepy. It wasn't the thin ale they gave to slaves, made from the leavings of the mash. It was rich red ale, fresh and thick. These were stunningly kind people. Gentle, sweet generous people, with no distrust in their hearts.

It was a miracle their neighbours hadn't massacred them yet.

AFTER the midday meal, the men and women of Imleach went back to their chores. Morgan followed Béfind. She felt like lying down and sleeping for a year. But she was a guest. And she wanted to ask about the world.

Morgan peeked at Béfind's right hand. Her fingers were splotched with black. Ink stains! Ink meant writing. Béfind would be in contact with Britannia. But Morgan couldn't ask about Britannia. Not yet.

"As the daughter of a chief," Béfind said, "I suppose you can do the most delicate needlework?"

Morgan's heart dropped. Her mother had done that kind of work. As a child, Morgan had worked a child's loom while her mother stitched the most elaborate silk embroidery across her father's tunics. It was a skill that any chief's daughter would have spent half her life mastering. Would her lie be exposed so very quickly?

"I'm sorry, but I can't set you to embroidery," said Béfind. "It would set you apart too much. Here we are all equal in the eyes of the Lord."

"I understand."

"Oh, I doubt that very much," said Béfind, with an amused grin. "But you will."

Béfind assigned Morgan to work with Luan, pulling weeds out of the garden. Morgan knew all about weeds, of course. But she let Luan tell her which of them were good for salads, like the young leaves of dandelions and purslane. "We prefer to eat what God plants," Luan said with delight. "Like the lilies of the field." She was a strange girl, full of grand enthusiasm for small things. "I'm glad you came here," she added. "There's no one else my age. Everyone's older. Except for the little kids."

"How old are you?" Morgan asked.

"Six months," said Luan. Morgan stared at her. Luan giggled. "In Christ, silly!"

EVENING came, and with it the evening meal. No one asked her any more questions. Morgan was surprised.

At night the women and men split up and went to sleep in the round houses, eight or ten to a house.

In the women's house, Luan gave her a bundle of fresh straw to lie down on. They lay down near each other. The women began praying. Morgan let the Latin words roll over her. It was nice to hear Latin. They were giving thanks…just for the day? The druids made invocations only at great ceremonies. If Buanann had wanted something in particular, she asked a god and sacrificed a rabbit. Nobody gave thanks just for the day.

"I'm giving thanks that you came to us," whispered Luan.

"Nobody asked me any more questions," said Morgan, kicking herself that she'd brought it up.

"We don't care about your old life. Just your new life," said Luan.

"Oh," said Morgan, relieved and surprised.

Her old life? There was something she had forgotten to do.

She burrowed her hand under the hay and scraped aside the old straw beneath it until her fingers were touching the earth. The earth had protected her, back in the lake village. It was the earth to whom she had called out when she was in chains, and the earth that had made the chains rust away a hundred years in the time it takes for bread to rise.

Would the earth hear her in this place? The Christians hated the heathen gods. Salvatus had banished the druids' magic.

She reached out with her soul. Her soul became larger than herself, and stroked the heart of the earth. And there it was, comforting, reassuring, bearing her high up above the subterranean rivers that flowed back and forth beneath her in vast slow tides.

The earth was still there. It was a cradle. It rocked her to sleep.

MORGAN was safe. At the lake village, she had lived in a state of vague floating dread, punctuated by occasional fright. Not a week had gone by without a fight. Here, nobody even raised their voice. Actually, once Petrán had shouted at one of Matha's boys, the five-year-old, when he was about to fall out of a rotten tree. But then Petrán had knelt and apologized to the boy, who hadn't even been upset, and had only wanted to run along. She had forgotten what it was like not to be scared.

But she was itching to find out about Britannia.

Morgan made an excuse to go visit Béfind in the great hall. She was writing letters. She didn't stop writing. Morgan stared at the letters, trying to read them over Béfind's shoulder. They were in Latin!

Suddenly Béfind looked up at Morgan sharply. She snapped, "Can you read?"

"Just the alphabet," Morgan said modestly. Then she realized that Béfind had asked in Latin.

Béfind tilted her bench back, eyeing Morgan. Airily, she said, "I just know so little about the Corco Duibne. See, my people aren't from around here. So I had to ask around. And you know what? Apparently nobody knows very much about them. Isn't that funny? Some people say they're fierce warriors. Other people say they've got two heads and one foot. You could say practically anything you like about them, and no one could really contradict you. And yet, somehow, I never thought of the Corco Duibne as speaking Latin."

Morgan swallowed. So Béfind had seen through her lies. She had just taken her time bringing it up.

Yet Béfind didn't seem angry. She seemed amused. "Do your people speak Latin?"

Morgan was bewildered. Should she run? But Béfind didn't seem to be calling for guards, not that there were any. She didn't know what else to do, so she tried to lie her way out of it. "I...I just guessed you were asking if I could read."

"And I am the Queen of Bactria, where the camels come from," said Béfind, with a hint of irritation.

Morgan sagged. She felt bad for insulting Béfind's intelligence.

"You know, there are two kinds of people who come to us, Morgan. One kind has found a peace in Christ that they never found anywhere else. They know that He has redeemed them, and so long as their faith in Him is strong, they're going to Heaven. They're in love with God, and they know that He loves them. They are happy, happy people." She smiled ruefully. "The rest of them *want* to come to Christ. Something haunts them. They have a hollow in them. They know only Christ can fill it. They don't have perfect faith. They want to. But faith is a faraway lamp that they sail toward in the dark. The wind drives them off, and they beat back against it. Are you following me?"

"I guess I'm a doubter," Morgan said, hoping it would do the job. She was walking on eggs, waiting for them to crack.

"That's the thing, though. You're not." Béfind shook her head, a wry smile on her lips. "You believe. You just don't believe in Christ."

"Yes I do!" said Morgan.

"I've been organizing this faith for some years now. I have a little experience with sinners and saints. You're not a saint. But you don't think you're a sinner either. A sinner is off balance. You're not off balance, you're just trying to figure out your next move."

Morgan certainly felt off balance just now.

"The thing is, your faith doesn't make you happy. Does it?"

Morgan winced. Her faith? She had never thought of herself as having a faith. Faith was when you believed in things you couldn't touch or see. She had felt the powers within the earth. But they didn't make her happy. That wasn't their job. They had saved her life. They gave her power beyond what a fifteen-year-old girl could have in this world.

If she told the truth, she would have to leave. Wouldn't she? This was a community of the faithful. But Béfind knew things about faith. And if she lied, Béfind wouldn't tell her those things.

"No," said Morgan.

"Then maybe it's not a true faith."

"Why should the truth make you happy?" Morgan asked.

"My god loves me. Does yours love you?"

"Love" was too strong a term. "God" was too sharp a term. The powers of the earth just *were*.

"Do you want me to go?" she asked. She was terrified.

"Do you have somewhere to go?" asked Béfind.

Morgan looked away. She had no place to go. That was why she was here. "I'm from Britannia," Morgan said.

They would send her out alone into the dying year. But she could survive in the woods if she had a knife and a flint and a pot to cook roots in. They would let her keep the bloodstained cloak she had taken, and the boots. Wouldn't they?

"I think I should ask no more questions." Béfind shrugged.

Morgan was stunned. She wouldn't be sent away?

Béfind was smiling at her and shaking her head as if she knew what Morgan was thinking.

Morgan's resolve broke. Fear poured out of her like water out of a bucket. She was suddenly sobbing uncontrollably. Béfind got up and held her. Morgan hid her face behind her hands, embarrassed. "What do I have to do?"

"It's free," Béfind said. "Like the lilies of the field." Morgan was dizzy. If Béfind let her go, she might fall down. "Do you know what you're feeling?" asked Béfind.

"Thanks," whispered Morgan, but it was more than that.

"Grace," said Béfind. "You've never felt it before, have you? This is only *my* grace, and that's a tiny mouse of a thing. Imagine a thousand times that. That's God's grace."

Morgan's head swam. She was relieved, and embarrassed, and miserable. She was still crying. "Why are you doing this?"

"To put you in doubt," Béfind said, smiling.

Morgan was confused.

"There's something great within you," said Béfind. "I saw it when you came here. There's something in you that cannot be stopped. You could be a great leader in the Church one day."

"But I'm not a Christian."

"Yet," said Béfind, simply.

Morgan let go of Béfind. She sat down on the dirt floor.

Béfind was watching her intently.

And what if she embraced Béfind's god, she wondered? Would she be happy? What if she never went back to Britannia? What if she chose an entirely different life, and a new name?

She had been reborn out of the sea when she had reached Ireland. She could be reborn again. She could call herself Mary. Mary would copy books, and write new ones, and teach a new faith to the barbarians. Mary would have nothing to do with vengeance against the faraway king of another land. "Call no man thy father," said the Christians. What if she became Mary?

Morgan had a sudden impulse to ask to be baptized right away. To throw everything away and become someone entirely new again, someone who didn't owe anything to anybody or any place.

Béfind smiled. Morgan stood up.

And then she felt the earth under her calloused feet, moist and soft. She thought of the land, and how it had once told her, "Be like me," and how it had cradled her when she had had no one else. She gasped in surprise, and felt the air she inhaled. She thought of the power she had summoned to rust her chains off, and the spirits of the land that whispered to her through all the years of her captivity. She had been exiled from Britannia and reborn in the Irish Sea, in an ocean of tears, and then she had escaped under the water of the village's lake, and fire had kept her warm.

But here there was no captivity, and no need for tears. There were no chains. Why did her story have to be written in blood? And hadn't Salvatus' faith been as powerful for him as the spirits of the land for her?

Morgan opened her mouth. She didn't have the slightest idea what she meant to say.

"I can write," she said.

"Ah." Béfind seemed disappointed.

But she didn't dwell on it. "We barely have any books. I wrote to a decurion in Bannaventa." That was a place in Britannia! "He promises to send us some books, but we must return them within a year. But in a year we could copy them." Morgan could see that the prospect of having books was already wafting away the disappointment in Béfind's face.

Books, Morgan thought. They would be Christian books, full of praise of the Lord. But there would be news of Britannia from time to time, even if it was old news.

"I could copy them," she said.

Béfind gave her a twisted smile, as if she were trying to stay disappointed that she was getting a scribe instead of a convert, but couldn't quite do it. She half snorted, and nodded her head. "I want you to teach Luan."

Morgan smiled and nodded. Luan would like that.

Morgan went to the door. But something made her stop. "What kind are you?" she asked Béfind.

"Of Christian?"

Morgan nodded.

"Which do you think?"

Morgan looked at her. She'd never really met Béfind's eyes. They were beautiful. Her face was faintly weathered, but lovely. There was great wisdom in her eyes, wisdom Morgan wondered if she would ever have herself. She had taken Béfind's wisdom for faith. But she could suddenly see the tension in Béfind's bearing. Béfind was sure of nothing. She was fighting to believe, Morgan realized.

Morgan nodded to Béfind, who smiled hopefully back. They understood each other.

Chapter Fourteen

THE STONE GUEST

In the beginning was the Word.

In the eating hall, Morgan pored over the slightly mildewed parchment of the Gospel of St. John. She and Luan were huddled near the doorway for light, while sheets of rain swept across the settlement. Morgan was copying the book out on another parchment. Her handwriting was nowhere near as elegant, but it was readable. It was slow going, which gave her plenty of time to try to teach Luan what the Latin meant. Outside the hall she could see Erc the shepherd out in the rain with the soggy sheep. She heard the dull thud of axes wafting in and out with the wind; Fergus and Ioseph building another corral, she guessed. She had seen Aillean and Sodelb heading out to the woods to pick berries. By now the rain would be dripping through the thickest trees.

Morgan whispered to Luan, "The Word of God will keep us dry."

"It will?" said Luan, with that hopeful look. She was always ready to hear new good things about the gospel.

"If we weren't copying this, we'd be out in the rain."

Luan smiled, chiding. "You shouldn't make fun." Luan's name meant "radiance." She had plain brown curly hair and a plain freckled face, but she did have a radiance. Béfind spoke of Christ as a lover, but Luan really seemed like a girl in love. She was a devout student too, listening so intently that Morgan would get rattled and lose track of what she was saying. "But you're right," said Luan, laughing. "The Word is keeping us dry today. And I'm so grateful." She embraced Morgan, hugging her tightly with the sheer joy of being able to serve God in such a fun dry way.

Morgan found it utterly mystifying.

TꞮE next day they finished reading St. John. The rain had subsided to a dull drizzle. The two girls went over, beaming, to where Béfind was talking with the blacksmith.

"We finished!" said Luan.

"Already?" Béfind said mildly.

"It's pretty simple Latin," said Morgan.

"Luan understood it completely?" asked Béfind, even more mildly.

"Of course," laughed Luan. "I know the story, after all."

"Of course," said Béfind breezily. "How hard can it be to learn Latin?"

Oh. Béfind was irked, Morgan realized. The milder Béfind got, the more trouble you were in. "Maybe we missed some things. Maybe we should go back."

"Oh, don't worry about that." Béfind smiled. "I've got something else for you. And it won't be any trouble for you two, since you're both so smart."

Uh oh.

"I want you to move the ram from the field to the corral Fergus and Ioseph just built. You can get a rope from Dara."

Morgan looked outside. The rain looked cold.

"I'Ve never caught a ram," said Morgan. "Is it hard?"

"How hard can it be?" asked Luan.

The ram was in the middle of the field, munching grass. He glanced at the two of them and tossed his head. He was larger than any sheep, and his horns were bigger. He looked like he weighed more than Morgan, and the soggy dirty wool that covered him everywhere except his black hooves, eyes and nose didn't make him look a bit cuddly.

"If we have faith…" said Luan, but for once she didn't seem convinced. The ram tossed his head and trotted away. "Maybe we should try to get him into a corner."

"Get him cornered? Is that a good idea?" asked Morgan.

"Otherwise he'll outrun us."

They split up and closed in on him. Morgan spread out her arms, and Luan grabbed her skirts and held them out so she'd look bigger.

The ram looked at them, then trotted back toward a corner of the field.

"See?" said Luan.

When the ram got to the fence, he turned and faced them. He lowered his head and pawed the long grass. "Does he look angry to you?" asked Morgan.

"What does he look like when he's happy?" asked Luan.

They moved in until they were about twenty-five feet from him, but he didn't back up anymore. Morgan flexed the rope they hoped to get around his horns.

They edged closer. The ram huffed, and his breath puffed white in the drizzle.

"Should we rush him?" Morgan squatted down. She had cunningly brought along some oats and she held out a handful.

"Come here, boy. Don't you want a treat?" The ram just stared at her. Morgan waddled a step forward, still holding out her handful of oats.

The ram charged right at her. Terrified, she threw herself to one side as he nearly ran over her. "Damn it!" shouted Morgan, running after him, oats spraying. Luan chased him too. The two girls sprinted after the ram, but he zigged and zagged every which way, trotting easily, while they exhausted themselves.

"Go around those bushes!" yelled Morgan, as she tried to herd the ram around a stand of low berry brambles.

The ram took the bait, heading right for Luan. Luan shrieked, suddenly realizing that four horns were headed straight at her. She tried to flee but slipped on the slick grass and slammed face first onto the soaked ground, sending water flying everywhere. With a terrified shriek, Luan squashed her face down into the mud, cowering with her hands over her head. The ram galloped over her, leaving muddy hoof prints on her back. Then he headed right for Morgan. Morgan yelled and threw her hands out wide and jumped into the air, trying to look threatening. Her dress billowed on the way down, and the ram bolted for the other end of the field. Morgan kept shouting.

Luan got up, her face red, her hair sopping, screaming at the top of her lungs. Morgan caught, "Son of a bitch bastard!" and, "My father will break your legs!" and, her voice rising, arms flailing, "...break your ribs myself!" and, hysterically shrieking, "...cut your balls off and feed them to you roasted!" Luan kept screaming curses, fiercer and fiercer, until her voice became a squeak and she stood there choking with outrage.

Morgan laughed and laughed. Luan glared at her furiously. But Morgan couldn't stop. She had to sit down. Luan opened her mouth, but no sound came out, and that only made Morgan laugh harder.

Utterly defeated, Luan sat down on the grass and wiped her tears. She managed a sad little smile at Morgan, and after a moment, a real smile. She started laughing at herself, a low, quiet chuckle. "Um," she said after a while, "maybe we should ask the shepherd how you catch a ram?"

Morgan realized she liked Luan a great deal.

ERC the shepherd had Luan lead a ewe into the pen. He'd put an odd leather apron under the ewe's stumpy little tail. The ram trotted right over and mounted her while she stood there eating grass. Luan led the ewe off to the new pen. The ram followed her, bumping away furiously and uselessly at the leather apron. When they got him there, Erc threw a rope around his horns and held him still while Luan pulled the ewe back out of the pen. Finally, Erc let him go. The ram hurled himself at the gate, but it was too sturdy even for him.

As they led the ewe back to the sheep pen, Luan sighed. "I'm sure there's a lesson in this."

"No doubt," said Morgan. It was probably: don't send two girl scribes to do a shepherd's job.

"The moral is," said Erc, "if a man thinks he's going to get lucky, you can lead him anywhere you want. Remember that, Luan, when you leave here."

"Why would I leave?" asked Luan.

But Erc just snorted. He shot a curt nod at Morgan as if to say, "You remember that too."

LATER that night Luan stared into the fire, her faced scrunched up in thought.

"What is it?" asked Morgan.

"It's the animal urge that dooms us," said Luan. "We think we're free, but as long as we follow our urges, we're just slaves. It's only when we do virtuous things we don't want to do that we're really free."

Morgan frowned. That made no sense. Uter had been nobody's slave; he'd done what he wanted. And when Morgan had been a slave, it had been her urges, her will, that had saved her.

But Morgan did like the way Luan searched for a moral in everything. The people of the lake village had lived out their lives eating and drinking and bearing children and dying. Only the druids asked why, and they never shared their answers.

Until now Morgan had thought of Luan as a simple girl who believed everything she was told. But what if she was wrong, and Luan knew important things? What if Morgan was missing something?

"How did you come to Christ?" Morgan asked.

"There was a coppersmith. Well, he wasn't very good at fixing pots. I guess he said he was so he could visit my father's village."

"Your father's village?" asked Morgan.

"No, I mean…" She sighed. "It *is* my father's village." She made a face, embarrassed. "He's the chief. This is his land."

"Oh!"

"See, that's why I liked you so much right away. Because you're a chief's daughter too! But I didn't want to just say that."

"No, of course not," said Morgan.

"I was a bad daughter. Willful. Spoiled. Not like my brother, Conall. You should see him going off to hunt with Papa. They're

proud, and they're tough, and they won't step aside for any man."
Her eyes lit up. "But I was pigheaded."

"You?" Morgan asked, but then she remembered Luan cursing
the ram.

"You didn't know me then," Luan said, laughing. "Anyway, this
coppersmith, he always took his time fixing things. And I wanted
to hear about the world. And he was so good at talking. He told us
about Christ, and his words pierced my heart." She smiled again,
that radiant smile. "He baptized eleven of us in the stream, and the
moment I came out of the water, I knew everything had changed.
And you know who the coppersmith was?"

"Who?"

"Salvatus!" said Luan. "Same as you!"

"What did your father say when he found out?" asked Morgan.

Luan frowned. "He had his men shut Salvatus in a barn. He
kept yelling that he was going to burn it down. But Conall talked
him out of it. He said why burn down a perfectly good barn? So
Papa told Salvatus to leave our village and never come back."

"That was kind of him."

"Salvatus was so brave. I wanted to follow him, but Conall told
me it would break Papa's heart. But I told my mother all about the
Lord. And together we worked on Conall. But he just poked fun
at us. He said our neighbours would come and kill him while he
was turning the other cheek."

"The Romans were Christians." Morgan shrugged. "And they
did all right."

"Exactly!" Luan said, a little petulantly. "Anyway, later on,
Béfind came to my father. We hold this valley by ancestral right,"
Luan said, slipping easily into the language of privilege. "But no
one had farmed here for a generation. Conall told Papa to give it

to her, because otherwise one of our neighbours might come and claim it. So Papa granted Béfind a leasehold on the land, with no rent for seven summers, because of the work of clearing it. Papa's a good man," she said, "even though he's a pagan."

Papa's a clever man, thought Morgan. Béfind's Christians were all outcasts from their own tribes. They were clearing his land for him, but any time he felt like it, he could raid the settlement, take the land and sell all the Christians into slavery. And no one would say a word.

"He didn't want me to come here. But I think he was afraid I'd convert his lords. They kept coming around asking me about Our Lord Jesus Christ."

I'll bet, thought Morgan. She imagined warrior lords in fine silks and gold, listening to this beautiful girl babbling about some foreign god while they tried to figure out how big a dowry she would come with. Was Luan really so naive? Or did she just not see things she didn't want to see?

They watched the fire for a while.

"Have you ever been in love?" Luan asked.

"No!" Morgan said, and was surprised to hear how harsh she sounded.

"Me neither," said Luan. "Except with Christ."

"Do you ever wonder what it's like?" asked Morgan.

"Not anymore," said Luan.

MORGAN woke up alone. It was an odd sensation. Luan was a foot and a half from her, snoring. The whole room was awash in the breath of a dozen people. But she was alone.

The land. The land was not there. When had it gone?

She suddenly realized that she had not felt the land for some time now. How long? Weeks?

They were heading into spring. On Imbolc, the feast day of the goddess Brigid, the Christians had lit candles in the great hall and prayed to the eternal light of Our Lord. She had felt a faint glimmer in her soul, but then it had gone. Even at the lake village, shoved to the back of the crowd with the other slaves, when the druids lit the fires of Imbolc in front of the entire village, she had always felt a part of something ancient and vast. She had felt the great wheel turning beneath her. She had felt the warmth of the returning light. Here at the monastery they celebrated the light without celebrating the darkness. They called it Candlemas.

She missed the darkness.

Morgan got up. Outside, the rain had finally stopped. She left the house. The air was dry and chill. She shivered. She slipped through the gates of the settlement, out into the wilderness.

In the still, wet meadow, she called out to the darkness.

Nothing.

She took a few more steps away from the gates. She called out again. The land was glistening wet. The moon was full. You could read in moonlight that bright. The rain had cleared away the peat smoke that lingered over the settlement. Morgan strained her inner voice and shouted out to the ancient land around her, the waters of the lake, the stones of the ridge, the still breeze and the fire within her soul.

Her voice echoed hollowly within her.

She looked within herself, troubled. She had not done even the smallest spell in a long time. She hadn't had to.

Did she need the land? The darkness? Today she slept in comfort. People loved her. People had hopes for her.

Luan would be horrified by what she was trying to do. She would have thought that Morgan was lapsing back into the Devil's embrace.

Morgan was frightened. She touched the moist earth. It felt like nothing but soil. There was no one there. She closed her eyes. She tried to listen. But all she felt was the pulse of her blood in her veins.

And what if the land did speak to her? What would she say to it?

MORGAN shoved the gate door open again and went back into the settlement. She shoved the bolt shut behind her. She felt safer inside the gate. The monastery was hallowed ground.

She felt even safer inside the house, where the other Christians were sleeping.

Not all of them. Luan was awake. She seemed worried. "Where were you?"

"Outside."

"What about wolves?"

Morgan turned away from Luan, and ignored the gentle tug Luan gave her shoulder. She shivered, though the house was warm.

She lay down by the fire. Luan pulled her close, put her arm around her. For Luan's sake, Morgan forced herself to stop trembling. Eventually she found sleep.

THE wheel of the year spun, and the land warmed up. Morgan had been at the settlement almost four months when a procession appeared from the east. It moved slowly, a two-horse chariot, slowed by the dozen or so men following on foot. This time, Béfind called everybody in from the fields to greet the visitors.

It was Béfind's overlord, Oengus, Luan's father. Conall, his black-haired son, drove the chariot with easy grace. Behind them, Oengus' full retinue followed: his druid Maelgenn, his poet, his healer, his harper, his steward, his charioteer, his groom, his huntsman and six lords in attendance. Luan hurled herself at him, and he lifted her up into the chariot and whirled her around as if she were no more than a six-year-old girl. Conall had to leap out of the chariot, grinning, to calm the horses. They seemed reassured the moment he touched them.

Then Oengus got out of his chariot and received Béfind's formal courtesy as his free client and leaseholder. "You're just in time for our evening meal, my lord," Béfind said. "Will you do us the honour of eating with us?"

Everybody followed Béfind into the great hall. Oengus seemed surprised when Luan sat next to Morgan at the long dinner table, rather than at his side. But he quickly recovered his spirits. As the food came out, he kept smiling fondly in Luan's direction, but only, Morgan noticed, when Luan was looking somewhere else.

After the meal the Christians sang their songs. Then one of Oengus' lords started a song about a farmer in love with a sheep. Oengus frowned at him and the man stopped. Morgan was impressed with the discipline Oengus had instilled in his retainers.

Conall was full of fire. "You should have seen the feast we had for Brigid, Luan! The candles burned all night." He turned to Béfind. "We sacrificed a beautiful white ox to Her. What did you sacrifice to your god?"

Morgan liked him. He had his father's piercing eyes and strong nose. And his smile was brave and generous.

"We don't sacrifice to God," Béfind explained. "We pray."

"Oh, don't think too highly of him, then, do you?" asked Conall, with a grin. Luan frowned. Oengus shot his son a mildly amused, mildly reproving glance. Morgan remembered her father shooting the same look at one of his centurions.

"He sacrificed himself for us," said Luan.

"I can understand why you don't respect him." Conall was enjoying ribbing his sister.

"He redeemed our sins," said Luan.

"What sins?" asked Conall. "You folks sin? You seem like such nice people."

"There's always pride," said Luan.

"Pride is a sin?" asked Conall, honestly bewildered. "Shouldn't I be proud of myself, of our father, and his father?" He glanced at his father, who nodded. "Pride makes men do great deeds in battle."

And with that Conall launched into a long story of a raid he had led into his neighbour's lands, stealing a flock of goats and one truly magnificent horse, killing half a dozen men, burning half a dozen houses and getting his men home safely. It was a great story, though the Christians didn't seem to appreciate it. Conall even poked fun at his own mistakes, and played up how he had nearly got himself killed several times.

Morgan liked Conall. He had Luan's fire, but he didn't even try to hide it.

Conall was about to go back out and attack his neighbours unprovoked a second time when Petrán interrupted him. "If you want to be proud," Petrán said, "be proud of your sister. She's truly strong in Christ." Pride was always an issue with Petrán. He couldn't stop talking about how humble he was. "She's so young, barely old enough to marry, but she prays as long and as devoutly as a saint."

"What's a saint?" asked Conall. "Is that like a high druid?" Morgan had to suppress a grin. Conall obviously wasn't impressed with Luan's ability to pray extra long.

"A bishop is like a high druid. A saint," said old Dara, "is a very holy person. She may know many things, but she only needs to know one thing well. She has found God."

"Where do you find God?" asked Conall. And suddenly, instead of telling an unwilling audience about his adventure, he was really talking to them. "Or how? If you pray all these long hours, does he come?"

The room fell silent. Luan didn't say anything. Béfind was surprisingly quiet. Even Petrán seemed to be struggling to figure out what to say.

Conall eyed Luan. But Luan didn't look back. She seemed nervous and flighty, not the self-assured girl Morgan knew.

"It's not just praying," said Morgan, and was surprised she'd jumped in. "You have to listen."

She had listened to the earth, and it had spoken to her. But now it didn't. Should she try to listen to Luan's god? Morgan pushed the unwelcome thought out of her head.

"I think it's time for Luan to come home," Oengus said, as if it were a perfectly reasonable response to Conall's question. Luan blanched.

Oengus' eyes roamed around the company, without looking at her. "Time she married."

Luan was thunderstruck.

"I told the chief of the Uí Drona about my daughter's beauty," said Oengus. "Luigdech is his name. For those of you from strange lands, the Uí Drona are the tribe to my east. Fierce boys with a spear, and rich. Their chief is prepared to give me three fifties of cattle, along with the land they graze on. You should see it. The soil is black and rich, and there is room for another two fifties of cattle should the gods grant us increase. We've been fighting them there for two generations," he said. "I got the better of them these past few years, and now they don't dare graze there anymore. But they don't want to give it up for free; they're not cowards. So Luigdech will give me the land and the cattle for my beautiful daughter. A good bargain, right?" He chuckled.

So that was why he had come here now. Oengus had never intended to let Luan stay here. He had indulged her religious whims only until he could marry her off. And at a religious community, there was little danger of her falling in love with the wrong man.

Luan was staring at Oengus, her mouth open. Morgan was suddenly, painfully aware what a lovely mouth it was.

Conall was watching his sister, worried.

But Oengus was smiling at the Christians, avoiding Luan's eyes. "I like to avoid a fight when I can." His fighters all laughed, and Morgan noticed him fingering a fresh scar on his neck.

Morgan reached out to comfort Luan, but she was frozen, rigid.

Oengus kept explaining in his soft-spoken, reasonable tone. "Oh, you should see Luigdech in a battle! Hasn't he killed dozens of my men with his own hands? And haven't I fought him in single combat, practically to a standstill? And his wisdom! He always listens to his druids, they say, and he's never made a false judgment. When his own foster brother stole cattle from one of his farmers, did he go easy on him? He killed the man with his own hands. And his riches!" Oengus was waxing grandiose. "He never wears any cloth against his skin but silk, and he never wears any metal but gold. His cloak is so white it dazzles you. He wears a gold neck-ring as thick as your wrist, Luan, and he has another one like it for you."

Morgan thought unwillingly of a slave collar. Luan looked like she was in shock. Even Conall looked nervous. Maybe all his bravado had been nervous energy.

Oengus kept talking. Morgan realized he wasn't trying to justify his decision. He only wanted to give the Christians time to accept it, lest one of them say something he might have to get angry about. He kept talking, and no one else spoke up.

"Your father really is a great chief," Morgan said to Luan, under her breath.

"You can have him," murmured Luan, looking pale. "I'll take your father instead."

"You don't mean that," said Morgan. Would Luan really trade an unwanted marriage for exile in a foreign land, her father slain and her mother taken as a trophy?

Yes she would, in a moment. If she were Morgan, Luan could live forever at the monastery and become a saint among the Christians.

And if I were Luan, Morgan thought, *I would become the wife of the chief of the Uí Drona.*

She would help him win victories. As a child she had dreamt of helping Ciarnat become High Queen of Ireland. Maybe she could even persuade Luigdech to take his warriors across the Irish Sea to Din Tagell.

But if Morgan were Luan, she would have no need for vengeance. There would be no Uter in her life. Her father would be a neighbour, an ally in war, someone to visit. But Oengus wasn't her father. And even the Enchanter couldn't make her into Luan.

Oengus looked at Luan. He waited for silence at the table. "We won't have to fight our neighbours anymore. We'll finally have peace." Oengus knew Christianity was a religion of peace. Oengus smiled hopefully at his daughter.

Luan burst out of her chair and rushed out of the eating hall, looking pale. Everyone watched her go.

Béfind said, "Dáire, why don't you see to Luan. She seems ill." Dáire, the monastery's healer, got up. Morgan followed.

To Morgan's surprise, Conall followed them both to the sick-house. Luan was bent over, her face buried in her arms, sweating and moaning. Conall knelt down by her side.

"Are you going to be all right?" Conall asked.

Luan didn't answer. She just gave a little whimper.

Conall nodded and made a small frown. As if that whimper had told him what he needed to know.

Morgan said, "She's too sick to travel anywhere!"

Oengus was just coming in, trailing his healer. "Who said I was travelling today?" He barely raised his voice, but it was hard to meet his gaze. "Would I risk my daughter's health?"

Then Oengus turned to his healer. "Give her a remedy."

Dáire said, "Bog myrtle," at the same moment that Oengus' healer said, "Marsh rosemary." And they glared at each other.

Dáire said, "Bog myrtle calms the stomach."

"Calms the stomach, brings on the menses, aborts the fetus, in large enough doses kills the patient. But here we have possible food poisoning; what's needed is marsh rosemary—"

They went on, both of them trying to prove what clever healers they were, while Luan sweated.

Morgan was worried for Luan, but not because she was ill. She had a pretty good idea it wasn't food poisoning.

Morgan suddenly noticed that Conall was grinning. It was a sincere, honest grin, as if he too suspected that Luan wasn't really sick. Morgan glared at him, and he smiled boldly at her. His teeth were straight and white, and he had all of them. She didn't want to like that smile, but for some reason she did.

Conall shrugged and kneeled by Luan's side again, and took her hand. He half-smiled encouragingly. Luan pulled her hand away weakly. "Maybe we just need to get some sleep," he said, the way you'd talk to a baby.

Oengus nodded. He obviously listened to his son. "Let me know if she gets any worse," he said. "Don't give her any medicines. I think she'll be better in the morning."

He strode out of the hut. Conall stayed. Oengus came back to the doorway and shot a look at Conall. Morgan could see that Conall wanted to stay at his sister's side. But Conall sighed and kissed his sister on the forehead, and got up.

Then he looked straight at Morgan. His intensity took her aback, his dark eyes and his long black hair glimmering in the light of the rush torches. He was just as beautiful as Luan was. Just as intense. But it was a man's beauty, not a girl's. She suddenly felt embarrassed. She made a silly little smile. "I'll look after your sister," she told Conall, or might have; she wasn't actually sure if she'd made a sound.

Oengus jerked his head with finality, and Conall headed out the door after him.

Morgan followed them out. A few minutes later, she caught a glimpse of Oengus grabbing a spear and striding off toward the gate. Conall raced after him, Oengus' lords and retinue following him.

"I hope they find something to kill," Dáire said.

Morgan nodded, and she went back into the sick-house.

"I'm feeling a little better," said Luan.

Morgan kneeled, put her hand on Luan's forehead, and whispered in her ear, "I'm not surprised."

Dáire harrumphed. "I'll be the judge of that." She came over and felt Luan's forehead. She made a face, gathered her robe about her and stalked out.

Oengus' healer winked at Morgan. He was a small man, balding and pudgy. "Luan's always been my best patient," he said, squatting by Luan's side. Luan buried her face in the bed straw, avoiding his look. "I can't tell you how many times I've cured her without doing a thing."

Luan moaned, and covered her head in her hands.

"Except the headaches. She gets terrible headaches, and she sees pixies. Well, she used to see pixies, but now she sees angels." He got up. "Do you think there's still some of that ale left in the eating hall?" Without waiting for an answer, he trudged out the door. Luan made another petulant whimper.

"They're all gone," said Morgan. Luan lifted her face out of the bed straw. She wouldn't meet Morgan's eyes.

Béfind came in and nodded her head at the door. Morgan made to leave. But Luan put her hand on Morgan's. "Please?" She gave Béfind a tortured look. Béfind shrugged at Morgan.

"You will have to do as your father says," said Béfind. "I know you don't want to. But you have to."

"The Evangelist says, 'Call no man thy father,'" said Luan.

Béfind shook her head. "Our Lord said, 'Render unto Caesar.'"

Morgan felt betrayed on Luan's behalf. Luan had never asked for anything for herself before, not since Morgan had known her. Who was Béfind, of all people, to throw Luan to these pagans?

"She belongs here," said Morgan, and she was shocked at how sharply it came out.

"Maybe so," Béfind said. But she didn't take her eyes off Luan. "Your faith is strong," she told Luan. "I don't fear for your soul."

"I wanted to be—" Luan started, and stopped again, her voice choking.

She wanted to be a great Christian holy woman, thought Morgan angrily. *She wanted to be a saint. Now she has to be a wife.*

"That's pride talking!" said Béfind, as if she'd read Morgan's mind.

"It is not!" snapped Morgan, surprised at her own fervor. "Luan was given a gift by God—"

"By God? Really? Did He mention that last time he spoke to you?" She glared at Morgan.

"If I could make him not want me," said Luan. "If he wouldn't want me…"

What did that mean? Who wouldn't want Luan? Luan, who, even sweating and sick as she was now, made you want to hold her and comfort her and love her? Morgan had never cared about Luan as much as she did now.

Béfind got up. Paced. Sat down again. "Don't even think of doing something like that," she said.

What did that mean?

"What is a face? Nothing to the glory of God," said Luan, her voice getting calmer and more confident. Morgan felt like Luan was slipping away from her. Her voice felt cold and distant, and it scared Morgan.

"You have too much faith," said Béfind to Luan, sharply. Luan's eyes snapped wide open with shock. "God gave you gifts for this world. Don't destroy them for the sake of the next."

"Béfind!" said Morgan, and Béfind looked at Morgan with torment in her eyes. Morgan could see she was reeling. But what was their faith about, if not the next world at the expense of this one? "You can't mean that!" She took Luan's hand, but there was something hard in Luan's eyes, something withdrawn and pebble-hard.

Maybe she really was a saint. Maybe she could become someone like Salvatus. But her father was stealing that from her.

Morgan didn't believe in Luan's God. But she believed that Luan had faith. It was a pure strong thing, and it made Luan more beautiful inside than she already was outside. Béfind's faith was words and hope. But Luan's faith was magic.

"Be brave," Morgan said to Luan, getting the words out before her courage failed her.

"What do you think your father would do to this monastery?" Béfind shouted at Luan. "He'd blame me for anything you did!" What were they arguing about? "Your salvation is not the only one I have to think about."

Luan's head sagged.

But Béfind was right. Oengus suffered the Christians to live on his land because it provided a solution to a problem he had. If they interfered with his daughter…where would the Christians go?

Where could Morgan go? Morgan couldn't worry about that.

Luan's face was pale. Her radiance had dimmed. Maybe she'd faked being sick, but now she really was sick. "Is it God's will, then?" Luan asked softly.

Morgan couldn't bear to watch her submit. She turned away. Luan was holding onto her hand like a child, so she couldn't go.

"Yes. It's God's will." Béfind's voice was firm. "If it weren't, your father wouldn't have come."

Luan clenched her jaw, struggling for the strength to say something. "Then I'll go with my father." She sighed.

"God will protect you," said Béfind stiffly, and then, more softly, "You'll bring the True Faith to the Uí Drona. Isn't that worth doing?"

Luan didn't say anything. She seemed terrified. And Morgan thought she understood. She'd seen petulance in the way Luan wouldn't look at Oengus' healer. There was another side to Luan, wasn't there? A spoiled child who pulled stunts like feigning sickness to get her way. A Luan who screamed threats at disobedient livestock. Maybe she had run to the monastery not just to learn about Christianity but to run away from who she was. In the monastery she would be encouraged to be brave and humble and generous and pure of faith. Would she be such a brave and good Christian once she was the wife of the chief of the Uí Drona? Or would her pride return, and her anger? And sloth, and greed, and gluttony? And then she'd ask herself what the point was of being a bad, guilty Christian when all her excesses would make her a perfectly fine Irish chieftain's wife?

Salvatus had had pure faith. He had worked miracles with it. Morgan opened her mouth to tell Luan she could be strong like Salvatus.

But Salvatus had died the triple death. Morgan kept silent.

WHEN her father helped her up into the cart for the ride back, Luan did her best to be gentle and modest. She smiled at everyone. But her eyes were hollow. Their radiance had dimmed.

Oengus and his retinue slowly moved off, Oengus leading in his chariot, his druid Maelgenn and his bard riding, the warriors walking behind. Conall looked back, the chariot reins in his hands. He turned and stared at Morgan, his dark eyes troubled.

His look tugged at her. Suddenly she wanted to run after him. She wanted badly to give him a reason why it was important for him to stay.

But his chariot rolled away, and he turned away from her to guide his horses.

Chapter Fifteen

A LEAP OF FAITH

A chill ran down Morgan's back. It was cold here in the beehive-shaped stone hut, even with the rawhide door pulled shut. But she wanted to be alone, and she didn't want to upset anyone by straying outside the gates. The stones of the hut were unmortared, and starlight filtered in through a few cracks where rain had melted away the mud caulking. It was damp and musty. She kneeled and touched the dirt, felt it in her hand.

What was she doing here?

It would be so easy, wouldn't it, to disappear into this life. Who was waiting for her return? The people of Din Tagell? Who was she to them? Her father was long dead. Her mother was another man's wife.

Morgan remembered her old dream. Her mother was watching Uter's five-year-old son dueling other boys with sticks. She was watching him with love, and if she had any thought for her long lost daughter, the one she had put on a boat and given a new name to, Morgan hadn't seen it in her face.

If Morgan never came back…who would she be betraying?

She knew what Béfind's answer would be. Stay here and become a great holy Christian woman. Turn these huts into buildings, copy out a library and make the settlement into a great place of learning and peace and prayer.

Could she do that?

The Christians came here to pray for wisdom. Did they ever get it?

Morgan didn't have the obsidian blade her mother had used long ago to draw her sacred circle, or even Buanann's gnarled bit of rowan wood. With nothing but the twig of an ash tree, she inscribed a sacred circle along the stone walls of the tiny cell. With her will, she made a wall to contain the power she was intent on bringing inside the circle…

…but the place was already alive, like the air before a thunderstorm. Luan had prayed here. So had the other Christians. They had woven their prayers into this place, and their prayers lingered in the air, in the stones, in the dampness.

Give me wisdom, she prayed. And she reached out to the land, waiting for an answer.

The land seemed to shrug. I CAN GIVE YOU POWER, it said.

But—should I stay here? Or go? And go where?

NOT MY FUNCTION.

I was hoping you—

IF YOU DON'T KNOW WHAT YOU'RE SEEKING, YOU WON'T FIND IT.

But no. It wasn't the land speaking, Morgan realized. It was all in her head. She was talking to herself.

The energy in the cell was real. She could sense it. But magic couldn't give you advice. The wind could not tell you where to sail, nor fire tell you what to burn.

She lay back on the damp earth. She could feel the currents swirling, the latent energy like lightning coiling within a cloud before it strikes. But it didn't tell her anything.

Gently, she released the circle she had made, and returned to the solid world.

MORGAN worked alone now, copying Augustine's tract against the Pelagians. She enjoyed writing, moving her fingers in the minuscule strokes of the letters, occasionally scraping wet ink off the vellum with the dull blade of the penknife when she made a mistake. When she was writing, she didn't have to think about anything else.

Then the dogs started barking. It was the only thing they were good for.

Through the open gates, she saw a chariot bumping along the meadow at a good clip, a proud young man working the reins effortlessly.

Conall was back.

"I'M worried about Luan," he was telling Béfind in the great hall, as Morgan came in. "Luigdech is coming to marry her at the end of the month," Conall said. "She says she's not worried about it. And then she laughs."

"She laughs?" asked Béfind.

"It's creepy. I don't like it." He imitated Luan's laugh. It was odd, cheerless, from the back of his throat.

"When she prays, does it seem to console her?" Béfind asked.

"Console her? No. She prays and she sleeps and she doesn't eat anything. Sometimes she's up praying in the middle of the night."

Béfind shot a worried glance at Morgan. "She must be praying for strength."

"She's getting weaker every day," Conall said. "She won't even talk to me."

"She's scared she'll lose her faith," Morgan said.

Conall and Béfind stared at her.

"She thinks if she becomes a chief's wife, she'll go back to being spoiled. She's been someone else for almost a year. Someone she likes better. But if she leaves, it won't be like here. Or like at your village, where everyone humoured her. She's scared that if she becomes Luigdech's wife, she'll forget how to be her."

Conall's eyes were wide. And Béfind was looking at her with surprise and admiration.

"She's not a saint yet. She just wants to be one. She hasn't given up her pride. She struggles with it every day."

"You have a strange god that turns pride into a sin," said Conall. "Why does Luan love him so? Can you explain him to me?" Béfind took a deep breath. "I don't know if your father would approve if I—"

"Not you. Her." He was looking straight at Morgan. She tried not to shiver. He had never looked at her this long, this intently. "Maybe you can explain it better than my sister did."

She was supposed to explain Christianity to Conall? She looked at Béfind.

But Béfind only smiled and nodded. She kissed Morgan on the cheek. "I know you can do great things," she said, in Latin, so Conall couldn't catch the meaning. She smiled. "You might be the only one here he'll understand."

"ƮႬє Lord gave us grace," Morgan said. Conall was guiding the plow as it ripped through the rich soil. It had rained the night

180

before, and the soil was heavy. The air was thick and humid. Conall had his tunic off, and his body was drenched in sweat, his muscles tense. Morgan urged the ox on, and it leaned its head forward, tugging the ropes tied to its horns, pulling the plow. "His mercy drops out of the sky, for free. You can let it drop onto the ground, or you can hold out your cup and it will be filled."

"Mercy for what?" he asked.

"Mercy for all the sins we've committed against Him," she said.

"What have I ever done to your God?"

He was right. What had he ever done wrong? The ox had stopped. Morgan whipped the willow branch at it, stinging it, and the beast leaned its head forward, and the plow began cutting the soil again. She knew Conall was still waiting for her answer, watching her with his deep brown eyes. She watched the ox. How had he sinned? His eyes never left hers, and she felt naked.

"Haven't you ever felt like life is too hard? People die in war, or they're taken from you…?"

"I don't whine about it."

"But in the next world, with God's mercy, you'll see them again, and no one will die."

"Why would your God do that for me?" Conall had a small shy smile on his face. It was strange. In the eating hall, Conall had been loud and comic, but here, alone with her in a field, he was actually listening. More than listening. He was looking into her eyes.

Morgan was embarrassed. She felt like a fraud. "Because he loves you," she said.

"Why?"

"Why do you love your sister?"

"Because she's my sister."

"Why does your father love your sister?"

"Because he's her father—oh." He smiled, taking her point.

"God is our father," she said.

Conall's strong arms kept the plow on course as it ripped through the thick soil. He seemed lost in thought. "They're beautiful, the things you're saying. Maybe I should become a Christian."

She knew what Béfind would want her to say. But instead she told him, "Your father would be pretty angry."

"I am not afraid of my father," Conall said. But he seemed thoughtful, and they did not discuss it again that day.

THAT night Morgan wondered about the things she had told Conall. She had lost her father. Twice. Once when he was killed, and then all over again, over the years. She did not feel like his daughter. Her father had been a governor, a civilized man. He hated war. When he spoke of honour, it was something that had to be maintained, like a roof. She had never heard him speak of vengeance.

Then why did she need vengeance?

For what had been done to her mother, of course.

But she heard in her head the words she'd been saying to Conall, about grace, about forgiveness, about love.

She had always distrusted those words. They might make her weak.

Conall did not seem to think they'd make him weak.

What if grace was real? What if she opened her hands and let God pour mercy into them?

Wasn't that what her father would have wanted her to do? To give up a fight she'd already lost long ago, against a man who'd probably forgotten she existed, who for all Morgan knew was already dead?

What if she accepted grace? What if she surrendered to it?

What if she accepted grace, and converted Conall? Would he stay at the monastery? She could teach him and work with him, like she had with Luan.

She had once thought about being baptized. *If Conall is baptized*, she told herself, *I will get baptized too.*

What was she thinking? Conall was a chief's son. His place was in his village, leading his father's raiding parties.

Then would he take her home with him?

She shook her head, trying to clear it of all these confusing thoughts. Béfind had sent her with Conall to help him understand his sister. So he could speak to his father on Luan's behalf.

Or had she sent Morgan with Conall so Morgan would begin to doubt?

Why was she even thinking of going back with Conall? She probably meant nothing to him. He was just there to understand his sister. Wasn't he?

"Ðið it change you?" Conall asked her. They were plowing again. The sun seemed hotter than the day before. "When you became a Christian?"

The ox had slowed and stopped again. It shook its head, irritated at the ropes tied to its horns.

The monastery was changing her, wasn't it? And she wasn't even a Christian.

But Morgan didn't want to scare him off. "Maybe it wouldn't change you," she said.

"Why not?" he asked.

Because he was so strong and brave, she wanted to say. So brave that he had opened his heart to her, a total stranger, because she was his sister's friend, because his sister had gone away to a strange faith, and he wanted to understand where she had gone. Would Christianity change him? No. He would make it his own.

Not sure how to put it all into words, she reached down and took up a clump of damp earth. The earth was real. Long ago, she had felt it, felt its strength.

"Your bones are the bones of the land," she said, and she wasn't sure where the words had come from.

Conall shook his head, struggling to understand her. He was looking right at her, into her, and strange sensations were rippling through her. "Are you sure you have faith in the god of the Christians?" he asked.

She tried to calm herself. "Not like Luan. She's a saint, I think. The rest of us are just praying for faith."

He cocked his head at her. "You're a chief's daughter, aren't you?"

How did he know?

"You don't look down when I speak to you," he said. "Even Béfind does."

"My father led eight hundred trained warriors into battle," she said. There was no word for *soldier* in Irish.

"Well, I can leap from my chariot onto my horses, and back, with a shield on my arm and a spear in my hand."

She liked how his eyes flashed. "Teach me that."

He grinned some more. "Is that part of your spiritual education?"

The ox was standing still, but everything seemed to be moving fast. Morgan held the willow rod in her hand. The sun was hot and bright. The air was perfectly still. Far away in the fields, other virgins of Christ were labouring. They would be murmuring prayers, but they were too far away to hear. She wavered a little on her feet. Conall's eyes were dark and deep. She could see sweat trickle down his bare chest.

"Are you all right?" he asked, and she remembered to breathe.

He smiled again. It was a softer smile, and it was not exactly a friendly smile. There was laughter behind his eyes, and she wasn't sure if he was mocking her, and if she should be mad.

She wanted to kiss him. She came toward him.

It seemed to confuse him that she had come so close.

What if he didn't want to kiss her? Maybe he thought of her as a sister.

She snapped the ox on the rump with the willow rod, and it lumbered forward. The plow jumped out of the furrow, and Conall leaped to right it, and Morgan kept her eyes on the field ahead of them, not looking at him.

She wanted to tell him about herself, how she really was—the way the land had once spoken to her, how it had protected her, how it had broken her chains for her.

But she didn't dare say anything more. They went back to the settlement for prayers and the evening meal, and then he went away to the guest house.

SɆE lay down in the great hall with the other novices. The moment the rush candle was snuffed, everyone else fell asleep immediately, exhausted from the day.

It was dark, the night too chill to leave the door open. Nameless shapes swirled across the blackness. The faint smell of peat smoke lingered in the walls, but there was no fire, the room warmed only by the sleeping men and women.

She was sweating. Her skin felt alive. She realized she hadn't been aware of her body since she had reached the monastery.

Before that there had been pain, and when there wasn't pain, the pleasure of food and drink and the loveliness of sleep. When she moved she noticed the touch of her tunic against her skin. The drip of sweat between her breasts.

She needed air.

She opened the door and went outside. The air was still. The stars were unaccountably bright, sparkling, like myriad campfires flickering on a great plain at night.

She found herself walking to the settlement gates. She felt uncomfortable on this holy, sanctified ground. There was great goodness here, a well of goodwill and friendly love. But something about that goodness tugged her down.

She was on fire.

She slid the bolt on the gate back and slipped out, shutting it behind her.

Outside the settlement the world was wild. She walked out into the night.

She let the darkness of the woods embrace her. She walked until the trees opened out into a small meadow. She was alone. But she felt invincible.

She threw her arms out wide, and it was all there. She could feel the heat of the land again. She knew the dampness of the ground and the freshness of the breeze.

The crickets were loud, owls hooted and the wind rustled the trees. Everywhere, beneath everything, the land pulsed, strong and silent. And she was as ancient and mighty as the bones of the land.

She knew the spell she was casting. She did not even need to draw the circle in her mind. It was there as she thought it, and she drew aside the Veil, and she was between the worlds.

ŦꞪЄ sky was spinning around the Pole Star like a chariot wheel.

A man was coming toward her. She couldn't hear or see him, but she knew. She began to withdraw herself from the circle between the worlds, to meet him in his world. But then she decided to leave the Veil open. She could stay in both worlds at once.

The man came softly, like a hunter tracking dangerous prey. He paused from time to time, but he never faltered, never broke a twig or stepped on crisp leaves. He was steady on his feet, moving with grace and speed.

She waited for him in the meadow.

He paused in the shadows of the trees, watching her for a long time.

"Come here," she said. She did not want to leave the place she had sanctified.

He came out of the shadows into the circle. He was between the worlds with her.

"You shouldn't be out here, alone, at night," he said. His breath was hot in the chill air. "The woods are dangerous."

"There are wolves," she said, and smiled.

"You're not afraid?"

"No," she said.

He seemed to like that. He reached out and touched her shoulder, and her entire skin was on fire, from her toes to her thighs to her breasts to her ears. He pulled his hand back, shocked. She wanted him. She put her hands to his cheeks, and pulled him toward her and kissed his lips. His arms and chest were hard, but his lips were soft, and he held her with amazing tenderness, and that didn't stop him from kissing her with an intensity that shocked her. He moulded her with his fingers.

She had no idea how long they kissed before he tugged himself gently away.

"You spoke a great deal about love," he said carefully. "The love of Christ for all men. Loving each other as we would be loved. But none of you are married…"

"They call themselves virgins of Christ." She had a wild fever in her blood; she was impatient with having to use words.

"And what do *you* call yourself?" He frowned, as if that wasn't what he had wanted to say, not at all—he who could walk silently through a wild forest at midnight.

"I'm a virgin too," she said, and she laughed from nerves.

Conall nodded, confused. Even in the starlight, she could see he was blushing. "Maybe we should go back," he said.

It was too late for that. "I'm not a Christian," she said.

He stared at her. His mouth moved in a strange way, and she was afraid that he felt betrayed. But a bewildered smile was on his lips.

She wanted him very badly now. She pulled him down onto the grass, the still-warm earth.

Then they embraced each other, but that wasn't all of it. It wasn't just the rhythm of their two bodies discovering and demanding each other. She had never known a greater tenderness or a greater hunger, and now they were combined in one moment, but that was only the human side of it.

They were between the worlds, and she was rising. She was lighter than the wind coursing through the trees. If Conall let go of her, she might blow away like steam. She was the warmth rising from the land into the night air. She was the sap rising into the crowns of the trees around the clearing. She was the land itself, the very earth and stones of Ireland, floating on an ocean of heat.

She had never thought it could be like this. She could feel Conall's breath on her skin, feel his pulse in his muscles, feel his desire, all rising like a river flooding toward its banks. But that wasn't all of it. There was a goddess within her, a god in him, and they set each other on fire.

Later, there was a lull in the world, and a contentment she had never thought possible, and she was empty, and yet she was full.

She kissed him on the lips, gently, letting the power drain out of him into her, and from her into the land. The grass was moist against her skin, but she was not cold, and they slept.

Chapter Sixteen

CONALL

They walked back silently, holding hands. The crescent moon rose from behind the trees, a bow aimed at the still-hidden sun, and the world seemed impossibly bright. Several times, Conall seemed to be about to ask her something, but he always caught himself. She knew if she said anything, it would reduce everything to words. The magic still lingered around them. He must feel it.

They slipped inside the gate and bolted it. She kissed him one more time. Every kiss had been different, but this one was different from all the rest. Now, within the fence, they were only man and woman. There was no magical power in this kiss, but somehow it seemed stranger and newer than all the others. It was all she could do not to look back at him as she went back to the women's sleeping hut.

It was quiet there, a dozen people breathing, their breathing rhythmic and reassuring. She found her bed in the darkness, and sleep embraced her.

DAWN woke her. It always did. That was something from the lake village she had carried with her. Morgan lay back, listening to the settlement wake up. The roosters were staking their claims. The milk cows were lowing for someone to milk them. She heard the little boys shrieking with laughter, and their giant puppies barking. It would not be long before morning prayers.

Morgan got up. There was a little blood on her dress. She knew that when you were with a man for the first time, you bled. She didn't hurt, though. Her body was glowing all over. And the land beneath her...

She felt like laughing. There it was, the land, as if it had never left her.

Morgan had not meant to make a sacrifice. But she had spilled blood, and the land had come back to her.

With a shock, she thought of Luan. What would she think? Luan would forgive anyone their sin. But she would be hurt. Morgan winced at the thought.

Transgression. Oh. She suddenly understood something. Why Uter had made war on her father. If he had felt *that*...yes. If there had been walls between her and Conall, she would have smashed them. She could forgive—

No. She couldn't forgive it. Uter had taken her mother by guile and force, and murder.

She winced. Why had she even thought of Uter? She had known him in another country, a couple of lives ago. She couldn't remember Uter's face. She didn't even want to. Couldn't she just forget he had ever existed?

She got up. She needed to see Conall before her past dragged her into a welter of doubts.

Morgan went outside.

Fog had welled up from the valley floor. It was chill. She thought she felt raindrops.

191

"Where's Conall?" she asked. Fat Lí Ban pointed at the westernmost house, the guest house. It was the lodging of honour because, with the wind blowing out of the west most of the time, you almost never had to smell the privy at the farthest east.

She knocked gently at the guest house door, but there was no answer. She opened the door and slipped inside.

Conall was inside, sleeping.

She thought of shaking him awake. She wanted to hear him say what had happened last night. She wanted him to say that it had been as strange and powerful for him as it had been for her.

But what if it hadn't?

Morgan heard Béfind ringing her hand bell for morning prayer. The Christians stumbled out of their houses. But not even the bell could get Conall out of the guest house.

A little before noon, a caravan came out of the east. It was Oengus and his retinue. Oengus rode ahead of his men, alone, standing rigidly upright in his chariot, his cape pulled tight around him against the chill rain. His men walked alongside a cart. Morgan thought she saw Luan in the cart. But they were all going too slowly. Something terrible had happened.

Morgan's heart dropped. Luan had a bandage around her eyes. Morgan started to run out to meet them, but Béfind grabbed her arm. Morgan yelled and wrenched free.

She ran up to the cart. Oengus didn't even turn or slow. He ignored her, staring straight at the open gates of the settlement.

Luan's bandage covered her eyes, but blood had soaked through the wool. It was dry now, but there had been a lot of it. Morgan reeled back in horror. Luan didn't move, just held onto the cart, rolling from side to side as it took the bumps of the path. Her lips were moving. She was praying, with a sad sweet smile in possession of her face. Morgan had seen that smile so many times before. But what had happened to her?

"Luan!" she cried.

"Morgan?" asked Luan, holding out her hand. "Give me your hand, sister." But Morgan couldn't bring herself to take it.

"For the love of God, what happened to you?" asked Morgan, hoping desperately that it had been an accident.

"For the love of God, I did what Saint Lucia did. So I could see Him better." Morgan and Luan had copied out the story of Saint Lucia. She was being forced to marry a pagan, so she had cut out her eyes. Morgan wanted to scream, to weep, but she was too shocked, and the cart kept rolling. She took Luan's hand. It was still bloodstained. "I won't be much use copying manuscripts anymore," Luan said, "but there's more than one way to spread God's word."

Morgan felt sick. She collapsed on the cold wet meadow grass. The caravan of grim-faced warriors, the healer—his own eyes red and haggard from weeping—all walked past her as she lay on the cold ground. The poet came last. He looked at her, ashen-faced. His tunic was ripped. He, too, had been weeping.

Morgan struggled to her feet. Her vision was blurry. She stumbled after the caravan. They passed through the monastery's gates.

"Béfind!" Oengus called out. His voice was commanding, and frightening.

The Christians were in shock. Dáire, the monastery's healer, ran up to the cart. "Help me with her! Help me get her into the sick-house!"

193

Two of the women helped Dáire get Luan down. But the warriors stopped them from taking her away.

"I'm fine, really," Luan said. "The Lord will heal the wound. There's nothing to cry about. It is the Lord's will."

"Béfind!" Oengus cried out, his voice cracking. Morgan could hear his anguish and bewilderment.

At that moment Conall ran up and stopped dead, staring at his sister. Then he shoved the Christians aside, ripped Dáire away and took Luan's face in his hands. "What did you do?"

"He won't marry me now." Luan smiled sweetly. "Now I can come home to the Lord."

Conall trembled. He embraced his sister, folding her head onto his shoulder. He moaned as if wild beasts were gnawing at his gut. Luan tried to comfort him. "I don't need eyes to see God," she said.

That did not comfort him.

Oengus stared at his son for a moment. Conall hung his head. Then Oengus shouted again. He still hadn't got out of his chariot. Béfind fell to her knees, tears streaming down her face. "Heal her," he said. "If your God has the power." His voice trembled. "She spoke of miracles."

"Her eyes!" said Béfind, choking out the words. "Are they—"

"She stabbed them with a knife," said Oengus. Morgan felt like when Gabrán had hit her, over and over, but this was inside of her.

"I...we...I...the Lord has the power...but I..." Béfind stammered. Oengus stared at her, waiting, but Béfind just shook her head. "There was one among us...who might have...his faith was so strong...but he was martyred."

"He was what?"

"Killed. By druids. They gave him the triple death."

Oengus nodded slowly, stony-faced. He had allowed himself to hope. Now his last hope was betrayed. He turned his face away, and Morgan could see his shoulders quake. He was weeping. It was terrifying to see such a strong man weep.

Oengus gathered himself together. He got out of his chariot. He walked over to Béfind. He took her hand and helped her up. It seemed like a friendly gesture, and Béfind reached out to embrace him. But Oengus pushed her back with his other hand. "Is there any reason why you and your people should be allowed to stay on my land any longer?" Oengus asked quietly.

Béfind, stunned, searched his face for any trace of mercy. "You want us to leave our homes?"

"I could blind you," Oengus said. His words were measured but terrible. "My warriors feel that you should pay for what you did to my daughter." Béfind paled. "But you did it without malice. And it would not bring back my daughter's eyes."

He sighed. Even in this crisis, he had thought it all through. "If you could pay my honour price…"

If one man dishonoured another, the dishonoured man had to take revenge; the only way out was for the man who had wronged him to pay his honour price. Morgan could see that Oengus was holding onto the law with all his strength, desperately trying not to unleash the rage he felt. His warriors were staring at the Christians with rage and contempt. One word from him and they would slaughter everyone.

"But I know you don't have that much gold. Even if I were to sell all of you into slavery, it would not equal my honour price. So there will not be peace between us."

Béfind nodded.

Oengus turned to his son. "So this is where you went."

Conall straightened up. He put his grief away. "I wanted to know what this faith of hers was."

Oengus nodded. "Are you a Christian now too?"

Conall shook his head.

"Will you speak for them? Can you defend them? What did you learn from them?"

Conall looked around at the Christians with a great sadness. "They said a great many things, and I thought some of them made sense. But against this…" He shook his head.

He shot an intense look at Morgan. She had wondered what he would say to her when he awoke. There was no mistaking the love he had for her in his eyes.

But he looked around the monastery. "No. They mean well. But their god has no power."

She had told him about Salvatus' miracle. But Conall had felt the power of the land, bringing him to her. How could what she had told him compete with what she had done?

Unwillingly, Morgan looked at Béfind. Béfind stared back at her, bewildered.

Oengus nodded. "In three days my warriors will come here. Go back to the lands where you were born, go to someone else's lands, I don't care. If any of you are still here in three days, my men will slaughter you like milkless cows at Samain."

He turned to the warriors guarding Luan. "Help her back into the cart." He turned to Conall. "Let's go home."

Conall came over to Morgan. He looked into her eyes, sad, but with longing. She could feel the bond between them. He wanted her to come too. She wanted to go with him.

But when she looked over at Luan, she saw that Luan was resisting the warriors. She wanted to stay here.

Of course she did. She had sacrificed her eyes to be here. There was one thing Luan had wanted. One thing above any other, above comfort, above the love of her family, beyond pain, beyond darkness. She had done the one thing that would give her back the love of her god.

Morgan wanted Conall to kiss her again. She wanted to leave the Christians and go with Conall and his father.

But Luan would lose everything.

Morgan had to speak up. And she knew, as she looked at Conall, what it would cost her. "You can't take her home," she said to him. She turned to Oengus, and shouted, "You can't take her home, my lord!"

Oengus stared at her. His hands gripped the side of his chariot. His fingers crushed a piece of its wickerwork, but he kept his voice level. "Men do not say to me what I may or may not do, except for druids, and they say it quietly, out of the earshot of other men."

"If you take her home, she'll just be a blind girl no one will marry. She can't weave; she can't knit. No man will have her." Oengus stared at Morgan. "Here she's a saint. She has the most faith of any of us. More than Béfind, more than the best of us."

"What does that mean to me?" asked Oengus, trembling.

"If you leave her here, she'll become a great"—Morgan struggled for the right word—"chief among the Christians. Here she doesn't need to see."

Conall was staring at her in stunned betrayal. "You're taking their side?"

"It's your...faith"—Oengus choked the word out—"that took the light from her eyes!"

"IF you take her away from us, then she did it for nothing," said Morgan.

Conall turned away. He couldn't bear to even look at her.

Oengus stared at Morgan. No one dared speak.

Slowly, Oengus shook his head, no.

So I've lost everything. Both Conall and Luan.

Oengus grimaced. "Béfind? What this girl says…"

"Luan is a great holy woman," said Béfind, though Morgan could see she was still struggling with what Luan had done. "If you let her go with us, we will care for her for all the days of her life."

Oengus weighed her words. His lips were trembling with emotion, but his hands no longer clutched the sides of the chariot. He was fighting sorrow, not rage. He understood the choice.

"Luan. Go with your people." Dáire darted forward to the cart, and the warriors stood back to let her help Luan down and guide her away.

Oengus drew himself up, rigid. "Three days. I will not come myself. I'll send warriors with hearts of cold iron."

Conall shot one last stricken glance at Morgan. Then he got in Oengus' chariot, took the whip and snapped it. The chariot shot forward, Christians scattering out of its way. It circled and raced out of the enclosure. The cartman led the cart ponies around, and Oengus' retine left the monastery without another look back.

MORGAN spent the rest of the day in a dull numb haze. The Christians were packing up all their belongings. Morgan had nothing of her own except the cloak and boots she had come with. It was not yet time to gather the cattle, sheep and pigs.

The Christians had no destination yet. Béfind gave the one pony to Petrán, to ride up north to the Delbna. Though the chiefs of the Delbna were pagan, they had many wild valleys, and were hard pressed on all sides by their neighbours. Maybe they would welcome settlers.

All around Morgan the Christians wept and prayed. It was the worst time of year to resettle. The crops were planted. They had only saved a little seed, to make bread until the harvest came in. But if they ate that, what would they plant? And if they planted it, would they be able to harvest it before the frost? Would there even be fields where they were going? They would have to slaughter their flocks and herds just to survive.

One of the villagers suggested they burn the settlement. "Why should Oengus profit from our exile?"

Béfind was firm. "Would Christ have burned the settlement out of spite?"

The man slumped. "No."

The only one who wasn't worried was Luan. "God will provide," she said.

But Morgan had nothing more to say. Luan had torn her own eyes out, and torn Conall from her. Morgan ached for him.

BÉFIND came to see Morgan. "Come, take a walk with me."

They walked out into the fields. The sun was setting somewhere behind the overcast sky. There was not even the whisper of a breeze.

"It was very brave, what you said to Oengus."

"I had to tell him," said Morgan.

"You told an unwelcome truth to an angry man with a sword. And you changed his mind. I couldn't have done that."

Morgan didn't know what to say to that.

"Do you think Luan is…not right in the head?" Béfind asked. They walked for a bit in silence. Morgan thought about the headaches the healer had mentioned. Béfind sighed. "And so Peter denied Our Lord." They walked a little ways more. "What happened between you and Conall?"

Morgan wondered if she could just lie her head off. She hadn't lied to Béfind, not since the week she'd come to the monastery. If she put all her strength into it, Béfind would believe her, maybe.

But she couldn't do it. Not here, on the land she and Conall had made holy. "How did you know?" she managed.

"Before…what happened…I thought he was almost tempted to come to Christ. Almost," said Béfind.

Had he been?

No. He was a warrior. He was proud. He wanted what he wanted. Morgan shook her head.

"I thought you might be, too. I thought you were beginning to doubt your pagan gods. I thought maybe the two of you would convert each other." She shook her head sadly. "I shouldn't have gambled with everyone's lives for your sake."

"I'm sorry," said Morgan. She had never thought of Béfind as a gambler. She had thought of her as wise. She wondered what Béfind had been like before she'd become a Christian.

"Did he seduce you?" asked Béfind.

Morgan had to shake her head again. He'd come to her. She had summoned him.

Béfind was looking at her with surprising concern. "Have you been to see Dáire?" she asked softly.

That was odd. Morgan wasn't sick. "Why?"

"Have you talked to Dáire?" asked Béfind again, pointedly.

"Why?" Oh. Oh, God. Dáire, the healer. Béfind was asking if Morgan was in danger of being pregnant. She hadn't even thought about that. "Oh, God." Morgan might have asked the magic to protect her from that. Maybe it could have. But she hadn't been thinking. She had let her emotions sweep her away. Stupid. Stupid. Stupid.

"You should have gone with him, maybe," said Béfind.

And it came home to her in a rush of horrible shame. Morgan couldn't even look at Béfind. She had betrayed the monastery, hadn't she? She could have given Conall the faith he was asking for. Instead, selfishly, she had given Conall something so much stronger, so much more urgent than Luan's faith. Morgan had put a god into him. And then she had rejected him, in the name of his sister's faith, the faith that had made Luan rip out her eyes.

Morgan doubled over, sick to her stomach. She had ruined everything for the only people in Ireland who had ever been decent to her.

"Dáire can do many things, with God's help. Maybe she can tell you if you're pregnant." Her voice was kind, and utterly without accusation. "And if you are, we will provide for you and your child."

Morgan couldn't bear her tenderness. She wanted to flee.

"Are you...do you know if you are...?" Béfind went on.

"No. I don't know," Morgan said, and she was crying. Béfind reached to comfort her. "I'm sorry. I'm so sorry."

"Good," said Béfind. "From repentance comes forgiveness."

"Forgiveness?"

"We're all sinners here," said Béfind, matter-of-fact.

Morgan was bewildered.

Forgiveness?

"Surely God had a hand in this. Maybe He punished me for my pride in wanting buildings of stone, when we should have been preparing for His Second Coming." Béfind's voice trembled. "I still have faith in you, Morgan. You're braver than I am. *I* didn't speak up for Luan today."

Morgan stared at her, mystified. How could Béfind still have faith in her?

"God will forgive you. You only have to ask Him."

Forgiveness, for free. Grace. All Morgan had to do was hold out her cup and let Béfind fill it.

But *forgiveness?* For touching the power of the land? For being fire and water and earth and air? Morgan shook her head. She hated that she had betrayed the monastery. But she couldn't regret what she had done in the forest. She could not betray the land.

"I can't," Morgan said.

"Are you trying to punish yourself? You have nowhere to go!" Béfind was mystified. "I know how you feel. You did a wrong thing, and you don't deserve mercy. But don't you understand? Grace is mercy when you don't deserve it."

There it was again. Grace, tugging gently at her, so much harder to ignore than the hard pull of fear, or hunger, or pain. But she could not bear it if the land was silent again. If she prayed for forgiveness, she thought, the land would never answer again.

She shivered. It was suddenly much colder.

"Sleep on it," said Béfind. "You could be a great leader among us. You have strength of will, and you can change people's minds. But if you aren't even trying to accept Jesus Christ, then we can give nothing to each other. Think, Morgan. Think before you reject the gifts of God."

"I will," said Morgan. But she knew what her answer was.

MORGAN spent some of the three days finishing up her copying. At least she could do that for Béfind, while she tried to figure out what to do next. It was an excuse to stay in the empty great hall and concentrate on a task that involved no one else.

She peeked out from time to time. The Christians had more possessions than they had thought. Morgan watched them shovel the precious supplies of wheat, barley, rye, oats and millet out of the storage pits, filling all the baskets they had, wrapping the rest in spare clothing. It was warm enough for people's cloaks to be sewn up for sacks. They baked as much into bread as they dared, extra hard and dry, so that it might last two weeks even in the moist weather. The baskets that were not tightly woven enough for grain they used for dried peas and beans. They had wheels of cheese, and pottery jars full of salted meat or butter. Maybe it would all last until they could reap a new harvest. It was a lot to carry. But it was not much to own.

They were crying as they worked, and praying as they cried. They had left their homes to come here. For some of them, it was the first place they had felt at home.

Morgan knew she had to leave. She couldn't go back to the Eóganachta. The Christians were headed north. East was Oengus' land. That left the Muscraige to the west.

But she couldn't motivate herself to go. Not yet. The longer she stayed, she knew, the less food she would have. What was she waiting for?

Morgan went into the sick-house to see Luan. She was on her knees on the bed, praying without cease. Morgan wanted to hold her and cry with her. But Luan thought she had nothing to cry for. Morgan couldn't cry for her if she wasn't crying for herself.

"Morgan?" said Luan.

Morgan went and took her hands. Luan embraced her. "I was afraid you weren't going to come." She embraced Morgan tighter. "I know I'm hard to look at. But I wouldn't be here at all if I hadn't done it. And if you hadn't made my father listen!" She pulled away, but she put her hand on Morgan's face, gently. "I owe you my life."

"I'm not going with you," Morgan told Luan.

Luan clutched at her hands. She would have closed her eyes, if she'd had eyes to close. "Do you think he'll come back for you?" she asked.

"Conall?" asked Morgan, but as she asked it, she thought, *is that who I've been waiting for?*

"You never know with him. He can be so pigheaded," said Luan.

Morgan had been expecting a lecture on grace. But now she was off balance. Had she been waiting for Conall?

"Do you really love him?" asked Luan. "Because he's so easy to fall in love with. All the girls in our village want him. Do you really know him?"

Morgan wondered. Yes. She felt like she knew him. He had been so easy to be with. He had looked right into her, and she'd seen him, and…

She realized she was crying. Luan felt it, and pulled her in tightly. "I don't know. I…" Morgan's mind was awhirl. "I don't think he likes me anymore. You should have seen how he looked at me." The words choked off in her throat.

"He'll come for you. I know it." Luan embraced her very hard. "When you see him, don't let him forget how much I love him."

Morgan held her tight. "Oh, God, I'll miss you."

WHEN everything was ready, the cowherds gathered up the cattle. The shepherds gathered their sheep and lambs, with a lot of familiar jokes about Lambs of God. The swineherd moved his pigs out of their pen. The oldest sow trailed her twenty-pound six-week-old piglets behind her, squealing and grunting. If they couldn't keep up, they would be dinner along the way.

The Christians hadn't heard from Petrán or any of the other messengers. Their best bet was heading north to the lands of the Delbna, travelling slowly and praying for a miracle.

Morgan watched their caravan roll slowly away. Luan was on one of the carts with the baggage, kneeling and praying. For a moment she looked like she was a statue of the patron goddess of the tribe of Christians, and they were carrying her with them as a household god.

They moved slowly. It was almost sundown before they were finally out of sight.

IT was strange to be in the settlement alone. Morgan missed the sounds of people breathing.

She wasn't tired. She had the place all to herself. If she wanted, she could clear a circle within the great hall and give the consecrated ground of the monastery back to the spirit of the land.

But that spirit would be here soon enough. There would be owls nesting in the thatch, and weasels sleeping in the storage bins. If Oengus' men didn't torch the place, the land would reclaim it within five years.

And Morgan couldn't ask the land to call Conall. Not this time. If Morgan summoned him again, he would know what had brought him here. He would know it was her witchcraft, not love, that made him come. He would probably kill her if she did that. She would have to go to him.

She sat up, watching the fire in the middle of the great hall, the roof beams throwing a great black shadow of a cross on the roof. When she felt tired, she pulled the logs apart so that the fire died. Then she curled up next to the embers and went to sleep.

MORGAN did not have much to carry. Béfind had given her provisions for a week, hard cheese and bread baked extra-hard.

She left the gates to the settlement open. She wondered if she had made a mistake. She thought of that other, imaginary Morgan, now called Mary, walking alongside Béfind, full of trust and hope and faith.

And grace. Mary would be full of grace.

Morgan had given up grace. But she had the land.

She started walking.

The longest journey begins with a single step.

The weather was fine and clear, with billowy clouds sailing across the blue sky. She walked toward the east, wondering what she would say to Conall.

With a sudden pang, she wondered if she was horribly wrong about him.

What if he was fickle? What if he was all of the moment, falling into passionate love with one girl after another? What if he was arrogant and spoiled like his sister? What if he had never really loved her? What if he had only wanted her, and now that he'd had her, he lost interest? Wouldn't he need to marry a chieftain's daughter, a real one, for some alliance, now that his sister was useless for that?

Morgan was suddenly angry at him. Why was she walking toward Conall? She had defended his sister. He had had no call to be angry at her. She had been more loyal to his sister than he had.

Maybe she was going in Conall's direction only because she was scared.

Maybe she didn't need anyone. She had the land. She had the power. She didn't need to be a runaway slave. She could be an Enchanter, living in the woods, summoning men when she wanted them and dismissing them when she felt like it. And if she *was* pregnant, she would have the baby and raise him alone. He would be her champion, her warrior, a great king among the Irish...

A chariot was coming over the rise, dust blowing in front of it.

Morgan froze, stricken with fear. It was the third day. Oengus had promised slaughter. If there were more chariots...

But there was only one. It was moving fast, the ponies pulling it full speed, and only one rider in it. His cloak blew back in the wind, like his long black hair, so that he seemed to Morgan to have the wings of a raven.

Morgan shrugged off her sack of provisions, and waited for him.

Conall pulled the chariot to a halt with a flick of his wrists, as if the ponies were an extension of his will, and hopped off. He walked right up to Morgan, his dark eyes blazing.

Her heart leaped. He seemed as fine to her as any man had ever seemed. "I came back for you," he said. He moved toward her as if he wanted to kiss her.

That was all Morgan wanted. Oh, how she wanted to be swept up and carried off and forgiven and loved.

But she didn't like his cocky smile. "I didn't need rescuing."

That seemed to shock him. "You didn't?"

"I was heading to the woods. The Christians are headed that way." She gestured toward the north. It was a ridiculous thing to say. But she was proud. As proud as any spoiled fickle boy like Conall.

He looked around. They were clearly on the path to the lands of Conall's father. Morgan jutted out her jaw, daring him to point that out. "You said a brave thing to my father," he said, a little worried.

"I'm glad he understood, even if you didn't like it."

Conall seemed utterly taken aback.

"Did he send you to make sure everybody got out?" Morgan's heart was thumping in her chest. She couldn't seem to stop herself from provoking him.

"I came to get you!" he said, flustered. "To take you back to my village!" Obviously it had sounded better in his head.

"Why would I want to go to your village?" She needed him to say it. She needed to know what he thought this was, between them.

"To be my woman!" he blurted out.

"To be your woman? Just because we…we…had sex once? Do you think that makes me your woman?"

He stared at her, taken aback. He actually seemed worried she didn't like him.

"I love you, I think," he said. And she almost tore into him for saying "I think," but a feeling was surging in her that she couldn't suppress. She wasn't sure if she could wait until he kissed her. He took a deep breath and said, "I want you to come and be my wife."

They stared at each other. He seemed startled that he had said it. She thought she might fall down if she just stood there. So she threw herself into his arms. "All right, then." And then they were kissing, and it was an entirely different feeling than it had been in the woods when they had come together, or later when they'd come back to the settlement.

Morgan got into Conall's chariot. He flicked the reins, and the ponies leaned into their harnesses and the chariot rolled forward.

They whirled around on the grass. It was no more than a few minutes before they reached the top of the pass. They plunged over the ridge, and another valley appeared beneath them. The path continued on down the hillside, flew across the valley and went over the next ridge. Morgan looked at Conall with a wild wonderment. He laughed, and she laughed, and they kissed again, while the horses sped onward and home.

Chapter Seventeen

SOVEREIGNTY

As Morgan and Conall came over the low hills, a valley spread out below them, wide and green, with a narrow river snaking through it. The wooded hillsides were dotted with meadows full of sheep and cattle. The banks of the river were golden with fields of wheat.

The village was large, maybe fifty houses. It didn't seem to be in a natural defensive position, but then Morgan noticed that the river bowed away from it. So it must be built on a slight rise. And as their chariot bumped and rolled down the grassy path, Morgan noticed that she never lost sight of the village's tall fence of sharpened stakes. That meant its people had a clear view of anyone coming. She could already see a boy running up toward the wide-open gates.

Conall grinned at her. She felt good. Neither of them said a thing, or needed to.

THE moment they rolled through the gates, they were thronged by villagers. A man grabbed the bridles of the ponies and the chariot jerked to a stop.

A boy ran off into a house, shouting, "Conall's brought a fairy woman back!"

Conall raised an eyebrow at her. "Fairy woman?"

"I get that a lot," said Morgan. "Big nose. Big mouth."

So he pulled her close and kissed her on the mouth, and everyone cheered.

Ŧⱳꝺ of Oengus' lords kept the throng of villagers from following Conall and Morgan into the great hall, so they all crowded at the door instead, blocking the sunlight. As Morgan's eyes adjusted to the darkness, she could see Oengus at the far end of the smoky hall, slumped over his high table.

"Is he all right?" she asked.

Conall squeezed her hand and pulled her a little farther in. He seemed a little nervous. "He's been like this since Luan…" Conall let her hand go and went to his father's side. "Father?"

Oengus didn't move. He seemed dead to the world.

"Should we take you to your bed?" Conall asked.

Oengus' head shot up. He stared at Conall. Then he glared over at the crowd in the doorway. "What are they all staring at?" Oengus shouted at his lords. "Get them out of here!" He gestured to his lords, and his lords started pushing the villagers out of the entrance.

As the room brightened, Oengus grabbed his brass cup and downed its contents. "Where the hell did you go?" he asked Conall.

Conall gestured for Morgan to come near. She could see that Oengus' eyes were bloodshot.

"We left something important at the settlement," Conall told his father.

"Your sister? Our honour?" Oengus squinted at Morgan, obviously hung over. "Dagda's sack! What's *she* doing here?"

"You told me to find a wife," said Conall.

Oengus stared at Conall as if Conall had lost his mind. Then he looked at Morgan. Then back at Conall. He shouted, "I told you *I* was going to find you a wife!" and then cringed at the loudness of his own voice. He glared at Morgan. "Why haven't you gone off with the rest of the Christ-worshippers?"

"Because she isn't one of them," said Conall proudly. "She doesn't worship Christ."

Oengus grabbed his cup and looked around, frustrated. Morgan spotted a pitcher on the floor. She picked it up, put her hand softly on Oengus' arm to steady it, and poured Oengus more ale.

Oengus' eyes narrowed. "You! You're the one who contradicted me. In front of everybody."

He seemed to expect an answer. Did he want her to apologize?

"I meant no disrespect, my lord," she said.

"You told me what to do with my daughter."

"And you agreed with me."

Oengus frowned. Then he smiled slightly and turned to Conall, intrigued. "She looks you in the eye, this one."

"Yes, she does."

"Whose daughter is she?"

"My father led eight hundred men into battle," said Morgan.

"Where are your people?"

"Across the Irish Sea."

"Sure you're not of the fairy folk?"

Morgan laughed at first, but then she realized it was a serious question. "My father was the lord of Trigos, in Britannia, until Uter slew him by treachery. My mother is a Roman from Brittany."

Oengus raised his eyebrows, struggling to absorb that. "And you swear you're not a Christian?"

"I swear by the Morrígan, Great Queen of Shadows."

Oengus shuddered. "Dagda's Sack, woman. Swear by Her all you like, but would you mind not speaking Her name? What if She shows up?"

"Forgive me," said Morgan.

"How about we just tell everyone you're one of the fairy folk," Oengus said. "Simpler."

Conall looked amused.

Oengus stood up, a little wobbly, and gestured to one of his lords.

"Fetch the druid! And fetch my wife, and Conall's brothers," he bellowed. "My son has a wife!" And his villagers pushed past his lords as they flooded into the great hall.

MAELGENN the druid blessed Morgan and Conall with salt and smoke, and they were married.

Then there was a lot of drinking, and men wrestling, and Oengus' bard singing soppy love songs. He made up a song in Morgan's honour that said she was a princess of the fairy folk, and everyone asked for it so many times that she knew all the words to it by the end of the evening. Everyone congratulated Conall on his good luck, and warned Morgan that he would be a handful, over and over. The ale was very good.

Conall shouted to Morgan above the din, "It's not a real wedding yet, you know."

"Why not?" Morgan shouted back.

"A fight hasn't broken out!"

But then there was a commotion in one corner. "Oh, there we go," he said. People were clearing out a circle so two lords who had been shouting at each other could hit each other properly. In a few minutes they were rolling bruised on the floor, weeping and embracing one another as brothers.

There was more singing and drinking. Every time Morgan looked at Conall, she wondered if she was dreaming. It must be a dream. Someone else's dream. She had never dreamt anything like this.

Then Oengus grabbed both of them and pushed them out of the great hall. "I thought you two liked each other," he said, and released them into the quiet darkness.

In the moonlight, Conall led Morgan by the hand to a large house near the end of the village. A crow flew off the thatched roof as they approached.

"Shhhh, She's watching us," Morgan said, giggling, meaning the Morrígan. Conall looked at her, wide-eyed, shocked at her bravery, and pulled her inside the house.

WHEN Morgan woke up, it was the middle of the night. It was pitch black. She had a horrible headache and a bad taste in her mouth. She wasn't sure where she was.

There was a man next to her. She could barely see him in the dark. He wasn't moving. He seemed to be watching her.

"Ow," Conall mumbled. "My head."

She was his wife!

She didn't *feel* like a wife. "Ow," she said. "My head."

He reached over and poured a cupful of water from a pitcher. The water was cool and sharp in her mouth.

She couldn't see Conall. She wondered what it would be like to kiss him now, when she couldn't see his expression.

So she leaned over and kissed him. His lips were very soft. His shoulders were very hard.

Her head was spinning, but she wanted him. She pulled her dress off. It got tangled in the many strings of beads and chains of gold that had somehow wound up around her neck. She managed to disentangle the dress. She kept the gold chains on. She liked how they felt against her breasts.

She caressed him and kissed him. And then she felt him inside her, and this, too, seemed too good to be her own dream, and she hoped she wouldn't wake up anytime soon.

T٩ celebrate his son's marriage, Oengus took thirty of his favourite warriors to steal cattle from the Laigin, his neighbours to the east.

While they waited for him to come back, Morgan asked Conall the same question she had once asked Eochaid of the Déisi, what felt to her like lifetimes ago. "Why just steal cattle?"

"We take slaves too, when we can."

"Why not take land?"

"Well, it's hard to *carry* land."

"I'm serious."

"What would we do with land? Land is a lot of work. Someone has to farm it. And the more you have, the more you have to protect. Meanwhile your enemies are starving to death, so they're really hot to come back at you. It's not worth the trouble."

Morgan tried to put into words how the Romans conquered peoples. "You could tell your enemies they can have their land back, but only if they join your tribe," she said.

"How can they join my tribe?"

Conall just could not grasp it. Wasn't it obvious that it was better to take the land with the farmers *on* it, rather than steal a few score of cattle?

She was still trying to explain it when a great wailing started up outside.

They both ran out.

One of Oengus' lords—Crimthann?—was getting out of Oengus' chariot. But where was Oengus?

Conall hung back. Morgan ran to the chariot.

Oengus was strapped to the chariot pole. His face was pasty white, bloodless. Morgan didn't dare touch him. She remembered her father's face, on the day Simon and the other boy had brought him back dead from the ambush.

Crimthann was talking, but Morgan didn't need to hear what he was saying. There was a savage gash on the side of Oengus' neck. There was a lot of blood on his tunic. A spear, probably. His skin was clean, though. His men must have washed the blood off once they got him away.

Morgan whirled around. Conall. He was pale, shaken. He'd seen dead men before, but this was his father.

Everyone was running up to the chariot. Men and women and children were wailing and shrieking. Conall's mother screamed and tore at her clothes. Conall's little brothers were crying out of confusion and fear, not sure what they were seeing.

Conall needed to do something. But he was still trying to grasp that his father was dead. The bottom had just fallen out of his world.

"My lord," Morgan said, looking Conall in the eye, "shall we move your father into the great hall?"

"What? The great house!" He was looking straight at her. She guessed he didn't dare look at anyone else, and he didn't know what to say. "Yes, let's do that..."

Morgan held his gaze. "Which of his lords should have the honour of carrying him?"

That was it. Focus on the simple questions. Conall looked around. He said a few names, and the men he chose helped him lift his father gently off the chariot and carry the dead chief into the great hall.

THAT night the women bathed Oengus and laid him out in white. Morgan did not join them. Conall needed her.

Conall and Oengus' lords were gathered around a bonfire well away from the thatched roofs of the houses. Morgan watched them from the shadows.

"We should go and teach them a lesson," a thin scarred man was saying. "We can't let them kill our chief without paying for it."

"That's crazy," said a fat man. "We raided *them*. They're probably thinking about paying *us* back. This isn't the time to go raiding. We should bring in the stock from the outlying settlements."

"That would be showing weakness," said a tall wiry man.

"We're weak! Let's be honest. We're just about to bury our chief," said the fat man.

Morgan was worried about Conall. He was listening to all the arguments, nodding along with them. Didn't he realize he needed to lead these men?

She remembered how she had been swept along when her father was killed. She had been swept like the tide all the way out to sea. The village would dissolve into factions if he did nothing. The

217

factions would have their own leaders, and the winning faction would make its leader chief.

Say something! she wanted to shout at Conall.

"I'll take the men back out, and teach those Laigin a lesson," said the scarred man.

"I should lead them," said Conall quietly.

But his voice shook as he said it. Morgan watched the men eyeing Conall, weighing him.

He was coming up wanting.

"This isn't a raid for fun," said the scarred man. "This is serious business. To make sure they leave us alone while we figure out who's in charge here."

Morgan gasped. That was a challenge. Would Conall—

"I should lead them!" said Conall, missing the challenge, or ignoring it. "He was my father!"

"You should stay here and bury your father," the fat man said.

"I don't know how the men will feel about you leading them," said the tall man. This was getting worse and worse.

"Just what is that supposed to mean?" asked Conall angrily.

"How do we know you're not one of those Christ-worshippers?"

"If my father were alive, you wouldn't dare ask me that."

"Maybe your father would still be alive if he hadn't betrayed bright Lugh by letting those freaks worship their foreign god on our land," said the scarred man.

"Careful who you're calling freak." Conall was trying to be commanding, but he was confused, not knowing which point to confront first, and his voice was getting shakier.

"Leave his poor sister out of this," said the fat man.

"Fine," said the scarred man. "We'll leave her out. But what sort of judgment do you have, if you married one of them?"

"Yes. How can we trust a man with a Christian wife?" asked the tall wiry man. "They're a religion of peace." He spat the last word out. "Their god is a coward."

"My wife is not a Christian!" Conall insisted.

"I heard what she said to Oengus about your sister!" said the fat man. "Why would she say that, if she worships our gods?"

Conall seemed stumped by that.

So Morgan walked into the firelight. She had to. The men stopped talking. Conall stared at her as if she were one more problem he just couldn't handle.

"I said she would be better off with them," Morgan said. "I said it because it was true. Who would marry her now? You?" The fat man took a step back, as if he was not used to hearing arguments from a woman. He opened his mouth, but she cut him off. "If you ever catch me on my knees—" she paused for effect "—praying to a god of peace, then do me a favour and kill me on the spot."

"We're all happy that young Conall has chosen a woman..." started the tall man.

But Morgan didn't dare let him finish. "Anyway, who cares if I'm a Christian? Honestly. Am *I* leading you in battle?" She laughed at the ridiculous notion. "You need a leader who can win battles. Has Conall lost one yet?" She hoped Conall hadn't been exaggerating when he boasted of his victories. "From what I've heard, my husband has done nothing but win since he began leading raids."

"This is hardly the place for a woman—" interrupted the scarred man.

But Morgan shouted him down. "Conall has to avenge his father. Would you steal that from him?" The scarred man looked embarrassed. "If he dies in battle, you can pick yourself any new chief you like. But if he brings home cattle, and the heads of your enemies, then he's your rightful chief. Or do the Osraige pick their chiefs by how well they can talk?"

Conall was grinning. "Does she sound Christian to you? She doesn't sound Christian to me." The men, nervous at having to listen to a woman, all chuckled, and Morgan took that as her cue to exit.

THAT night in their house, Conall was in a strange mood, by turns elated and worried. "You made me chief," he told her.

"Weren't you going to be?"

"It wasn't going that way."

"Are you mad at me?"

"I'm just…surprised."

Morgan didn't know what she was supposed to say. Had she done something wrong?

Conall laughed uneasily. "I really have to win the next battle, don't I?"

Morgan was shocked. "You told me you always win."

"That may have been an exaggeration," said her husband, a bit sheepishly.

He was scared. But hadn't his father taught him what being chief was like? To rule was to know fear. A soldier only had to know how to fight. A leader had to win the battle before it began.

"They'll be expecting us," Conall said.

At that moment Morgan knew how Conall would win the battle. She would have to teach him how to fight Roman-style, for victory, not for glory. It would take some convincing.

She smiled. Then she took his face in her hands and kissed him.

FROM the hilltop Morgan could see Conall fighting for his life. His men were outnumbered. He only had two dozen men, while the Laigin had fifty or more. She could hear the clang of spears on shields.

The fat man had been right: the Laigin had sent their own raiding party to pay the Osraige back. They were hot for battle, pressing Conall's men back.

Conall was in front. Morgan's heart was in her throat. He was trying so hard to prove himself that he alone wasn't retreating. If the Laigin on either side noticed him, they'd have three on one. Then he would come back to the village with glory and a spear wound, like his father. She would be a widow.

Morgan was barely breathing. Had her plan gone wrong?

At that moment Conall seemed to lose heart. He shouted to his men, tore himself free from the Laigin. He broke and ran.

His men saw their leader running. They broke and ran too, dropping their shields, sprinting away up the ravine toward the place where Morgan was hidden.

The Laigin pursued them, close on their heels. This was the time of battle when men died if they ran from the enemy with their backs exposed. As the Osraige men pulled away, the Laigin pursued, throwing away their shields too, in order to catch up with them.

Morgan could hear the Laigin shout, "We've got them bottled up!"

There was dense forest on all sides of the steep muddy ravine, and the Laigin knew the ground even better than the Osraige.

Morgan gripped the horn tightly. She hadn't seen a battle in four years, and that one hadn't seemed real. This was real. The slowest Osraige man went down suddenly, a spear in his back.

The Laigin were stringing out along the ravine floor, dodging the low bushes that dotted it, their fastest men catching up with the slowest Osraige. They wouldn't catch all of them. But if they did catch them, they would have heads to take home. Conall might make it—he was the fastest runner, and there was no Osraige man ahead of him.

Wait for it...

Another Laigin threw his spear, but missed. He ran up to it and worked it out of the soft earth.

The Osraige men were slowing down as they ran up the sides of the ravine. Any farther and the men would have to scramble on all fours, perfect targets for the Laigin javelins.

"Now!" yelled Conall, and his men picked up the shields they had hidden along the sides of the ravine earlier in the day. They turned, and suddenly they were a ragged line.

The Laigin came up short. They must have been thinking, *Where did those shields come from?* Then Morgan raised the horn to her lips and blew.

Suddenly twenty Osraige men whom Conall had hidden in the bushes surged out to ambush the Laigin with joyous battle cries. The enemy warriors turned, startled, to see armed men running down the slope at them. Two of the Laigin died on spears before they could react. The others screamed, "Ambush!"

Conall yelled, "Charge!" and his men, too, charged down on the Leinstermen.

The enemy was trapped, muddy slopes to either side of them, warriors in front and behind them. The Osraige men had shields; the Laigin didn't. Some threw their spears away to try to scramble up the slope, but they were cut down before they could get away. The brave ones found themselves shoved together in a confused mob. The more bunched up they got, the more they interfered with each other's spears.

Conall was roaring happily. Morgan saw him stab two Leinstermen in a row, clean shots to the ribs. Both staggered and fell. The mud beneath their feet was turning slick with their own blood.

The killing took a surprisingly long time. Or maybe it just seemed like a long time. Maybe it was all over in two minutes. But in the end, the Laigin all lay dead, or were bound as prisoners, and a bright rivulet of blood was trickling down the stream bed in the middle of the ravine.

Now they came to the hardest part of the plan. The men wanted to round up as many of the Laigin cattle as they could find and take their prisoners home for ransom. Conall had to explain again and again why he wanted to do more fighting.

But the men were listening to him. It had been hard to convince them to make an ambush; where was the glory in that? But now that they had won, there was no doubt that he was their chief. They were only giving their chief the usual bellyaching.

The men settled down to wait for nightfall. They cut down trees and hacked the branches off, leaving stubs which poked out from the long trunks.

Conall snuck away to Morgan's side. "Are you still sure this is a good idea?"

"How was my first idea?"

"What if I'd fallen while running away?"

"Then you would be in the Halls of the Valiant."

"People would have called me a coward for dying with a spear in my back."

"The gods understand tactics better than your men do."

"Do they know what's in our hearts? Or do they only watch from on high?"

She couldn't answer him, so she kissed him.

THAT night they pushed the trees up against the fence that stood around the Laigin village. Conall and his four strongest men scrambled up the trees, using the branch stubs as ladder rungs. They disappeared over the fence into the village.

Moments later she heard shouting. Then the gates opened.

The Osraige men poured into the village. One of them shut the gates behind him. She had told Conall to insist on that.

She could hear more shouting, and then screaming. The thatched roofs of the houses started to burn, fire roaring into the clear night. Morgan could guess what was happening inside the village. There might be as many Laigin warriors as there were Osraige men. But the Osraige men were armed and awake. "Ten soldiers outnumber any mob," her father had said once.

Morgan shuddered at the slaughter that must be going on inside. She felt the thrill of victory. She almost wished she were a man, so she could be there.

But it was her victory.

MORGAN and Conall drank Laigin mead outside the great house of the Laigin village, and ate roast Laigin mutton. Morgan had insisted that the Laigin women, rounded up by Conall's men, be gathered inside the great house, not left outside. She had told Conall it was to prevent escapes. She didn't tell him of the night she had spent with the Déisi women, outside, while the Eóganachta men caroused inside.

"The men are restless," Conall said. Morgan had noticed that none had taken off their sword belts. Many had their shields nearby. "They're wondering when we're going home."

"I can make you a king," Morgan said.

"What?"

"You have to decide whether you want to be a chief, or a king," she told him.

"Ireland doesn't have kings," said Conall. "Not since the time of the fairy folk."

"Don't burn this village. Keep it," Morgan said.

"Keep it?"

"Fortify it. Build walls, high ones, twice as tall as these. Build them with a walkway behind them, so that you can post warriors on them, who will be able to throw stones down on the enemy. Build a tower, even taller than the walls, so you can see your enemies from miles away." He was staring at her. But not in total confusion. More like a child listening to a fairy tale, his eyes wide in wonder. "My father's castle"—she had to use the Latin word, *castrum*, because there was no word for castle in Irish—"had walls as tall as four men. No enemy ever took them, except by treachery."

"He was a king, then?" asked Conall.

He was a governor. But it would be hard enough explaining what a king was. "He was a great and wise king," she said.

"You think I could be a king?" Conall asked, bewildered.

Morgan smiled, and kissed him. She hoped she wasn't wrong about him.

THEY made love in one of the empty houses. Conall was on fire. He had risked his life, and she had given him a victory beyond anything he had ever imagined. She had offered him a throne. And she gave herself to him as if she were giving him all of Ireland.

And then she shuddered with a pleasure she'd never felt before.

So this is what it can be like? she thought, as they lay on the straw of the strange bed they had conquered. *Is this what all the songs are about?*

MORGAN woke up. She felt uneasy; she couldn't put her finger on why, but there was something…stirring. What was wrong? She knew how to reach out to the land, to feel its invisible pulse, the currents that flowed within it. But this was inside *her*.

She sat up. Conall was sleeping by her side. They had made love.

If they kept doing that, she would be with child soon enough.

WHAT would that mean? She had told Conall she could make him a king. She knew about walls, and ruses, and fighting through to final victory. She knew how a land could be governed.

And she could make the land help him. There was power here, and it listened to her. She had broken iron with it, and she had summoned Conall. There would be other things she could do with that power.

But could she be a mother?

She wasn't a mother. The word couldn't mean her. Mothers stayed at home, and shouted at their children to keep clear of the cliff's edge. They didn't join their men on campaign. They didn't go to battles and blow horns.

Ygraine had never worked magic, except to make the bad dreams go away. She hadn't even worked the magic the wise women had asked her to work, to save Din Tagell.

Morgan thought of the Enchanter. He had strange powers, but no family, no wife, no children. Men were never pleased to see him, even if they needed his help in battle.

Morgan's mind was spinning. Conall was sleeping. What would he think? He would want a child. Every man wants children. She was already sixteen, more than old enough to become a mother. And every wife of a chieftain wanted to bear him children.

Did she?

Did she have a choice?

She wasn't ready to take care of a child. Not yet. Being with Conall was strange enough.

Maybe she wasn't pregnant yet. Maybe it hadn't happened yet.

She reached within herself. Inside her was fire and earth, water and air. And there was darkness.

Her body was soft earth that lets a fallen seed plant itself and grow in the sun and the rain. But it could be stone.

She reached with the darkness inside her and became stone.

Then, exhausted, she let herself sleep.

In the morning she was bleeding.

Had she made that happen? Or had she been worried about nothing?

Conall was still asleep. Morgan knew she could never talk to him about it.

She went outside and looked at the sallow sun hiding behind the clouds, and shivered.

She was crying. She couldn't even tell why.

Chapter Eighteen

THE BATTLE OF THE CROWS

Two years later Morgan was looking out from the top of a hill toward the enemy. She watched the sunlight creep down the dew-streaked hillside. It was already warming up at the top of the hill. Her breath didn't puff white anymore. The rising sun had crested the distant ridges only a few minutes ago. From here it almost looked like she could see the sea, far to the east. But she knew it was only the grey-blue haze lying across the land.

Down below, the enemy was waiting for them.

Conall had four hundred men and a dozen chariots in position. He had seized the hilltop the evening before, daring the enemy to attack. The enemy had as many men as they did, but Conall's men were two hundred yards uphill. The enemy would be charging upward; Conall and the Osraige men would be charging down. Morgan had little doubt who would win that clash. Battle among the Irish was all about momentum. There would be a few casualties, the enemy would break, and it would be slaughter from then on.

They had raided deep into the lands of the Eóganachta. Not because Morgan held a grudge against them. They were in her past. But the Osraige lands now reached those of the Eóganachta. When she had met Conall, a man could have walked across the Osraige lands in a single day. Now it took two days going north to south, and three days east to west. She had promised Conall she would make him a king. After two years of lightning victories, he was the strongest chief of all his neighbours.

Morgan had been content to stop at the Eóganachta's borders. She didn't want to expand southwest. It felt like going backward, going in the wrong direction, away from the sea.

But the Eóganachta had raided some of the villages the Osraige had recently acquired. You couldn't ignore a provocation like that.

She had taught Conall to be patient, though, and wait until he had won the battle before going off to war. Instead of retaliating right away, Conall let Morgan do her work. Morgan had Conall's bard compose an extravagant praise song in honour of Cú Meda, chief druid of the Eóganachta, and she made sure wandering harpists learned it. She knew they would play the song to Cú Meda sooner or later, and the Eóganachta chief, Flannchad, would resent the attention his druid was getting. He would take every chance he could to cut Cú Meda down to size. When a chief and his druid are at odds, their clan is weak. Only when they were confident Morgan's ruse had worked did Conall and his warriors slip across the Eóganachta frontier. Now they were camped on a hill, two days' march from their own lands, three days' march from home.

Morgan tapped her fingernails on the golden greaves on her forearms. She would rather have worn a sword and helm, but it would have confused Conall's men to have a woman dressed for battle. So she wore a pure white dress, and a white cloak, and her greaves of gold reminded men, in case they needed reminding, that she was as warlike as they were, in her way.

It was still dark in the valley below. Morgan could make out the hundreds of enemy warriors in the shadows at the base of the hill. Out of those shadows, a grey-haired nobleman was guiding his chariot up the slope toward them. As he crossed into daylight, his red cloak and blue silk tunic blazed up, the sun flashing on the gold trim of his chariot. He carried no spear, and his sheath was empty. He held his hands up and open, to show he carried no weapon. Conall's warriors pointed him the way to their leader.

"Do you think they'll surrender?" Conall asked her.

"I hope not," Morgan said, grinning, because she knew it would make him smile. She walked back to the command tent.

Maelgenn held out something steaming in a wooden cup: an herbal drink. He had an honest face, with laugh lines around his eyes, a rare thing among druids; but he was a rare, honest druid. She took the cup, blew the steam away and sniffed. It smelled good.

They watched the old enemy nobleman head his chariot right at Conall, reining in his ponies just three feet from him. Conall never flinched, or even drew his sword. The old nobleman lowered his hand. "I bring a message for Conall, son of Oengus, chieftain of the Osraige people."

Conall said, "So long as you are in your chariot, my lord, you have not accepted my hospitality, and until then, my men may take it into their heads to kill you."

A chuckle ran through the men.

The old warrior dropped the reins and got down from the chariot. Erc took the ponies' bridles.

"Are you Conall?" the old man asked.

"I am, and Oengus was my father. Welcome to the lands of the Osraige people."

The old warrior made a twisted half smile. "I am Finn, son of Crunn, and this hill is Flannchad's hill."

Conall smiled broadly. "Then you are doubly welcome. I am always pleased to meet my new vassals."

More laughter from the men.

The old man smiled and shook his head. Why was he so confident? Or was it just bravado?

"My chief, Flannchad, has sent me to tell you that if you wish a battle, come down off the hill you are hiding on and fight us in the valley below. There is an excellent meadow, wide and dry, and may glory go to the valiant."

"We like it up here in the sun," said Conall.

"It would be the brave thing to do," said the old warrior, "instead of hiding on top of a hill."

Conall smiled, and for a moment Morgan was worried that he would take up the old man's offer. He could be reckless. But not this time.

"If we're on your land, come up here and push us off."

Morgan sipped the herbs, smiling. The enemy had to fight them here or call themselves cowards. They'd rather die; and she would give them the chance to die.

The old warrior shrugged. "Proud words, Conall, son of Oengus. But true glory would be to fight us in the valley."

He climbed back in his chariot and went riding down the hill.

IT was strange, the waiting moments before a battle. Nothing was happening, and yet every gesture, every breath, every moment, seemed to take on an immense power, just because men would soon die on the hillside.

Conall came over to her and kissed her. He was always in a good mood before a battle. She felt the wild fury inside him. She loved how he melted into her, how he was strong, yet he could be gentle as a wolfhound puppy.

But she pulled away. There would be time for more kisses after they won.

Conall's lords were watching. He nodded to them. They started barking orders to their men. The mass of men on top of the hillside began to form into columns and ranks. Morgan had taught Conall that. They wouldn't fight that way, that was too much to be expected of barbarians, and anyway she had no idea how men fought in formation. All she knew was how they marched. But she knew that when Conall's men started in good order, they stayed in good order for as much as half a minute longer than the enemy did. The solid ranks of Osraige men would charge, and the enemy would run at them, the fastest warriors arriving first, and these fastest ones would be cut down by the Osraige line before the slower ones closed. The slower ones would see their brothers die, and they would hesitate, and more than once that had made all the difference.

The ranks were forming up on the hillside, gold flashing in the dawn sun, cloaks rippling in the dawn wind. It always thrilled her. She let Conall go, and he smiled that joyful smile at her, and they walked over to his chariot together.

Already Conall's bard was in front of the men, exhorting them, telling them of the great deeds they had done in the last three years, of the great deeds they had done before that under Oengus, of the great destiny of the Osraige people. That was her idea too,

233

giving them something greater than cattle and gold to fight for, giving them a dream.

Morgan wondered if she was growing too fond of war.

Below, in the valley, gathered the enemy. Dozens of chariots spread out in the meadow, the sun glinting off beaten gold on their shields. Behind the chariots, there were maybe five hundred men on foot, same as she had. But the Eóganachta were not in formation; they were just a mass of warriors in tattered lines.

As far as Morgan could see, they had no druids exhorting them to combat. So Cú Meda was sitting this one out. Morgan smiled. She was always impressed when one of her stratagems worked.

Then a murmur spread across the Osraige lines. Men were pointing. She strained her eyes. It was hard to see, but something was moving in the woods by the meadow.

Men. Maybe two dozen of them. And chariots, rolling alongside.

No, three dozen. Now four or more, pouring out of the woods. They began taking up positions on the right side of the meadow.

"Who are they?" she asked.

"I don't know," said Conall.

"How many of them are there?" They kept coming, beginning to fill up the right side of the meadow. At least a hundred so far.

"We should attack immediately," said Conall. "Before they're formed up."

She thought about that. "We're not ready. Look at our men." Conall's eyes ran across the ranks of his men. They were confused by the new arrivals. They were not ready for battle, not yet.

More men were pouring out of the dark woods below, leaving the road for the chariots. There were already five of those.

"There are too many of them. We'll knock them back a bit, then it'll be man to man and they'll win," she said. If the enemy didn't break at the first charge, it would be all over. Conall had no reserves. They had brought every fighting man along. That had been his idea. He had cowed all his neighbours into submission; they were leaving his borderlands alone. They wouldn't even know about this battle until Conall was home again, so he had left no one to defend his strongholds. If they lost this battle...

She shuddered, and thought of how Ciarnat had doomed her people through her stupid misunderstanding of the enemy's strength.

The enemy was forming up in a loose line. There might be as many as five fifties of the newcomers. Not a crushing advantage, but it would make them feel they ought to win the battle, and that was worth another few hundred men. The enemy wouldn't break if they knew they outnumbered the invaders. And if they didn't break, their numbers would eventually tell.

"We need to retreat. Now," said Conall.

"We'll lose the high ground."

"If we get to the stronghold we'll be safe," he said.

Morgan had made Conall build a fortress on the border. That was a Roman thing, building fortresses on the move. It had walls of reinforced pine, and towers. If only they could reach that! None of Conall's enemies had ever taken one of his strongholds. In her second year with the Osraige, she had even lured enemies to attack the strongholds. No one attacked her strongholds anymore.

But they wouldn't reach the stronghold. The enemy was fresh; they knew their land. It would be a rout.

Maybe the new arrivals were too tired to fight well.

Morgan looked at the trees around the gathered armies. Black fruit everywhere, but it didn't dangle, it stood upright and cawed. How did the crows know the battle would be down there and not up here?

"Is there anything you can do?" asked Conall.

She thought of all the advice she had given him, all the half-remembered lessons her father had given her, and the stories of great battles she had learned from the Greek, and from the scraps of Roman histories she had found among the Christians' books. She had told him about strongholds, and about formations, and about making sure the men minded their sandals when they marched. Was there anything else she had missed?

"Is there anything you can do?" asked Conall, and now she knew what he meant.

It made Conall uncomfortable when she used magic in a battle. It stole from his glory; it made him feel like a fraud. He had only gradually come to terms with what she could do.

But he needed her magic now.

Morgan looked down at the men assembled around her husband, and then down at the mob of warriors waiting at the bottom of the hill. They were clanging their shields and spears together and yelling. She remembered the day the Déisi broke.

"I'll need some privacy," Morgan said. Conall nodded, and glanced at the men around him. They moved away from her.

THE night before, Morgan had prepared a circle. She did it to calm herself, and to feel the land. When she travelled to new lands, she felt disconnected until she scribed a circle and reached into the land. It would not work for her until it knew her.

She went to the circle she had made.

While the armies shouted defiance at each other, she held her arms out low at her sides. She felt the sun on her eyes. She felt the chill, dry clear wind that blew across the grassy hills. She felt the heat of the campfires, and the sun that warmed the land. She felt the river at their backs, whose hidden courses ran underneath the hills they had marched through. Most of all, she felt the earth.

Morgan thought of how Cú Meda had made a hole in the world. She needed something that powerful. But she needed the opposite of what Cú Meda had done. She needed to fill the world.

She let fear into her heart. She let fear and desperation become an empty vessel inside her, drawing strength into her. She thought of her years of slavery, and the destruction of the Déisi, and Gabrán and his cruel iron collar. She thought of the storm that had tried to sink her boat before she reached Ireland. She thought of the man with Bretel's face, and the torches in the woods outside Din Tagell, and how her mother had cried with passion.

Fire rushed into her from nowhere and everywhere. Her breath was the air and her veins were fire, her blood was water and she was part of the earth she was standing on. She was angry, and scared, and she would not let her lover's people lose this battle.

She opened her eyes. The crows and rooks and ravens were a black blanket across the trees down in the valley. They would gorge themselves soon. They would be too fat to fly.

She looked at Conall. She knew what she would do. She had raised the power to do it. He saw her nod, and looked away from her. She saw him raise his sword.

His men fell silent too. It was time. Morgan flung all her strength down the hill.

In the valley, night erupted from the trees. Thousands of black birds whirled up into the air, a maelstrom of wings and talons and beaks. They cawed a cacophony of death and vengeance. The men in the valley below looked up in shock and dread as the cloud of birds covered the sun. They lifted up their shields in fear. Then they were hidden from view as the birds fell on them like a black wave.

Conall yelled, and his lords flashed their swords in the sun, and his men roared as one. Then they were running down the hillside toward the enemy in good order, their feet shaking the ground with each stride. Morgan could not see the enemy anymore, just glimpses of men swallowed up by the living darkness which whirled among them, cawing and pecking.

The Osraige dove out of the dawn into the shadow of the valley of the birds, a joyful, dreadful cry in their mouths.

And through the shadows of the birds, the enemy saw the Osraige descending upon them. And they broke and ran, and as they ran, the Osraige cut them down like wheat in the fields.

ꝧꞪꞒ men were still killing the enemy wounded. As she walked through the battlefield, Morgan could hear moans cut short. She saw men pulling rings off dead fingers. She saw a few captured lords being bound for ransom.

The field was covered with fat black crows hopping around, barely keeping their distance. Conall's men never quite met her eyes. They weren't sure what "that thing with the crows" had been. They were grateful, but wary. Up ahead, they were crowding around Conall. They preferred to give him the victory, for he had led them down the hillside. They would swear he killed two dozen of the enemy by his own hand.

"I want to show you something," said Maelgenn. He led Morgan to the body of a chief, pinned face down in the blood-slicked grass by a spear through his spine. His woolen cloak was sewn with gold. Maelgenn turned the head to the side.

It was Ciarnat.

So it was the Déisi who had joined the Eóganachta at the last minute!

Morgan had reached out to Ciarnat at the beginning of Conall's campaigns, even though the Déisi chief had let her languish in slavery for four years. But Ciarnat had ignored her: Morgan was her neighbour, and therefore her enemy.

Now Ciarnat was dead. Morgan reached down and pulled the golden neck-ring off her neck.

She felt cold. Today she had defeated both the chief who had enslaved her and the chief who had left her in slavery. She should feel triumphant. Shouldn't she?

Morgan loved battle. When she watched battles, she often wished she were a man, so she could run at the enemy with a spear. Today she had flung all her power downhill with the men, and she had never felt more alive. She loved victory.

But she did not love viewing the dead. That much, maybe, she still had from her father.

She had seen so many battles. Toured so many battlefields. She wondered if she was losing her taste for war.

Morgan could continue this campaign. Flannchad and his men would flee to the lake village. No one could follow them there, they would assume. But there could be fog on the lake. Her men could sail rafts piled high with kindling toward the village, and light them on fire, and the enemy would see flames looming out of the fog. But her men would be coming from the other side, pushing logs through the water. Flannchad's men would panic, and be cut off from each other, and none would escape.

She had enough lands to the south and west. Only the east drew her.

She looked at the golden neck-ring in her hand. She had no desire to wear such a thing. A neck-ring might be open at one end, and made of gold, but she did not want its weight around her neck. It reminded her too much of the iron collar she had worn once.

Morgan wondered if Gabrán was somewhere dead on the battlefield. She was surprised to realize she did not care. She had already defeated him, long ago. This was enough slaughter for one day. And then Conall was coming toward her, with Corc and Erc, his faithful bodyguards. They were pushing a fat old man who waddled more than he walked.

It was the Greek! Morgan felt a rush of happiness. Had *he* been fighting? No. He was wearing slave's clothes. But clean, well-patched ones. He had clearly wangled himself a soft captivity.

Conall pointed at her, and asked the Greek a question. The Greek threw himself prone onto the ground.

"He said you would know him. But now he says he was mistaken," Conall said.

Morgan laughed.

"Please forgive me, my lady," the Greek said, in Irish. "I am an old, sad confused man."

"Look at me," said Morgan, in Irish.

The Greek got up on his hands and knees, but resolutely looked at her feet. "Forgive me, mistress, I heard that you were a foreigner...and you had the name of someone I knew."

"You're looking pretty fat," she said, in Latin. "You told the druids you were a famous philosopher, didn't you?"

The Greek's head shot up. He stared at her, and she could see he was trying to turn the twelve-year-old he had lost into the sixteen-year-old in white cloth and gold that stood before him.

"They…they have no use for writing. I told stories to children."

"I'm sure you did." Morgan held out her hand, and the Greek kissed it. "I'm trying to help you up," she said.

"Sorry," he said. "Habit." And he jumped up off the ground, grinning from ear to ear. He seemed a little dizzy. "Am I…am I…?" he babbled, and she guessed what he didn't dare ask.

"You're free," she told him.

He fell back onto the grass, sitting down suddenly as if his knees had given out. He was laughing, and looking at her and Conall, and laughing more.

"It's been a long time," she told Conall.

And then the Greek looked at her more seriously. "Simon's alive," he said.

WHEN the soldiers brought Simon to her, he fell on his knees.

He barely seemed to understand who Morgan was when she bade him stand. Then he tried to smile, but only twisted his face into a grimace.

"You're free," she told him.

He shook his head. He seemed almost angry.

"Come home with me," she said.

He shook his head even more angrily. "This is my home."

Morgan was stunned. *This* was his home? Had he become Irish?

And then she laughed. Hadn't she become Irish? Wasn't she a great Irish queen? What was left anymore of Anna, the British girl she had left behind in Britannia?

She shivered, and for the next hour she was irritable. She couldn't tell why, but she snapped at people, in spite of the great victory they had all won.

Morgan made Simon her charioteer. She did not ask him. She was a queen. He was someone from home, and she wanted him with her.

Тฦᴀᴛ night Conall's men burned their own dead in huge pyres of logs and kindling, broken shields and chariot wheels. The bonfires leaped into the darkening sky. The fire roared like a great beast.

Morgan dreamt of the Enchanter. It was a vague swirling dream, with times and places confused. The Enchanter kept walking away from her and she kept following him. Had he taken something from her? Or did she want something from him? She wasn't sure.

When Morgan woke up, the hut was dark and Conall was asleep. Morgan thought of the magic she had wrought that day. She wondered if the Enchanter would have been impressed. She wondered if he always knew what the magic was going to do, or if it was a surprise to him too, sometimes.

She felt terribly alone. This land was a strange place, with barbarous customs and a language she still had to make an effort to speak when she was tired. She was trying to reshape it into something her father might have recognized. But the bones of the land were not her bones.

In the two years she had been Connall's wife, she had worked miracles. Bards were making up proud songs about his exploits. Why did she still not feel she belonged here? Why did it feel like it was taking forever?

Was her mother sleeping next to that man? Did they have a son, like in her dreams? And was he learning how to fight?

She lay back on the bed, but she couldn't get back to sleep.

In the morning the battlefield was still black with rooks and crows and ravens. They waddled like ducks, pecking fitfully at the corpses. Someone had counted five hundred bodies after the battle, with only a dozen slain among the Osraige.

If ever rooks have deserved their feast, thought Morgan, *these are the ones.*

As the sun rose, she spotted half a dozen wolves eyeing the battlefield from the forest. They would wait until the men left. She spotted another bit of movement, fifty paces from the wolves. It was a wild boar. It grunted as it waddled back into the undergrowth.

She shuddered. Pigs would eat anything.

AS the men got ready to move out, a chariot came out of the south. The driver held a messenger's baton and took a leather sack and a bucket out of his chariot.

"I bring you honour on your victory from Cú Meda the druid," the messenger told Conall as he put down the sack and the bucket. He looked tired. He must have been driving his chariot all night. "Many have sung of your prowess in battle, and your wisdom as a leader. Your victory is immortal. We pray to the gods that the songs are equally true about your kingship."

Conall shot Morgan a look that said: *Where is this heading?* "Skip the compliments, messenger," he said. "What's in the sack and the bucket?"

"This sack is full of gold," said the messenger. "Cú Meda acknowledges that you are the rightful ruler of the Eóganachta, as foretold in certain prophecies that he has recently come to understand. He hopes that you will accept this tribute, and treat these lands as if they are yours."

"As opposed to enemy lands that I might pillage," said Conall, clarifying.

"You have it exactly," said the messenger.

"Does Flannchad agree with all this?"

"Why don't you ask him?" said the messenger. He kicked over the bucket, and a blood-slicked head rolled out onto the grass. Morgan remembered Flannchad's face from the day he had given out the Déisi slaves. The head on the grass was ten years older, and dead. But it was the man she remembered. "Cú Meda has come to understand that Flannchad was never properly selected as chief," said the messenger, "which explains why the Eóganachta were so unlucky in battle."

"Truly"—Conall chuckled—"Cú Meda is a wise man." He looked at Morgan. She knew he was thinking of her ruse to divide Cú Meda from Flannchad. It had succeeded beyond her wildest imaginings. "Tell my loyal druid that we accept his tribute, and I will treat my lands as, well, as my lands. Do you want the bucket back?"

"I've got a nicer one at home," said the messenger, and got back in his chariot and drove off.

A week later Morgan stood on the eastern ramparts of Conall's stronghold. "The Castle," people called it, mangling the Latin word. It was modelled on a Roman legionary fortress, with fifteen-foot-high ramparts of thick pine logs you could throw javelins down from, and twenty-five-foot towers on either side of the gate. She remembered being at the legionary fortress at Durnovaria. It had been just after Beltane. The trees had been in bud, the land waking up. She had been a child then. Now she was a queen.

A queen. Not a governor, or his wife.

She shivered. This morning the drizzle made the pine planks of the wall walk slippery. It muffled the distant sound of the boys clacking their hurley sticks together on the field below the western ramparts. Everything was dripping. All around the slopes of the Castle's low hill, cartloads of ash and elm leaves were laid out for winter fodder, waiting for the sun to dry them, if it ever came back. The peas and beans were already dried and stored away in pits. The fields around the Castle were muddy brown, the emmer and spelt wheat all harvested. Two dozen wild geese grubbed in the stubble, just out of bowshot.

In a fortnight it would be time to slaughter the cattle the land couldn't support through winter. There would be almost too much meat to pickle in brine, to dry and to smoke, because of the battles Conall had won.

The land was ready to sleep. But Morgan couldn't stop pacing.

CONALL gestured. The Greek unrolled the map on the wide table that Morgan had had made to hold it. It was her fourth map. She kept correcting them as she learned more, and this one was beginning to resemble a proper Roman map. She had quizzed messengers and tinkers and merchants, and even sent out a few brave young scouts with good eyes. It was another of her brilliant "inventions." Here, no one used maps, because who didn't know how to get to their neighbours? And who needed to go farther than that?

"Should I colour in the Eóganachta?" asked the Greek. Red pigment tinted the lands of the Osraige. Every year Morgan rubbed red pigment on more lands. The Greek's hair had, strangely, turned white as soon as she had freed him. But his blue eyes twinkled, and his ruddy cheeks were just as fat as ever.

"Who do we invade next year?" asked Conall.

Morgan looked at the map. She had always been drawn to the east. But whenever they took one village to the east, it would turn out to be dangerously exposed unless they also took the one south of it. Sometimes a chief in the west would die with no adult heir, and it would be foolish not to take advantage of that tribe's weakness, and she had no good reason to tell him why they shouldn't.

Looking at the map, Conall began enumerating the strengths and weaknesses of all the neighbouring tribes. She had taught him to do that. But Morgan couldn't focus. Her eyes traced a path east to the sea across the parchment. It was a hundred and twenty miles—and three tribes—away.

How many years? she wondered. What if Conall lost his hunger for conquest? What if she lost her appetite for war?

Conall glanced at the Greek. The Greek turned to Morgan. "If you don't need me, my lady…"

She shook her head.

The Greek bowed to Conall. Conall half smiled. The Greek liked to bow to people. It made him seem Continental. Conall knew better, so the Greek bowed just to amuse him. Then he scurried out.

"You weren't listening," Conall said.

"Sorry. Daydreaming."

"I said, 'or we could just make peace with everybody.' Usually that gets your attention."

The people were tired of war. Morgan knew that. They appreciated the victories and the plunder and the cattle and the slaves. But they would like to rest. And Conall still hadn't figured out how to bring the lords of the people he conquered into his tribe. They felt conquered. They obeyed. But they felt no loyalty to him. A few might fight for him, because it made them rich. But they would turn on him as soon as they could, out of habit if nothing else.

Over time the Osraige could become a bigger tribe, thanks to all the captured wives and slave women. But that would take years.

The land wanted to rest, she thought. It was blood-soaked and filled with death.

Morgan sighed, and sat down. "I'm just tired," she said.

"You wear yourself out," he said. "Women aren't supposed to go campaigning. It's exhausting. And the things you do…" He meant the magic. "You're always tired afterward. You don't admit it. But you are." He came over and began rubbing her shoulders. "I sometimes think that's why…" His voice trailed off.

That's why she was barren. There was no reproach in his voice. He loved her too much. She knew his lords talked about it behind her back. He was young, but who would succeed him if he died in battle? Or if he took sick?

"That's not why," she said. "Peasant women work in the fields until their water breaks."

"Maybe," he said very softly. "Maybe what you do is harder. Or maybe you're more delicate."

Morgan closed her eyes. She couldn't look him in the eyes

Conall began stroking her hair. "We're rich, you know. The people are happy. Our neighbours want desperately to make peace. There isn't anything we need that we don't have. Is there?"

His fingers slipped through her hair and caressed the soft skin behind her ear. His touch made her shiver. She shook her head, knocking his fingers away. "I'm sorry. That tickles."

"Sorry." He backed off, confused.

"Just a…just a chill," she said, lying.

He brushed the hair out of her eyes. She was in awe at the tenderness she saw in his face. He kissed her.

And suddenly she saw how it could all work. She could end the wars, at least for now. He wanted to. All she would have to do is give her permission. Conall could stay at home, and she could teach him to rule just as she had taught him to make war.

And she could give him the son he so badly wanted. She wanted to. And then she would no longer be a foreigner, an outlander. She would be the mother of the chief's children. She would belong to the clan at last, linked by blood to Conall. Then neighbouring tribes would send gifts and hope that now the fierce warrior Conall would no longer raid them. And they would live in peace. In time, Conall would become the first true king of Ireland since the fairy folk.

What was she waiting for?

She had dealt out so much death. Her body wanted to give life.

She kissed Conall back. She melted into him.

She took him to bed. He was so strong, so tough. She let herself be soft with him. She let him bend her, and take her.

Afterward she felt fulfilled. She felt like she knew what it was to be a wife. And she would know what it was like to be a mother. She felt safe. She felt good. She felt loved.

She lay in his arms, drifting off to sleep. For once she did not think of a fleet of ships, or of a fortress perched on high cliffs jutting out in the waves, or of a man who was not her father who had stolen her father's face, his life and her own.

Chapter Nineteen

PENDRAGON

Morgan dreamt.

She was her mother again. Her son was fighting Uter with his stick and wooden shield, and Uter was laughing, and batting the blows away barehanded, occasionally reaching through her son's guard to cuff him gently in the face.

Then everything in Din Tagell went quiet.

A small dark man got down off his pony.

Uter shot her a frightened look. Then he went to talk quietly with the small dark man.

Morgan could barely hear. But the phrase, "We talked about the price," wafted her way. And, "You chose this."

She shivered. Her son watched the two men argue.

Then the Enchanter got back on his pony. And Uter swept the boy up in his arms. Then he lifted the boy up into the saddle.

What?

The Enchanter spurred his pony around, and it cantered toward the gate. She had a terrible feeling. She ran after him, screaming.

Uter grabbed her. He was crying. She had never seen him cry. She screamed and fought him until the Enchanter galloped out of the gate. Then she collapsed.

IŊ her dream Morgan woke up. She was sitting on a chair at the edge of the cliff. Far below her the waves were coming in, rank after rank of them, to dash themselves on the cliffs. She had been sitting there for hours. She had been sitting there for days, looking out at the endless sea, waiting. She had dreamt of the Enchanter again. She had been Ygraine again, in her dream.

She got up and walked back to her house.

Din Tagell was almost silent. Only a few houses had smoke coming out of their thatch.

She went back into her house. On a table was a small portrait of a boy. Of her son, the day he had been taken away by the Enchanter.

She looked around. There was no sign of a man in the house. No shield, no sword, no helmet. The place had the disarray of an empty house, yet she knew, in her dream, that she lived there.

She was crying. She was alone.

STiLL Morgan dreamt.

And in her dream, black ships cut through the white sea. Banners rippled from their prows. They beat up the coast against the wind. She could see a promontory sticking out into the sea, a high long ridge that came out of the land like a neck. There was a fortress on it, and a wall that cut it off from the land.

Voices spoke in a strange guttural tongue she had never heard before. But she heard one sound she knew as a name.

She heard someone say, "Uter Pendragon." And she heard the sharpening of axes.

MORGAN was cold when she finally woke up for real. She was no longer crying, but her face was wet from tears.

Conall was looking at her. She loved him; she knew that.

She put her hand on the ground. The land felt alien. It had been feeling strange to her for some months now. It was not just the chill of winter. The land felt like a horse that wanted to throw her off, and she was getting tired of fighting it.

Conall didn't ask, "What's wrong?" He had asked that before, many times. She had given him many answers. This time he asked something else, in his softest voice, so soft she barely heard the question in it. "What would make you happy?"

What would make me happy? she wondered.

To be your queen. To be your wife. To be the mother of your child. To be the mother of the child that could have been, years ago. To be bearing Conall his second child by now, to be the wife of a rich and valiant chieftain living in peace with neighbours who did not dare to encroach on his lands.

To be someone else, she thought.

To be Anna, whose father was wise and her mother beautiful, Anna who would long ago have been married, the wife of another governor in a Britain empty of invaders, a Britain united and restored.

To be Luan, lost in her faith, praying to a god who loved her, surrounded by people who believed in her.

Or Mary-who-could-have-been, a leader in the church; not a saint, but someone who knew saints, and spoke to chiefs, and made druids listen.

To be any woman but herself.

She had been born of the sea, and the sea called to her.

She had been born of blood, and blood called to her.

She had been born of her mother, and her mother had been stolen from her, and the man who stole her had not yet paid for his crime.

She was not a queen. She was not a wife, not really, as she had never truly been a slave. She was only sojourning.

Conall was still looking into her eyes, and he was crying too. "I will give you anything I can, if it will make you happy."

But there was only one thing. It was something Morgan did not want to ask of him. There would be no more embraces after she asked it. No more soft questions. It would be the end of everything.

"Let's not talk about it," she said. "All I want is for you to be happy."

"There *is* something," said Conall. She could feel the intensity of his love. "Tell me."

"I can't."

"We have everything," he said, "and yet you cry every night in your sleep. What could I give you that would make you happy?"

She couldn't lie to him.

"Fifty men," she said, and her heart was breaking. "Fifty men with no land of their own, and no children, and no wives."

"Why?"

"To go on a raid. With me."

"Where?"

Morgan didn't answer. She had already told him about a man named Uter who had killed her father—she never said what Uter had done to her mother.

"We have all the gold we can use."

"This is about vengeance," she said.

He stared at her. And this time she told him everything. The man who had seen her mother across a room full of soldiers, who had convinced a sorcerer to change his face, who had destroyed all her happiness. When she was done talking, she knew he understood.

"Vengeance," he said, and nodded, for there was nothing more that needed saying. Any Irishman understood blood calling out to blood. It could not be ignored.

He leaned forward and grasped her hands. "There are better things than vengeance. We could be king and queen of Ireland. I believe that. We could unite the whole southeast. With my bravery and your—with what you do—we could bring peace and order to the island. Like Britain, in the time of the Romans. Isn't that better than chasing a man who may already be dead?"

She knew he did not really believe what he was saying. He was just repeating words she had once said to him, words he hoped would make her stay. "If I could stay," she said, her heart breaking, "I wouldn't even need that. I wouldn't need all of Ireland. I could be content with what we have. I could be content with just you, and one village."

"I've been holding you back," he said. "You've been pushing me to be greater than I am, and I've resisted, and I shouldn't have. I've been scared it wouldn't go well." He looked scared now. "I should have been scared not to live up to your dream for me. I need you. I need you to be great."

He still wanted to keep her. He loved her that much.

"I can't stay," she told him. She kissed him.

He was confused.

"Everything is ashes in my mouth," she said.

He stared at her until it sank in. "How long have you been waiting to say this?"

"I only knew it just now."

He shook his head. "No. You've never been content. You've always pressed ahead." It was true. She had always loved him. But he had never made her happy. She suddenly thought, what if she asked him to come with her. Just for the raid. Like heroes in a legend, they would take a fifty of men and cross the sea, and take vengeance. Then they would return in victory. She would belong to him and their children. She would be done with Britain.

"You can't take me to Britain with you," he said, as if he had read her mind. "I belong here. I belong to my people."

Morgan wanted to say he was wrong. But he wasn't wrong. And she couldn't lie to him. She couldn't leave him with a lie. She would never be done with Britain. She would stay there until she took Din Tagell, or died. And if she took Din Tagell, she would stay. She was the heir to Din Tagell.

"I think I've been a blade in your hand all these years. I think you've been sharpening me and forging me for this one thing."

"No," she pleaded. "I have always loved you." And she kissed him harder. She tried to show him her passion again. It was rising in her like hope.

He pulled away. "Maybe that's so," he said. The betrayal in his eyes made her feel sick.

All she could manage was, "It wasn't like that." She hated the sound of her voice. It sounded like she was lying. "I only wanted you to be great." She hoped she wasn't lying.

Conall got up. He went to the door. She thought he was going to leave without saying anything. But he rasped out, "I will give you the men you want." There was no harshness in his eyes, only a terrifying sadness. "In the spring. The sea is rotten in winter, and your boat will founder and sink."

He turned and went out.

Morgan winced, waiting for the door to slam. But he shut it gently.

She wept.

What she was giving up would have been the dream of any other woman.

But she could not be another woman, not even for Conall.

ᵀᕼᕮ sun was bright and hot, the air perfectly still. The Castle's courtyard was dry. Spring flowers lined the base of the rampart walls. Insects buzzed. Morgan thought of the sea. It would take them a week to reach the coast. It wouldn't be easy to pass through three other clans' territory unnoticed with fifty men. Then they would have to find boats.

The men gave her sidelong glances as she watched them load up the ponies. Men without land, men without wives or children, boys who hadn't proven themselves yet, who were ready for an adventure.

A dozen of the men were foreigners from neighbouring clans, whose lands and cattle Conall had taken, so they had nothing to lose. Morgan had sworn a great oath that they would never be asked to make war on their own people. None of them had any idea whom they were sailing to Britain to attack. She could have told them who Uter was, but they would only have asked her why she was trying to discourage them.

Morgan walked along the line of ponies. Now she did have a sword strapped to her waist. That had been Conall's idea. "The men will feel better following a woman with a sword."

Conall tightened a strap on one pony's harness, then headed over to her. In some ways they were closer now than they had ever been. They were friends, almost. He had taught her many things about leading men that he would never have told a wife. He'd helped her pick the men, and talked with each man to make sure he was ready to leave their homeland, led by a woman chief, and travel across the sea to fight British warriors. He'd even, bless him, told them all how good-looking British women were. He was her strong brother, looking out for her.

"About ready, I think," he said.

"Thank you," she said.

"I should have known better than to marry a warrior," he said.

"And if you had known better?" She was hoping to make him laugh. But his face clouded. She shouldn't have joked.

He looked over her face, intently.

He would have married me anyway, she thought.

"Do you want me to wait for you?" he asked.

She wanted to say *yes*. She wanted him to wait. She wanted to come back to him once she had slain the dragon in its lair. She wanted to bring him the dragon's heart in a gold box, so they could roast it and eat it together, and share the knowledge of all secret things.

But her place was in Britain, and his was in Ireland. His people did not sail, and her people looked to Rome.

"Don't wait," she said.

"Then I will mourn you." His voice was so soft she could barely hear it.

SHE stepped up into her chariot, and Simon snapped the reins gently, and the ponies moved into a walk.

The Greek grinned at her. They were going home at last.

The people gave up a great cheer for their men, going on a great raid across the sea. They had not questioned Morgan's leaving. She had never truly been one of them.

Maelgenn smiled as he swirled burning herbs in the air, giving the blessings of the gods.

Conall didn't move. He just watched her go.

Then Morgan turned, and she and her men headed off into the civilized east.

She was weeping.

But a strange calm fell over her. Her heart felt heavy for Conall. But it felt light too. She reached for her neck, and she realized she was reaching for a collar that was no longer there.

She was going home.

Chapter Twenty

BRITANNIA

They stayed as far away from strongholds as they could. The fifty of them made a large enough war party that so long as they seemed bent on raiding someone else's lands, the clans they passed through left them alone, merely shadowing them to make sure they kept moving.

They reached the coast in four days. The cliffs were barren, not a field in sight. Maybe the inhabitants were afraid of sea raids.

She set lookouts on the cliffs. Her men were restive. They had agreed to sail to Britain, but they had never seen waves before. Still, they didn't dare complain. If she, a woman, wasn't frightened of the water, they could not bear to show fear either.

They needed a boat. Fortunately, after two days, they sighted a Greek galley beating up along the coast. In secret, her whole war band paced it until night fell. The ship found a calm inlet and pulled up on shore for the night. In the morning, when the sky had barely begun to brighten, her men rushed the boat.

The Greeks never even tried to fight. As the men rounded them up, she smiled broadly at Aedan, the veteran warrior whom Conall had given her to take charge of the men. She could see a new respect in his eyes.

She would need it. There were forty amphorae of wine on the boat, and thirty slaves chained to the oars. Morgan ordered the jars of wine taken off the boat. The men were astounded. Each amphora was worth one girl slave; that's what the Greeks had come to Ireland to trade for, wine for flesh. In her mind's eye, she saw forty girls imprisoned inside the huge pottery vessels.

She knew her men would break into the amphorae and get drunk as soon as she was asleep. She had to make them smash the amphorae. Some of the men wept as they watched the red wine run out into the surf.

She kept three magnificent horses they found in the hold. One was a huge gelding, almost as tall at the shoulders as Morgan. He had three toes instead of one. He snorted at her. She called him Flaith, for his hide was red as *flaith*, the rich red ale of Ireland.

ᚦᚻᛖ winds blew gently off the coast the next morning, brushing the galley gently out to sea. They ran before the wind all day, and the men became convinced sailing was no big deal. They had nothing to do but sit, and the boat made the distance for them—the sail, and the thirty slaves in the hold, who beat the oars backward in rhythm. They sat in the sun, combing their hair, and watched the Greeks work the ropes, laughing as though they were watching performing monkeys.

But as the sun slipped behind them, the sky became dark with clouds. Darkness fell faster than night, and the wind rose, and kept rising. The galley began to pitch and yaw. She felt sick. The men disappeared beneath the deck, terrified of the rising waves. Only Aedan and two of his best men stayed to watch the Greeks, to make sure they didn't do anything treacherous. But the Greeks were desperately fighting to keep the ship turned into the waves. They heaved the steering oar to and fro, and yelled directions down into the hold for the slaves on the oars. As it got worse, they took down the sail.

The ship plunged deeper into each wave, its black prow disappearing into the charcoal grey water, coming up with water gushing off its deck.

She wasn't scared until she saw that the Greeks were scared. She'd assumed they knew how to handle storms. But ships were lost at sea all the time. Was this how it happened?

The wet salt air battered her face, while the galley's deck slammed up against her legs. The horizon was gone in grey confusion. The rigging sang a low banshee moan that rose and fell with the gusts. She heard the slaves cry out in the hold, frightened.

Suddenly she was angry. She had been born of the sea. She had given up her name to the sea, and she had given up her old life to the sea. She would not let it take her. So she reached out into the storm and lashed its fury to the mast. Morgan, once called Anna, was returning to Britannia to reclaim her destiny. She exulted in the gale that hurled her home.

THEY reached the British coast as the sun was rising behind it, and for a moment Morgan laughed at the sight of it. The sun would set on the water. She had not seen the sun set over the water in six years. She had missed that.

Keeping the coast in view, but not daring to get too close to its rocks, they turned south. They sailed south for two days with the wind running across the beam, as the galley slaves in the hold dipped their oars in unison and pulled.

Then they were across the gulf of the Severn, sailing along the Cornish coast. They were still far from Din Tagell. But she couldn't approach Din Tagell by sea. There were things she needed to know first. She ordered the crew to run the boat up on the nearest beach.

MORGAN knelt and touched the ground.

The land felt strange.

No. It wasn't the land that was strange. *She* was strange. The land was reaching out to her. It knew her, but it didn't know how it knew her. And now that she was back, its touch was so close that she shivered.

And she wept. She wept for Conall. She had wondered if she would land in Britain and realize her whole foray across the sea was unnecessary. She had dreamt of landing, and finding herself in a foreign land that had forgotten all about her, and turning back. She had dreamt of his joy, and her relief.

But she knew this land. She had always known this land. And she could feel a great pulse run through her, as a part of her that had been empty suddenly filled again.

She would not go back.

She was home.

"Milady?" said Aedan. "What do we do with the Greeks?"

They could not afford the news spreading that four dozen Irish raiders had appeared on the coast. She thought about killing all but a few of the Greek traders, and sending two of her own men in charge of the chained slaves to some distant place. But the Greek—*her* Greek—suggested that they chain the traders to the oars in place of the slaves who had rowed them there. They could put the slaves in charge. The Greek had a wicked sense of justice.

The liberated men were Numidians, brown as dry oak leaves, with black hair and noses as long as hers. Their leader was a small wiry fellow; she was amazed he had survived pulling the oars. He laughed, and called her "goddess," and kissed her feet, and if she understood his odd staccato Latin correctly, he proposed to sacrifice all the Greeks on the altar of his goddess, Tanit, the moment he was back home in Africa. He laughed again when she suggested they were worth more in the slave market. She guessed there was no danger of those strange dark men talking to anyone in Britain.

SHE had forgotten about roads. But here one was, stone laid next to stone, rising above the land on a bed of gravel. It was as straight as the hilly countryside allowed, and it shot out into the horizon in two directions. After ten years in Ireland, it looked to Morgan as if some giant had taken his belt and laid it down on the land. She put her sandal on the stone of the road. It was solid.

It felt good to step on a road.

She smiled at her men. They grinned back in amazement.

"Welcome to Britain," she said, and they cheered a mighty cheer.

NOW the men were investigating, of all things, the ruts in the stones of the road. They seemed to be trying to figure out why the road builders had bothered to carve channels for wagon wheels in the road: surely it wasn't worth all the effort with chisel and mallet, just so the stonework would look more like a chariot path. The Greek was grinning at them. "Wagon wheels did that," he explained. "Hundreds of years of wagon wheels, running over the road. They made the ruts."

"But surely all wagons aren't the same width," said Aedan, with great puzzlement.

"In Britannia they are."

"Why?"

"Because of the ruts," grinned the Greek. Aedan stared at him, trying to figure out if the Greek was joking.

"But who made the ruts, then?"

"The wagons."

"Which came first, the wagons or the ruts?" asked Aedan, with mounting frustration.

"The wagons, of course."

"Then why are they all the same size?"

"To fit in the ruts!" The Greek burst out laughing, and all the other men laughed too, although Morgan wasn't sure they could have said why it was funny. And with that she found herself laughing too, and everyone looked at her in amazement, as if they had never heard her laugh before.

MORGAN rode Flaith at the head of her men. The men were amazed that she would ride on the back of a horse instead of a chariot; but they had never seen a horse big enough to ride on, just the Irish ponies. She supposed that riding a three-toed horse into a place called Trigos had to be an excellent omen. She whispered it to the Greek, who was huffing and puffing alongside, knowing he would share it with the men.

She wondered where Uter was. When she had dreamt of her mother watching the waves from the cliffs, he had not been at Din

Tagell. Was he at war, in an armed camp? Had those dreams been true?

As they came over the next ridge, they saw a party of what looked like settlers a mile away. The people were travelling with their goats and cattle, and all their belongings in carts. But before they reached the settlers, the people scattered into the woods, abandoning all their belongings, and there was no finding them.

So they were not settlers; they were refugees.

After that, Morgan sent out scouts, always running one ridge ahead of the main body of men. After an afternoon's march, the scouts brought warning of another group of refugees, and Morgan set a painless ambush. When the dozen men, women and children came over the ridge, her men surrounded them. The men and women shrieked and brandished their wood axes and scythes. But when the Greek called out to them in Latin to put down their weapons, they realized they were not going to be slaughtered. They wept with relief.

Their leader was a woman in her very weathered forties. Sylvana, she called herself. Her hair was almost all white, but it was full, and she held herself proudly, though she was obviously fighting exhaustion. The rest of her party, deciding they were safe, immediately lay down and went to sleep in broad daylight. They had been walking for two days already, without stopping.

"Saxons," said the woman. "Running wild up the coast. Five boats of them, they say. They've burned two villages already." She pointed at two thin columns of smoke rising in the far distance. "And there's no one to stop them."

Morgan felt a tightness in her chest. Was she too late? The Greek shot an anxious glance at her. "What about the High King?" he asked.

"High King? You mean Uter?"

"Is someone else High King?"

"There's no High King at all, now that Uter's gone."

"What do you mean, *gone?*" asked the Greek.

But Morgan already knew the answer. She felt dizzy. She sat down on the grass, as Sylvana asked the Greek, "You sound like you come from here, but you don't know Uter's dead?"

"We've been away," said the Greek.

Sylvana nodded, asking no more questions. "Some say he took ill this winter, from a cold, and some say a Saxon put a poison mushroom in his stew. It was just after the solstice."

Morgan was having trouble breathing. She thought, *I almost reached him. When I had my dream, he was still alive. If I'd crossed the Irish Sea then, he would still have been alive when I reached Din Tagell.*

"Some say it was an old battle wound that festered," the old woman went on. "But I don't credit that, for the Lady Ygraine would never have allowed it."

"Then the Lady Ygraine is still alive?" asked the Greek, reading Morgan's mind.

"If Din Tagell still holds," said the woman. "But there are five boatloads of Saxons. And who knows how many behind them." The old woman's voice was choking. "One day they'll push us up into the mountains of Gwynedd and Powys," she said. "They're fierce, and they have good armour, and they sing the most bloodcurdling war songs. We'll become a wild people, living in the hills like beasts...." The woman shuddered and couldn't go on.

Uter was dead. She would never be able to make the world right.

She had given up Conall for this vengeance. She had given up love, and the children she would never have with Conall.

In dying, Uter had stolen from her yet again.

"Milady?" said the Greek. But she waved him away. She couldn't talk to anyone. She walked away, while he kept talking to Sylvana.

Could she go back? Could Conall forgive her? It was impossible, wasn't it? She had broken his heart. Had betrayed him. Had used him, even if she hadn't realized it. How could she go back to him now, in defeat?

And she did not want to. The land tugged at her. This was where she belonged. Already Conall seemed strange to her—a foreigner, a barbarian. She had been intimate with him, and known his secrets. But he had never known her, not like this land knew her.

The Greek was not going away. "Milady, the Saxons are said to be moving on Din Tagell. People have taken refuge there, but they say it won't be able to hold out for long."

The Saxons were going to finish the job Uter had started. That was something she could grasp.

What would her father have done? He would have rushed to the side of his lady. He would have been glad he was fighting barbarians, at long last, and not a fellow Roman.

Her mother was in Din Tagell. She could rescue her, not from shame and Uter, but from death and worse.

"The Saxons have a surprise coming to them," Morgan said, and she heard in her own voice an echo of her father, and pride thrilled in her veins.

ᛏᚻᛖ road southwest to Din Tagell was familiar, but strange. Morgan would recognize a feature—a crag, a stand of trees—but after a minute of walking she would see it from a different angle and realize that she had never seen it before, only one like it. She would see islets just offshore and remember them. Then she would wonder if she was trying so hard to remember them that she was creating her own memory. Had she ever taken the road up the coast to Aquae Sulis? It was so long ago, and she had been just a girl.

She sent her scouts out ahead, the two Fiachas, lithe runners, with knives but no spears, so they wouldn't be tempted to become heroes. They ran out like faithful dogs guarding sheep. Only, she smiled to herself, they were guarding wolves.

The two Fiachas came running out of the dusk, silent, their cloaks flowing behind them. They leaped like deer as they ran, and they grinned like madmen, and she knew they had found an enemy.

"Saxons!" Fiacha the Red gasped out.

"Foragers. A half dozen!" Fiacha the Black said. "Heading into the woods."

"About five miles from here," said Fiacha the Red, recovering his voice.

"Loaded down with traps and snares and sacks and things," said Fiacha the Black.

The men started to let out a cheer, but she shushed them. Her men could make a cry that travelled twenty miles when they were in good voice. She said quietly, "Let's go make some good Saxons."

MORGAN walked up to the last Saxon. He had put up a good fight. He had gone berserk, swinging his axes in tight arcs, dealing death. Or he would have dealt death, if Diarmat hadn't hurled a huge rock at him, staggering him. The Irish spears had made short work of him after that. Now he was propped up against a tree, grinning despite his obvious pain. He knew he was going to die.

She thought he might be more intimidated if she were beautiful just now, and made a cantrip she had done a few times at the lake village, to put Buanann in a good mood.

But this time she felt the land catch her cantrip and fill it with heat. Oh, it was powerful, the land here. It was familiar to her. It fit her bones. It knew her. She only had to reach out, and the elements were there. Everything she tried to do was so easy here.

The magic must have made her exceptionally beautiful, because the Saxon's eyes widened as she squatted down by him and ran her fingers gently along his face. He winced when she touched a gash in his shoulder, but his eyes never left hers. That was good. She let him fall into her gaze.

"What's your name?" she asked in Latin.

"Siegmund," he said. "You?"

She smiled. He had not earned her name, no matter how well he had fought. "You may call me the Lady of the Ravens," she said.

"Uter not help you now!" he said, and he laughed, though it obviously hurt his chest to laugh.

She smiled, because she knew it would throw him. "Good. I never liked him. Did you kill him?"

He frowned, trying to decide what that meant. He looked around at her men. "You folk not British?"

"Do we look it?" He looked around at her men, their capes, their long hair slicked back with butter, their mustaches.

He looked perplexed. "Irish?" he asked.

"Did you kill Uter?" she asked.

"Why you fight us?"

"Why should we leave all Britannia for you?" she said. "How many of you are there?"

"Ten thousands! Two hundred fifty men fight Tintagel alone!" he said, mispronouncing the name of the place. "We kill Uter!"

Two hundred and fifty. Sylvana had been right. Two hundred and fifty would have been nothing to the Osraige. But she had only fifty men. Fifty men, and surprise.

"How many horses?"

He laughed, though it hurt him. "Saxon not fight from horses," he said. "You from Ireland, not so?"

"Yes," she smiled. "I am from the sea. When will you take Din Tagell?"

"Tomorrow, day after tomorrow, thank Wotan."

A foraging party wouldn't be more than a few hours from the main camp. She didn't need this man anymore. "Did you kill Uter? You?"

"Me? No. Aelfred, son of Hewell, he strike Uter in battle. Truly Aelfred is in Valhalla now." So the Saxons believed that great warriors would go to the Halls of the Valiant too.

She said, "I came here to take revenge on Uter. You have stolen that from me."

The Saxon's face fell. That, he understood. Good. It was a good thing to know why you died.

ᚦᛖ moon was no more than a hook in the sky that seemed to grow thinner with every hour; it cast almost no light. They took precautions anyway. They filtered through the countryside in small squads, darting from bushes to hedgerows to stone walls. Conall had taught these men well. They had smeared mud on their pale skin so they were almost impossible to see. They spoke in hand gestures. A man looking in their direction might have seen a faint movement, and wondered if he had seen anything at all. He would not have seen a company of warriors.

Morgan breathed in the night air. She remembered these smells from her childhood. She could smell the smoke of wood, not peat. She could smell the sweetness of the woods. The pungent stink of cow and sheep dung in the pasture. Salt from the sea she had been reborn in. The smells of home.

She wondered what Conall was doing. Did he think of her? When he asked his lords for advice on how to handle the peace emissaries to the Eóganachta, did he try to guess what she would have told him to do?

Would he have found someone new? A slave girl? The daughter of an ally? She knew in her heart that he had not. He would be dreaming of her.

Morgan could not let herself dream of him.

She pulled her arms tightly around herself. If Conall were here, he would be standing a few feet away. They would be waiting together for the dawn to paint the clouds rose, the dawn breeze lifting strands of his hair. Or he would be walking with his lords among the gathered men, talking about the battle about to begin, and every now and then he would shoot her a look that said more than she would have thought a look could say, promise and longing and love.

Morgan's skin felt cold and dull. Conall had once brought it alive with his fingertips, his calloused palms, the rest of him moving against her. His touch had made her feel alive.

She hoped he would find someone else who would give him what she could not.

The sky was beginning to brighten. And there it was below them: the ridge of the headland. She could make out a grey line across the green top of the land bridge. That must be the Wall across the Neck. It was higher than she remembered. Had Uter built it up?

She could hear the distant crash of the surf, but from her vantage point on the low hill, the cliffs might as well be the end of the world; she couldn't see the sea below them.

She was seven hundred yards from home.

As the sky brightened further, she could make out the camp of the Saxons, and the men moving around in it. Her captured Saxon had told the truth. There were perhaps five fifties of men there. They hadn't bothered to pitch tents. They had slept in their cloaks, and now they were walking around warming themselves.

A horn blew in the Saxon camp. The men began to gather.

She knew what would follow. Their chief would rouse them to great deeds of valour. He would promise them the Halls of Valour if they died in battle.

Morgan wondered how many defenders there were at the wall.

Tӈє Saxons made good lines, every five men carrying a long ladder. They might be barbarians, but in war they were soldiers. Their horns were calling, and the men were singing. Quickly they marched forward into bowshot of the walls. But their shields and spears were up, and no arrows came down from the walls. The defenders—Morgan couldn't see them to count them—wouldn't waste their arrows on the iron hedgehog approaching.

The Saxons began to jog forward, and Morgan held her breath. She wanted to order her men to charge, but it was too soon. If there were no men on the walls, there was nothing she could do to stop a slaughter.

The Saxon line broke into a run, and arrows began to shoot out from behind the ramparts, but few Saxons fell. Then she saw the first few men plunge into a ditch in front of the wall; she hadn't noticed it, and she guessed they hadn't either. Spears began to soar out from the wall, and more Saxons fell. But they threw ladders over the ditch, and some scrambled down into and then up out of it, and soon scaling ladders were stacking up against the walls. Men on the walls began to hurl rocks down, but more and more Saxon ladders were going up.

She watched the wall. There were well-trained men there, men who fought in good armour and good order. She could see it, not because she could make them out, but because there was a rhythm by which the Saxon ladders were hurled down. A blur of red would speed to a spot on the wall where the Saxons were standing on the ramparts, and they would be hurled off, and the ladders would be thrown down. Someone was making an organized defence.

But it was taking longer and longer for the ladders to be thrown down.

Now was the time.

Morgan looked at her men. They had washed the muck from their bodies, and they were wearing their red and blue woolens. They were combing their hair up, straightening it with butter so that it stuck out from their bare heads like sunbursts.

She nodded to Aedan. He raised his spear high in the air, its point glinting in the dawn sun. Then he brought it down hard, and the men began to drum their spears against their shields. As one, the men gave out a high-pitched shriek that seemed to feed on itself, and then they charged down the ridge toward the wall.

Morgan reached into the earth, deep within herself, into a place she had made ready, and she pulled out clamour, and fear, and panic.

THE Saxons fighting at the wall did not hear Morgan's men at first. They were consumed with the ring of steel on steel, the shouting of men fighting, the screaming of men dying. It must have sounded like the land had taken up their cries and was echoing them.

But the Irish cries were high and uncanny, and the defenders on the wall had their mouths closed, grimly fighting, making a day's work out of the battle. This wasn't their cry. Something in it made your knees feel weak. It made you want to run.

Some of the Saxons turned to face the strange sound and saw a terrifying thing: tall half-naked men hurtling down the hill at them, shields glistening, their hair all on end. Who were these barbarians? A handful of men did run. But there was nowhere to run except over the cliff. The tall men raced forward. The Saxons braced themselves for impact.

Her attack failed. She could see it fail in the first few heartbeats. Irish warriors would have broken. But Morgan watched her ranks hit the Saxon line and stop dead. Oh, they were darting their spears forward, stabbing and cutting, smashing with their shields; but so were the Saxons. These raiders were hard men, harder than her Irish. They had not broken even when they were surprised from the rear.

Her men would fight like madmen, she knew, taking wilder and wilder chances to break the armoured men, to make them run. But the Saxons were backed up against a wall. They would not break. She had lost her bet. Even surrounded front and back, spears sailing out of the wall to kill them, strange warriors suddenly assailing them, these hard-shelled men fought like stone. Her men would smash against them like waves, and they would break, and run, and be lost in the countryside.

Morgan had only one hope left. Simon helped her up on Flaith. She spurred the horse down toward the gates of Din Tagell, Simon running as fast as he could behind her. She could see the Saxons pushing her men back. Some of them were already falling under the welter of steel. As soon as she was in earshot, she shouted, "The gates! Make for the gates!" She drew her sword and pointed at the gates.

At first nothing happened. It was a terrible thing to watch her own men fall, reeling back from the armoured men. One of her men broke and ran past her, not looking at her, and she had no time to stop and turn him around.

Then she thought to shout in Irish, "The gates!" Then again, in Latin, "Open the gates!" The Saxons stared at her; they barely knew what to make of her. Was she a leader? A warrior? A madwoman? They fought on, grim and hard.

Her men pressed toward the gates.

On the walls there was a flurry of movement. Men appeared, hurling javelins one after another, each one aimed and deadly. "The gates!" she yelled, over and over, in Irish, Latin and British, as she reached a knot of her men gathering in front of the gates, pressing hard against the Saxons bunched there. Javelins and arrows shot down out of the towers on either side of the gates, and here and there Saxons fell. Morgan plunged into the centre of her men, some of them fighting their way into a ragged defensive circle in front of the gates. Thank the gods she had made Conall teach her men how to retreat fighting.

All around her she could see her men fighting their way to the circle, stabbing and slashing with their spears. Fiacha the Red turned and died on a spear point. Fiacha the Black made it to the defensive circle, but took a bad blow from an axe on the way. He was still fighting furiously, but he might not survive the night.

The Saxons were swarming around the circle, hacking and cutting with their short axes. They were good at war. She could see their love for it on their bearded faces.

She turned and looked up at the gates. Through the ramparts she could see a great cauldron being readied on the right tower. A great lead-lined sluice was being deployed out of the tower, like a piece of some aqueduct made of moving parts.

The cauldron tipped. A dribble of something burning poured down the sluice and stopped. Then a rush of watery fire sluiced down out of the tower, arcing away from the gate, over her men, and splashing on the Saxons. They screamed in agony as the sluice pivoted, now right, now left, splashing them all with the burning liquid.

Greek fire.

The Saxons tried to retreat, burning and screaming. But the men behind them pressed forward with a roar. Still they came on, pushed on by the ones behind them.

The gates creaked open, one foot, two feet, three feet, and her men looked to her. "Inside!" she shouted, and her men darted into the safety of the walls of Din Tagell.

She would have waited for all her men, but Aedan took Flaith's reins and pulled her horse inside, shouting, her men forming a ring around her until she was safely inside. They followed hard on her heels, and then helped the soldiers shove the heavy gates shut and slam the bolt home.

Someone shouted from the tower in Latin, "They're pulling back! They're going! We beat them!" There were hurrahs from the soldiers all along the wall.

But there were far too few voices coming from the wall, and the Saxons' retreat was no miracle. Their lines were confused, their men demoralized. They had been surprised. They had nothing to gain by pressing their attack now. Better to retreat and regroup, and lick their wounds.

She had seen how those men fought. They would be back.

MORGAN looked around. Her men were surrounded by maybe thirty-five soldiers, all shield to shield, their spears pointing through. "Put your spears down," she said in Irish to her men. "It's all right." Reluctantly, carefully, they put their spears down on the ground, keeping their shields dangling loose from their arms. A few women ran up to them through the line of soldiers. They went for the ones who were bleeding, and started helping them away, those who could walk.

A tall man stepped down from the wall and strode over to Morgan. He wore a centurion's uniform, of course: the red cape, the embossed armour, the shock of red-dyed horsehair rising from his helmet. He saluted, bringing his fist against his chest. She nodded. He gestured to his men. "I apologize for the welcome, if it is not what you'd hoped," he said, in Latin.

Morgan smiled. "I'd hoped to break the Saxon line."

The centurion smiled. There was an endearing rough-and-ready honesty in his smile. "Still, it lacks something in hospitality, my lady," he said.

"I'd be careful too if I were you. You have no idea who we are."

"I was hoping you'd bring that up," he said. Morgan had forgotten what soldiers were like. Her warriors were wolves, their ferocity barely kept on leash, but this man was courteous and utterly lethal at the same time. "I am Gerault, son of Paterninus, centurion of this fort." He waited, sternly pleasant.

"I'm called Morgan. But my name was once Anna. My father was Gorlois, governor of Din Tagell. My mother is Ygraine, daughter of Ceinwen of Brittany."

Gerault took a step back, surprised. He stared at her. "There was a daughter," he said softly, after a long moment. "She was sent away."

"To Ireland." Morgan nodded.

"Nobody knew where. It was said that even Ygraine didn't know."

Clever, Morgan thought.

Gerault kept looking at her, as if he was trying to convince himself one way or another. "I saw Gorlois once. At the war council, when I was a boy. He had red hair, and his nose was strong…but you have your mother's lips…" He stopped. His eyes widened, as if he'd forgotten himself. So he had seen her mother in her. Gerault went down on one knee, and bowed his head. All around them were murmurs, and then slowly, the clank of metal and leather as the soldiers ringed around them also went down on their knees, perplexed. "You saved us, my lady," Gerault said.

And then he looked away from the wall, and rose. Morgan looked with him. The old round houses were gone. In their place was a great villa of oak, two storeys tall, its outlying buildings all laid out along a straight line with brick walkways between them. Then she saw her mother, a woman in white silk, coming out of the main building. Two village girls walked on either side of her;

maybe she was leaning on them. The woman's long brown hair was streaked with grey. But Morgan knew her.

Her mother drew near. Her face was still beautiful, but there was a fragility in her that hadn't been there before. The sadness: *that* Morgan remembered.

A wave of raw emotion surged through her, and she found herself swaying like kelp in the sea. She wanted to cry, she wanted to run, she wanted to weep with joy, but she could only sway. She had come home. Hadn't she? It wasn't the same. There was a Roman villa where her father's house had stood. But there was her mother. Morgan's face was flushed, and she wanted to hide it behind her hands like a little girl, but she kept her chin up high and looked her mother straight in the eyes.

Ygraine was squinting at her. Had her eyes gone bad? No. She was trying to figure out who Morgan was. Morgan had been eleven when she left.

Gerault stood silently by, watching Morgan and her mother. No doubt he was waiting for Ygraine to make her own judgment.

Ygraine, too, seemed to be searching for words. She looked Morgan over. She seemed to keep wanting to say something, but thinking better of it. Finally she said, "These are your men?"

"They follow me."

"I'm told you broke the Saxon attack on the wall."

Morgan didn't say anything to that. Why didn't her mother recognize her? Who else could she be?

Then her mother gasped a little, and looked at her with puzzled amazement. "Who are you?"

"Who do you think I am?" Morgan asked, and wondered why it came out so sharp, and why she and her mother were circling each other like fighters looking for an opening.

"I think you might be my daughter."

"What would make you sure?" asked Morgan, and she felt the moment slipping away when they would embrace, and she was frightened. Was her mother afraid of her? Angry at her? Should she never have come back? Was she supposed to have come back sooner?

"I gave you something when you left," her mother said. "What was it?"

What? A cloak? A boat? The Greek?

No. It was a trick question. Her mother was staring at her, hoping, wondering. Morgan thought of Odysseus' bed, that Penelope had asked him to move when he returned from his twenty years' voyage. But Odysseus knew it couldn't be moved because one of its bedposts was a tree.

"You gave me a name," she said.

Ygraine stared at Morgan with wonder in her eyes. Then she swept Morgan up in her arms and embraced her tightly.

Chapter Twenty One

DIN TAGELL

Ygraine embraced Morgan, and went back to bed. She was weak from some ailment Din Tagell's healer could not make sense of. She asked Morgan to come join her. But with an impending attack, how could Morgan leave her men? She couldn't, could she?

Nine of Morgan's men lay under the cover of the villa's gallery. Three of them were sure to die. Who would keen for them in this foreign land? She swore that she would, and she said she wouldn't need to. She told them brave lies, and they looked at her with puppy eyes, believing. Outside, she watched her men arguing with Aedan about the armour Gerault wanted them to put on, stripped from those of his men who were dead or too wounded to fight. Her men pointed out that it had obviously not protected the men who had worn it. Aedan countered that there was no fighting Saxons without armour on, and to put the Dagda-be-damned breastplate on before he had to go get Herself, meaning Morgan.

She had lost eleven men outside the walls. With nine men wounded, that left only thirty to man the ramparts. Gerault had another fifty-five. Eighty-five men to drive off four fifties of armoured foreigners.

Aedan came over and waited by her side until she looked at him. "I think we've got it under control now," he said.

"Good," she said.

"Working out well between them and us."

"I'm glad."

"They won't attack again before night, I think," he said.

She looked at him. He made a big show of not looking her in the eye. Just hooked his thumbs in his belt, and scratched his shoulder, and glanced at her with a brief smile.

"Yes?" she said.

"Well, I'm not entirely sure of the customs in Britain, of course," he said. "But when a band of warriors visits a lord in his stronghold, it is customary to visit with that lord a bit."

"You'd like me to go see my mother," she said.

He cleared his throat. "I wouldn't dream of suggesting anything between you and your mother. I'm speaking only of the customs of hospitality between a war chief and a village chief..."

"Fine," she said, and walked away from him, toward the villa, resenting him all the way, until she realized how anxiously she had been avoiding talking to her mother.

MORGAN put her hand against the doorway, and watched her mother sleep. The way Ygraine was hunched even in sleep made her seem like an old woman. So fragile. Was it just the illness?

What was holding her back from going to her mother's side? Morgan dropped her hand to her side, and forced herself to take the remaining steps to the bed.

Her mother opened her eyes and looked up at Morgan. "I was hoping it was you."

Morgan sat down on the edge of the bed. "Gerault thinks they'll attack tonight."

"I'm glad you came," said her mother.

"I got some of my men to put on armour. They weren't too happy about it."

"Tell me about Ireland," said her mother.

"Tell me about Uter," Morgan said, and she managed to say it softly.

Her mother didn't say anything for a while. Morgan waited.

Finally: "The Saxons ambushed him. I don't know if they were clever, or he was careless. He was getting careless, the last few years."

Morgan could see sorrow in her mother's eyes.

"Everything fell apart after you left, you know. After what he did to your father, no one would follow him into battle. They called him High King, but they always made excuses why they could not send troops. Those were bad years. Someone would win a big victory against a Saxon raiding party, but they would never follow it up, because it would have meant leaving their own lands. That's why our neighbours won't come to save us now. They're saving their men for when the Saxons show up at *their* gates."

Morgan found herself torn between a morbid pleasure that Uter had suffered for what he had done, and sadness for the land.

"He went out to surprise a Saxon camp, the day of the solstice. He didn't send out scouts. He was outnumbered. One of them stabbed him in the stomach." Morgan flinched. "Not even the Enchanter could heal him."

"The Enchanter is still alive?" Morgan asked.

"They say he never grows any older." The bitterness in her mother's voice reminded Morgan of the dreams she had had.

"There was a son?"

"The Enchanter took him." Her mother was choking, trying not to cry. "That was the price for his help."

"*Why* did he help Uter?"

Ygraine shook her head. "Who knows why the Enchanter does anything? They say he isn't even human."

One day, Morgan thought, she would have to find the Enchanter and ask him why he had helped Uter. And she would ask him *how* he had done it. He owed her that.

"I thought you'd never come back from Ireland," her mother said. "What happened there?"

And so Morgan told her mother the story of her years in Ireland. It was strange to tell the story by her mother's bedside. It almost didn't feel like her own story; it sounded like an adventure story set in a faraway land. She told of Ciarnat, and slavery, of the monastery, and most of all of Conall.

"And why did you leave him?" asked her mother.

"This is my home," Morgan said, because she didn't want to mention Uter, and because it was true.

"Have you come to die with us?"

Morgan shook her head. A fierceness was roused in her. "We will not die here."

Ygraine smiled. It was a sweet sad smile, but there was pride in it, and hope. "I will die here," she said. "But maybe you'll surprise me."

Morgan looked out through the window, through the slits in the heavy wooden shutters that had been bolted shut. Everything in this place was defensive. Uter had built well.

Outside, the sky was ablaze with the sunset. The clouds were glorious.

When it was dark, she kissed her sleeping mother on the forehead, and slipped out of the room.

THE men of Din Tagell and her Irishmen slept on the ramparts, their weapons handy, listening to the distant sounds of axes. But the enemy did not come in the night.

The Saxons came when the sun broke the horizon, the same as before, with the same songs and the same ladders, as well as a few newly-made walkways to throw over the ditch.

This time they stayed clear of the gates and their fire-spitting towers. They slammed one ladder after another against the wall, and hurled their throwing axes up at the defenders. The soldiers and warriors on the ramparts hurled down stones and curses and javelins.

The Saxons had numbers and ferocity on their side. The defenders had a high stone wall, and half of them had Roman discipline.

Morgan went among the old men, the boys and the strong women, and made sure they had axes and mauls and pitchforks. They would only get in the way up on the wall, but if the Saxons got through, it would be better for them to die fighting.

The battle flowed and ebbed. The Saxons would gain the ramparts in one or two places, and British countercharges would throw them down. They would retreat just out of bowshot, only to charge again, harder. Each attack could be blunted and then broken. But the Saxons whittled away at the defenders, and man after man fell to their sharp axes, especially the Irish, whose spears became awkward in a tight clinch. Gradually the odds were turning against Din Tagell.

At noon the Saxons gained the ramparts and broke the countercharges sent against them. They started to push out from their foothold, and the defenders had to fall back. The Saxons began to pour up the ladders, taking the wall by sheer weight of numbers. Now the fight was all man to man along the wall walk, and the Saxons had more men. Morgan ordered the women, boys and old men forward, to defend their stronghold against the murdering invaders.

It was time. Morgan went back to the villa.

YGRAINE was sleeping the heavy sleep of illness. Morgan bolted the door.

The box was there at the bottom of her mother's linen trunk. It still held the black glass blade wrapped in green silk. The blade was smaller than she remembered. But it had a tremendous heat trapped within it, as if the volcanic fires that had made it were still sealed inside.

Outside, the battle was feverish. Men were screaming and dying. The high piercing yell of the Irish: that would be their countercharge. She wondered how long before they broke.

She began to inscribe the circle. Three times she drew the line that would keep the forces inside, sealing it with a pentagram she drew in the air.

It was time.

But was there enough time? She needed to work a magic more powerful than she had ever worked before. Morgan felt the earth beneath her feet. She fell to her knees and put her hands on the ground. She was iron, born of earth in air and fire, running like water, then hardening into shape, unmoving, unbreakable.

She thought of her father. He had been solid, sure. He had spoken little and given away nothing. He had been the wall that protected his land. Her bones were his bones.

Earth *kept silent*. It was time.

Then Morgan reached up and found air. The room was still and quiet, but the air was only waiting for her. You could not hold air, but you could tease it. You could not command air, but you could tempt it to join you. She played with the air, her arms outstretched and dancing. She danced with the air, and then there it was, whirling, blowing her hair, swirling through her loose silk dress.

Air *knew*. It was time.

Fire was in her: hot skin, hot breath. There had been a chill in the room a moment ago, but she remembered Conall, his fingers moving across her skin, how they burned softly into her. She remembered Uter, and her anger blazed up hot, and the thought of the foreigners who had come to take her home away, and the room was suddenly hot like a bonfire. She pulled the fire into herself, weaving it, until all was ablaze.

Fire *willed*. It was time.

Water, loose and slow, rocked her gently. Kelp in a seabed, a boat plowing the Irish Sea at a good clip. The fire was still there, and the hot breeze that fed it, but she was cool and fresh. Water was all around her. The land was wet and good. She felt a memory of Buanann in the lake village, water surrounding her, knowing without thinking. She let the water take her and give her back, take her and give her back, until the room was thick with it, pregnant with it, ready to pour forth.

Water *acted*.

It was time.

Morgan heard women and boys shrieking. That meant the Saxons had broken through her men, and were killing her people.

Then time stopped. There were no more shouts from outside. The waves broke no more against the coast.

The circle was cast. She was between the worlds.

There was something else here. She felt it in her hand, pouring into her from the blade she held there. Not just from the blade. From the room. Magic had been worked in this room. There was a comforting presence around her, dancing, lithe, sweet, beautiful. Was it a young woman with long brown hair? Was it the smell of saffron? Was it a long ago kiss, a whisper, a promise?

But there was a spell to work, and Morgan had never been closer to the heart of the land. She was this land. She was immensely old. She knew how the land fought with the sea, seeking to rise while the sea tore it down. She knew that the sea had won a great and startling victory here, and that the land longed for revenge. It had bided its time, and now its anger was terrible. She felt the spirits that lived in this land, even the ones that slept.

She thought she might dare to ask a great and terrible boon.

ASK, THEN.

She asked.

And she pushed the circle she had made outward, until it took in the entire peninsula. All of Din Tagell was between the worlds.

GRADUALLY the breathing world returned, but she was in a dream. Not a sleeping dream. A waking dream. She saw not with her own eyes, but with the eyes of those fighting. She saw blades flashing in the rising sun. She saw blood on the grass, blood on the stones. She heard men gasping for breath. She saw them spin like dancers. She felt metal bend and wrench. It was easy to be fond of war. It was a power all its own.

She was Aedan, eight of his men hemmed in against the back side of the wall, fighting toe to toe with a dozen grim Saxons. They were his best men, and they were holding their own. But they were doing nothing to stop the enemy, and sooner or later some Saxon above them would notice, and then they would be dodging stones.

She was Gerault, fighting his way down off the wall with twenty men, trying to hurl themselves into the backs of the Saxons who were already headed for the villa. He wondered what formation he could create that would bring order to the chaos, though he knew it was too late to save their lives.

She was a Saxon whose name she didn't know, hacking with his twin axes at a mob of terrified, desperate women, his men at his side, singing a bloodthirsty song of love of plunder, of death and glory. It was a shame to be fighting women, for they would not be alive to enslave, but the man who pillaged Uter's fort would be a man worthy to be taken to the Halls of Valour by the Choosers of the Valiant riding their great black birds. The man who broke the neck of Tintagel's peninsula... wait.

There was no peninsula. Where was the sea? Where were the cliffs? The lands rolled out, gently rising and falling like waves frozen in motion. There was no end to the land. There was no sea anywhere.

And where was the villa? What were these strange domelike houses? What were the curving beams that made their structure? They looked like the dried ribs of a whale. Whalebones, this far from the sea?

And what was that singing, faint but growing? It was strange and savage, like nothing he had heard before.

Out of one of the dales of those lovely green rolling hills marched men with shields as big as small boats, and spears as thick and long as saplings. They were naked. They were giants. Their expressions were grimmer than night. Their faces were too long, inhumanly long, and they were grinning with mouths wider than mouths had a right to be, and their teeth were sharp like lizard teeth.

They did not stop coming. There was no end to the ranks marching out from between the hills.

"Shield wall on me!" the Saxon leader screamed instinctively. He took a step back from the women. His men pressed close to him. He wondered if maybe it was a mistake to fight the giants. But he could not bring himself to order his men to run for it, not in the middle of victory.

She was Aedan again, and the enemies in front of her wavered and stepped back. Fearcorb took one of them in the throat with a lucky stab. But something uncanny was in the air. "Hold back!" he shouted to his men. "Don't follow!"

They held. Good. The Saxons were looking away at something that he couldn't see. No...there! There were shapes coming out of the mist. No, there was no mist. There was land that stretched out as far as the eye could see, and there were also cliffs that fell away to the sea. It was a *shaping*, a very great one. The Morrígan had done shapings like this against the invaders of Ireland.

"Stay back!" Aedan screamed, and his men held firm as the Saxons ran to the centre of the peninsula to form a shield wall. "Let's go after them!" yelled Fearcorb.

"Don't you feel it?" Aedan shouted, and Fearcorb breathed in, and he shivered and looked around.

"Stay out of its way!" Aedan ordered, as Fearcorb and the other men lowered their spears in obedience, and wonder, and fear.

She was Gerault, and there was something savage in the air, and he felt chill fear in his back, he who never felt fear in battle, for the priest had shrived him, and he was strong in the faith of the Lord. But the air was wild like in a thunderstorm, and the sun was as dim as the moon, and he thought of seeing as through a glass darkly, and the enemy melted away from him and he did not even think to stab at them as they went.

She was a man who had died long ago in a great war, and he roared his anger at what had been done to him and his realm eons ago. The tiny men in front of him wore gleaming silver armour, but they were frightened, though they stood shoulder to shoulder, grimly shouting. The dead man slung his great shield off his shoulder, and nodded his head forward so that his bronze helmet fell forward to protect his face, and he couched his spear in his arm. He gave a great war shout, and his men added their voices, low and terrible, and they charged these strange little men in their strange silvery armour.

She was the Saxon leader, and there was no way these giants bearing down on his men were real. They must be witchcraft, an illusion. "They're not real!" he shouted, and strode out to meet them.

The lance ripped through his ribs, and as he died, he hoped the lovely Valkyries would come for him.

ЅԋЄ was an old man, watching the Saxons break and run for the cliffs. They must be thinking to outrun the tall warriors in bronze on those long rolling downs that stretched away into darkness. But he had lived at Din Tagell long enough to know where the cliffs were, even if he could not see them, and he could hear the Saxons stumbling on the cliff edge, and falling to the rocks far below, and he hoped they would be a long time dying.

Tꜧꜯý were tugging at Morgan, the spirits of the land. She was thanking them for their magical boon, but they wanted to be repaid.

WHAT IS IN IT FOR US? they asked. HELP THE SUNKEN LANDS RISE. GIVE US YOUR STRENGTH, YOUR FORCE, YOUR SOUL. Their hands were on her, pulling her down. She was sinking, and the sunken lands were rising, like a drowning swimmer who drags down his rescuer.

Morgan fought them, tore free. She ran. But it was like running through the muck at the bottom of a lake. She was sinking, and she was frightened. She had been powerful, but now she was weak and howling for help. The spirits of the earth would know her fear, and she knew it would give them strength.

She had come so far. But the dead were laying their soft hands on her, clutching her, binding her, drawing her to the sunken lands, sucking the life out of her.

She called on the elements. But this place between the worlds was an airless place, and there was no sun, no heat, no fire here. It was a dead dry place; there was no water here. And earth…the earth wanted her, longed to keep her. She owed everything, she had asked for a great and terrible boon, and now what did she have for payment but her body?

It hurt to fight them. It would be so easy to relax and let them take her. She was tired. She had saved her people. She had won a great battle. She had protected the land from these barbarians. She had done what her father had not. It would be a good day to die.

Her father.

Uter had taken everything from her father, and today she had taken it back. She refused to give it up.

She stabbed out with the blade in her hand.

It shattered. And suddenly there was blazing fire all around her. There was a whirlwind. There was the scent of saffron. There was a rising sea. There was a young woman with long brown hair dancing around her, and it was the dance of a fighter, spinning and slashing with bare hands, her hair flowing around her as she spun, her eyes fierce and sad and wise and strong.

The woman spun toward her, and Morgan knew her, knew her intimately, for the woman was flesh of her flesh. It was Ygraine. And Morgan suddenly knew the things that her mother had done, and all the things she had felt, as if they were her own memories. For a split second, they were one.

But Morgan did not dare stay. She took off like a glistening black bird and soared out of that place of darkness.

MORGAN was back in the world of time and space, holding her mother in her arms. Ygraine was almost unbearably light. "Thank you," Morgan said, the fear sloughing away from her.

"Is it done?" Ygraine asked, in a voice so faint that Morgan could barely hear her.

"It's over," Morgan said. "We're safe."

She helped her mother gently to the bed. There was shouting in the villa's hallway, but she didn't want to talk to anyone else. She opened the shutters and looked out on the peninsula.

The sun was clear and bright. The Saxons were gone, except some dead ones by the wall, and one lying on the ground surrounded by a cluster of soldiers and armed women. The sun streamed into the room. Morgan left the window and sat down on her mother's bed.

Ygraine looked at her softly, weakly. "You know, don't you?" Ygraine said. "You saw."

Morgan knew. She had seen everything in that moment when she and her mother were as one.

Her mother looked away. "Yes. I knew who it was, that night." The moment blasted through Morgan's mind. The man in her father's shape, making love to her mother. "I knew it was Uter. How could I not have?"

Morgan had thought the words would sear her. But now they just seemed like a confirmation of something she had guessed long ago.

"I knew it had to be the Enchanter's spell," said her mother, "and there is no fighting the Enchanter. I made him swear that he would do no more harm to your father. And he swore." She added bitterly, "He didn't forswear himself, for he had already slain him."

"Why did he come that night?" Morgan asked. "Why not after he'd won the battle?"

Her mother closed her eyes. "The Enchanter told him that a great king would be conceived on that night."

"Then where is my brother?"

"The Enchanter took him away." Ygraine shook her head in grief. "He took my son away. It was the price of his help. The Enchanter cannot have a child of his own. So he took your brother. I never saw him again."

Ygraine was silent for a few moments. She was sobbing quietly. Then: "I thought about poisoning Uter. After the Enchanter took my son. I almost did it, a few times. But I was weak."

Morgan shook her head. She knew her mother wasn't telling the truth. In that place between the worlds, she had known her mother in a way no child can, had seen into her heart and her memories.

And she remembered the look that had passed between Uter and her mother in the great tent, so many years ago. How her mother had looked frightened.

But not of Uter. She had been frightened of herself.

Her mother had wanted Uter. And even as she'd fled, she'd looked at him, and with her eyes she'd begged him to come after her, to pursue her.

"He didn't force you," Morgan said. "You loved him."

Ygraine closed her eyes, spent. Faintly, she nodded.

And Morgan realized to her amazement that she had already forgiven her mother. She knew how Ygraine had felt on that night. How she had not wanted to look at Uter like that. How she had tried to stop herself. But you could not always stop yourself.

MORGAN ran her fingers through her mother's hair. Ygraine was sleeping now, utterly spent. Morgan would send a message to their neighbours for a great healer. She would…

No. Her mother had worked a great magic with her. She had taken Morgan back from the airless place. Together they had saved their home.

And now her mother had nothing left. Morgan knew. It would not be long now.

Morgan, too, felt awfully tired. She would rest, and then she would decide what came next.

SOME time later there was a knocking at the door. Morgan went and opened it.

It was Aedan, grinning from ear to ear, with a wide amazed look in his eyes. Gerault was right behind him, and even he could not keep himself stern.

"I was sleeping," Morgan said. "My mother is sleeping."

"It's customary…" Aedan shrugged, and before he could explain about victories, Morgan just nodded and followed him out.

THE men cheered her. They almost lifted her up on their shoulders to parade her around like they had with Conall, but something held them back. Maybe there was an inkling of fear. That suited her.

When the men had gone to break out casks of Gaulish wine, Gerault took her aside. "What was that?" he asked. "Who were they?"

"I don't know," she told him, truthfully.

"Are you a saint?" he asked. "Was that a miracle?"

She shook her head. She had known a saint, once.

"Are you a witch?"

"Tell me what that word means, Centurion, and I'll answer you."

Gerault thought about that. Then he shook his head and smiled in that wry grave way of his.

"Maybe it was an illusion," said Morgan.

"That's what I thought at first," said Gerault, "but look at this." He walked her over to the dead Saxon leader lying on his face. "I ordered my men not to chuck him off the cliff with the others," said Gerault. He put the toe of his sandal under the dead man, and flipped him over. There was a gaping spear wound in his ribs. "No one remembers killing him. He was their captain. You remember killing a captain," Gerault said.

Morgan nodded. It had not been an illusion. She had taken Din Tagell between the worlds, where the giants lived on their rolling downs. She had summoned them to battle. And with the last of her mother's strength, she had dismissed them.

Gerault looked straight at her for just a moment. "I hope I never have to fight them."

Morgan shivered, and nodded.

EPILOGUE

Morgan stayed with her mother almost constantly for the next six weeks. A healer arrived from Drustranus Cunomorus, lord of the lands to the south—no one called himself governor anymore—but the wise woman couldn't do anything for Ygraine. But the weaker Ygraine became, the more content she seemed, as if death was a gift she had been long hoping for.

They never talked about Uter again. But one day she noticed that her mother was awake, and watching her with an oddly concerned look.

"You came back for vengeance?"

"Yes," she admitted. Her mother must have seen things in her too.

"You've won, haven't you?"

She had won. Uter was gone, and of his works there was nothing left. Even Uter's son was gone, stolen by the Enchanter. So Uter had paid at least some of his debt, if not to her.

She was the ruler of her father's lands. She was her father's daughter.

No. Her father could never have done any of the things she had done.

She wasn't her mother's daughter either. Her mother had given away her power when she came to Din Tagell. She had heard the spirits of the land. But she had only asked them to seal a room against a child's bad dreams.

Morgan had drawn on the powers of the land. She had summoned forth the old giants. And she had set things to right. Not back to what they would have been. But as they were meant to be.

She was the land's daughter. She owed it everything.

Morgan felt an incredible lightness in her own heart. She had given everything up for vengeance. She had given up grace. She had given up love. But it had brought her home. She was here on her land. She was strong, and the land and its people were safe, and its spirits lived within her.

And she forgave herself. She forgave herself for what she had done to Conall. She had needed to hate Uter, to blame him. She had needed her vengeance. And she had needed to return here, to be here now, safe and strong. The path she had taken had been the only one that could have brought her here.

Vengeance had brought her home. She no longer needed it. She cast it off. She owed nothing to anybody. She was free.

Her mother was already asleep again. Morgan sat by her side for a long time. There was no need to say anything at all, to anyone. There was no need to do anything. For the first time since she had gone to the war council with her father, she was content.

THERE was no trace of where Morgan's father had been buried. Ygraine had buried him in secret before Uter came to Din Tagell. With some misgivings, Morgan buried Ygraine by Uter's side, in the crypt deep beneath the villa, as she had requested. The villa itself was not to Morgan's taste, but it would have been childish to demolish such a cunningly built stronghold, and so she only had stone carvers summoned from Brittany. They carved its bricks with wild foliage and fanciful beasts interlaced in the Irish fashion. Now no one could mistake it for the grave of a Roman.

Years passed. From tradesmen and refugees, Morgan heard how the Saxons were roaming the land, raiding and burning. They steered clear of Din Tagell, which was rumoured to be protected by demons.

Word came to Din Tagell that a young man had found Uter's sword. The story was that Uter, mortally wounded, had sunk his sword into a cleft in a rock wall by a cave mouth, and that no one had been able to pull it out since. But the young man had pulled it out. In itself this might have meant nothing, for he was only a boy of sixteen, but the Enchanter had foretold that whoever drew the sword from the rock would become High King of Britain. Shortly after, with a dozen hotheads impressed by the act, the boy had surprised a small party of Saxons escorting three wagonloads of plunder, along with a dozen British slaves. He and his men massacred the Saxons and freed the Britons.

Moving quickly on horseback, he next surprised a Saxon village, burning it and killing the men, and taking their livestock. With every victory his war band grew, for he kept nothing for himself, but gave everything to his warriors. He made no effort to defend British strongholds; instead he harried the Saxon fringe on horseback, killing and plundering. The Saxons could not keep up with him, for they were always on foot.

People who met him, it was said, believed he was descended from some great mythic hero, Bran perhaps.

What made him easy to follow was that he came from no clan. No one knew who his father was, or who his foster father was. He did not answer these questions, saying only, "I am British." He spoke correct Latin and fluent British, and no one could place his accent. He was the favourite of no ruler, and none of the old quarrels applied to him.

With half of the war season already gone, a soldier arrived on horseback bearing Morgan a letter from this young war leader. He was raising an army against the Saxons. He made no claims to be High King, only *dux bellorum*, war leader. He addressed Morgan in excellent formal Latin as "governor of Trigos," as if the Empire had never died. He asked for her to bring Trigos' statutory ten hundreds to a council of war. She had nothing like a thousand fighting men. It was all she could do to keep her three dozen Irishmen at Din Tagell once they learned there was no gold to be had, only land and wives. But she would bring what she could, as befitted her father's daughter.

And so, a few days before midsummer, with all the men she could spare, British marching alongside Irish, she set off to the east, to meet the young war leader known only as Arthur.

Alex Epstein

is a screenwriter for film and television
specializing in science fiction and fantasy.
He lives in Montreal with his
wife and two children.